Where the Road Ends

by

Kathryn Beck

The Wild Rose Press, Inc.
PO Box 708
Adams Basin, NY 14410-0708
Visit us at www.thewildrosepress.com

Publishing History
First Edition, 2025
Trade Paperback ISBN 978-1-5092-5826-0
Digital ISBN 978-1-5092-5827-7

Published in the United States of America

Dedication

For Marley, Moline, Bridges, Lucidi.
And teachers everywhere who encourage students to
never let go of their dreams.

Chapter One

The imbalance of power in Wyoming's third district courtroom was uncompromising. Much like the aisle splitting the gallery in two.

The Haves. The Have Nots.

Two halves of a not-so-perfect whole.

Mara Sawyer tugged at her hair, ignoring both the spasms ripping through her gut and the bench in front of her. The lofty perch where the king or queen would take their seat and discharge their pearls of wisdom and judgment, determining fates of the less fortunate like herself.

Across the aisle, her ex and his lawyer laughed like twelve-year-old schoolboys. But schoolboys didn't wear thousand-dollar suits. Her own lawyer yanked at his neckline, looking like he'd made a quick stop at the local thrift store for court clothes today. Though she could hardly talk, with her faded, cotton jersey dress snagging with every shift of her hips on the splinter-ridden chair.

The only equalizer, the wood-soaked scent of aging lemon oil, filling up nostrils impartially at both tables.

The afternoon sunlight hit the dark wood, contradicting the dense shadows surrounding her. For anyone else, the elaborate interior contrived images of a big city municipal building, maybe a historic southern town, but this was Rock Springs, Wyoming. Population, twenty-five thousand, give or take. An authentic trading post town back in the day. A workingman's town in the here and now. Most people driving through were on their way somewhere else.

Anywhere else.

The judge settled and adjusted herself, peering down at her little kingdom. Normal busybody lurkers, with nothing better to do than get caught up in someone else's drama, scattered throughout the gallery. The imposing paintings of governors past lorded over the room, reminding Mara in stark clarity how far down on life's totem pole she lived. She gulped hard at the acid rising into her throat, waiting for words defining her fate.

The last time they gathered here, Charlotte—or Charlie, as her daughter preferred—had been awarded to the other side of the room. Visitation granted but supervised. Today, Mara's battle was for the right to take her daughter to the park by herself and eat frozen yogurt at their favorite froyo shop, after their prized mani-pedis, of course. Charlie may only be four, but she was a diva four, with everything that implied.

"Do you understand why we're here, Ms. Sawyer?" The judge spoke slowly, as if Mara did not understand simple English. The burn in the pit of her stomach sent tentacled fingers to the surface.

When her father was alive, he could stop the deluge of words she wanted to spout with an impressive lift of an eyebrow. Ranting came easily to her. It always had. There should be an acronym for people with poor impulse control—there was an acronym for everything else these days. Like a big card you could hold up and thrust in people's faces when you want to run your mouth.

"Judge. We're contesting unsupervised visits at this

time," the thousand-dollar suit lawyer spouted.

"On what grounds?"

"The incident was only three months ago. Mr. Owens is not convinced his ex-wife can take care of their daughter on her own."

Mara's mouth opened.

The judge raised a hand to silence her. Behind her, Rachel, her social worker and best friend, touched her shoulder and held her in place. They had discussed things that could be said. Hearing the assault in the courtroom was a whole different ball game.

Mara raised her hands to her lawyer. Stand, sit, speak. Something.

He finally jumped up. "Mr. Owen's claims are baseless. The home visits are going well."

"What about that?" The judge glanced at the other table. "The case worker has reported nothing derogatory."

"Because someone else is present, Your Honor."

"I need more. You know this," Her Honor said calmly. "She's working…"

"At a bar," Vivian, Chase's mom, sprang to her feet and blurted.

Mara huffed. "At least I work," she said louder than she intended.

The judge banged her gavel, the sound sinking and penetrating into crevices throughout the room. Her "poor person" lawyer grabbed at her arm.

Mara tried to count to ten. Hell, she'd settle for two.

"And we want a medical examination before the custody arrangements are altered."

"What? Are you insane?" She shook her finger at her former mother-in-law, matching the hammering beat her chest. "They made me drive. Because they want my daughter. That's what all this is about, all it's ever been about."

"Get yourself under control. Mr. Barnes, manage your client."

The room calmed for a quick second. Mara shook herself out of Rachel's clutches, hissed at Chase, and yelled again at his mother. "You know you made me."

The infuriating, all-knowing smiles silenced her.

"Ms. Sawyer," the judge said. "No one, not any one person, makes choices for you. You get to make grown-up decisions all on your own. You can point fingers all you want, accuse all you want, but you said, 'Okay, I can do that.' All I'm after here is a safe place for your daughter. Please be patient with the process."

Mara slid deeper into her seat, every word holding an element of truth. She needed to get herself straightened out, get her life straightened out. Become the mom Charlie deserved.

"As I was saying, we would like a medical examination. Charlotte is an active little girl; it takes a lot to keep up with her."

Mara rolled her eyes, grabbing her lawyer's arm. "Are you going to say anything? Anything would be great right here. I think we all know what he's implying."

"Judge, that's inflammatory."

"Maybe. It's a reasonable request if he's willing to submit to the same. How about it, Mr. Owens? Are you willing to get a physical?"

Chase stood, buttoned his jacket slowly, irritating Mara further with the dramatics. "Of course, Your Honor." His fingers slid down his tailored sides, raising his eyebrows. "I mean…"

Mara got his drift. Apparently, the judge did too.

Mara clenched her hands into tight fists under the table. Another verdict was making its way from the judge's lips. Another loss. Rinse, repeat.

"We will reconvene in sixty days. In the meantime, supervised visits remain in place. Both parties will get medical evaluations during that period. Do you understand my ruling, Ms. Sawyer?"

"I'm not a moron. Of course, I do."

The judge breathed deep and looked skyward. "Ms. Sawyer. Everyone makes bad choices. You made one. Own it. Accept the consequences. A little girl's life hangs in the balance. She does not get to make those choices at this point in her life. You can do nothing and give up on your little girl, or you can go back to the drawing board, figure out where you went off course. A DUI is a big deal. You work at a bar, for God's sake. Give me a new perspective."

"I have bills to pay," Mara blurted, forgetting again to shut the hell up. "A parent to support, a child to support, mouths to feed."

The judge held her hand up. "Seriously, quit making excuses." She leafed through the file in front of her. "You are less than a year away from your nursing degree. Finish that and—"

"I have people counting on me." Mara threw her hands up and pointed at her ex. "How about you talk to the unemployed at the other table? Tending bar is substantial money."

"Enough! Get. Your. Life. Together." The judge stood up from her lording-over-the-world position, leaning into her hands on the desk in front of her. "Find a job that doesn't have the optics yours does. A DUI doesn't speak well in custody arrangements. Finish your degree, get yourself a nice, clean apartment where you can live with your daughter so I can look at this and quit seeing a screwed up, entitled woman who wants to blame the world for every wrong turn in life. You're young. You can make this right, but your child is waiting for you to make that choice today. Not tomorrow, not next week."

Mara's head dropped, staring at the scarred wood of the table.

"Give your daughter a chance. More importantly, give yourself a chance."

The judge escaped through a door at the bottom of the podium. A bailiff called for the courtroom to be adjourned and rushed away.

Mara bounced her head on the table, trying to beat a measure of sense into herself. She'd lost her daughter for the second time. More infuriating, Chase only fought because of his mother. He had no more desire to be a good father than a rock.

"I'll see you next week?" Rachel said, reaching over the rail to squeeze her arm. "We'll reassess and make a new plan."

Mara nodded.

The room hushed into silence as people made their escape. Mara should have known to keep her mouth shut. Topping it off, the judge slung a little more mud and reminded her she had a going-nowhere career, and icing on the cake, she was a fat ass.

The sky outside was a dark gray. November was a good time for grays, at least in Wyoming. The thick clouds threatened to cry, but they, like her, didn't dare. She put that wrought iron facade in place before she lowered her head, her gaze meeting Charlie's caretaker, then traveling to the bouncing little ringlet-laced head clutching her hand.

"Mommy, I missed you so much." Charlie dragged the "so" out for an eternity, piercing Mara's heart. "Can I come visit you and Nana now?"

Mara crouched, pulling the mass of a squirming child into her, willing herself not to clutch too tightly, grip with too much pressure. "Not this time, baby. But soon, really soon. I miss you." Mara stretched her arms wide and wrapped them around her daughter again. "More than you'll ever know."

"Charlotte. It's time to go." Vivian prodded in her annoying way from behind.

Charlie rolled her eyes like the drama queen she was and hugged Mara tighter.

Mara stood, grabbing Charlie on the way up, snuggling her nose into her neck, drinking in the distinctive little girl smell. Somewhere between an open sky and fresh washed hair. "We're going to be together really soon, I promise."

"Shouldn't make those kinds of promises, Mara. Especially when you can't control yourself for a thirty-minute court session. Might work with the truckers you deal with at the bar, but obviously didn't work on the judge." The woman smirked while sizing up Mara from head to toe.

"Not around Charlie, please." Mara released her daughter to the caretaker, hoping her little girl's mile-a-minute escapades would divert her away from the confrontation.

"Got to say, though, it was pretty funny." Chase's mom put her hands on her hips and imitated the judge.

"Give me some new optics." She laughed loudly enough in her ridicule that people began turning their heads.

"Mom. Please."

Even Chase, immature Chase, knew this conversation was headed down a critical path. No one knew the meaning of entitled more than he did.

Vivian raised her eyebrows at her son and smirked yet again. "We need to get going."

Chase skulked behind his mother, following like the ball-less bastard he was, admonished by his mommy.

There were fifty things she wanted to spout at their retreating backs, but the ranting earlier left her depleted. The plug had been pulled; her words expelled. As her father used to put it, her very own reverse drain. Spewing water and gunk everywhere in its wake.

Chapter Two

Mara's mad worked into a bag of BBQ chips, chocolate bars loaded with nuts and caramel, and a two liter of diet soda. Then it took on a more practical approach when she determined she could tackle her bar job while her insides churned. Unfortunately, a trucker got a little too handsy with a coworker, and she shoved him. Drunk and stumbling, he fell onto another table, and they all fell to the floor in a heap. The truckers laughed. Her boss hadn't. Sending her home to practice her Zen, whatever that was. Not to mention losing a night's tips. She pouted, ranted at the contestants on one of the ridiculous reality television shows, and finished her pity party with a tub of cookie dough ice cream.

Something in there worked. When Wyoming went from gloomy to sunny, she decided two days off was better than one. Firewood got chopped, stored, and she even tackled a couple of wine stains on the carpet. Ending the somewhat productive day, she binged a season of the newest medical drama. Wishing, more than just a little, for their successful hospital lives to become her own.

Sunny got tired of hanging out in Wyoming and made an about-face into grisly. National news, hunker down, type of grisly.

Oil rigs shut down. Trucker momentum took a break from the roads.

At her bar.

A blast of cold air swept through the packed tables, causing Mara to glance up.

A new one. A new one out of his element and unprepared for the weather.

Oil field, definitely oil field. Thank God it wasn't another trucker. The bar remained full of them, locking down before the brunt of the storm hit. The heaters in their semi cabs would run full throttle in the parking lot tonight. Hell, she and Angela would run full throttle tonight. They made their bread and butter off the oil guys who wanted nothing more than beer to drink, more beer to forget about their backbreaking work. Truckers? Noisy, obnoxious. Angela called them the crude crew. But all of them tipped—and tipped well. Which was why she couldn't quite find her way out of the life. Hopefully she could make up for the last couple of nights off.

Angela hustled the other end of the bar, making her tips with low-cut T-shirts and her size four, maybe six, hips. Mara's tips were made with her stellar listening skills. The Rock was the best money an unskilled, uneducated girl could make anywhere in Rock Springs. The judge may not agree, but a girl's got to pay the bills. And her mother's bills. And her ex's bills.

The new one weaved through the crowd. Walked with an oilfield, my-shit-don't-stink, swagger. She wiped the counter and grabbed an empty, turning her attention to the guy in front of her. Swagger man would head to the empty stool in front of Angela's T-shirts. Guaranteed.

Running a quick rinse through the dishwasher, she put four shot glasses in front of her, filled them to the tippy top with vodka, and slid them across the counter to one of her best customers. She caught a finger raised and glanced at the end of her section, surprised to see new guy sitting there, eyes drooping, waiting patiently.

He smiled as she drew close, and the twist of his lips changed the angular shape of his jaw completely. All his harshness melted somewhere into the wood grain of the bar.

"What can I get you?" she asked as she put a bowl of stale peanuts in front of him.

"Whatever you have on tap is fine." The voice was low and sure, but soft, contradicting the severe angles of his face and tightness of his shoulders, and damn, all of him.

Pulling a coaster from under the bar, she put the glass down. "You're not from around here. Oil field?"

"Maybe." He cocked his head. "Is it always this bone-chilling cold?"

She laughed. "You are in Wyoming. It's empty, desolate, and for a good part of the year, yes, bone-chilling cold."

"Mara?" Angela hollered. "Can you get a couple pitchers to table four? I'll get their food from the kitchen."

She nodded at the new guy and hustled to table four.

"Man, you guys are hopping tonight," the new guy said when she returned and replaced his empty.

She scanned the crowd. "Truckers got to hunker down when the big storms roll in. The rest of them are our regulars. Are you just passing through?"

"Yes," he said simply. One word. The smooth voice begging to be listened to, but he didn't appear to be in the mood for indulging.

"Let me know when you're ready for another. I'll

run you a tab."

He nodded. "Did the other girl say you have food?"

Mara yanked a menu from under the counter. "If you want to call it that. We've got Hank in the back, manning a greasy kitchen. The food's not terrible, just not five star worthy."

He had sleepy eyes, weighted lids, making him a hard read. Especially when he looked down, which he seemed intent on doing.

She put his burger and fries in front of him, telling him to be kind with any online reviews.

He just smiled. And she tried not to melt any more than she already was.

After serving an ornery table of three old-fart truckers, she hustled back to the bar. One of them slapped her ass and found himself in one of her infamous headlocks. A better alternative than her shove the other night and having to navigate herself home minus a night's tips. Even in his half drunkenness, the old trucker knew he was no match and backed off.

New guy held up his finger for the fourth time in an hour.

She swept his plate and silverware into the dirty dishes bucket and pulled the handle to deliver him another beer. "Are you sure you don't want a shot of something?" She waved at the collection of liquor bottles behind her. "Your something unpleasant is going to get expensive at some point."

He ran his finger along the grain of the wood, up the condensation of the glass. His hands were large and calloused. Workingman's hands.

Refusing to bite, or speak apparently, he looked up and smiled.

Twisting around, she grabbed up one of their generic, bar-grade bottles. "You look like a tequila man."

"A tequila man, huh?" He raised one eyebrow, motioned with his finger for her to pour. "Are you sure you want to call that tequila?"

She glanced at the bottle, thought again, and grabbed up a bottle of Sagebrush, her mid-grade agave tequila, and held it up for inspection. "Better?"

"I'm impressed." He nodded as she was poised to pour.

"So, a man who knows his tequilas. A man not in his element with this weather." She glanced at his ambiguous touristy ball cap. "You're from Texas."

He extended a killer smile that swept all the sharpness away in an instant. "And how would you know that?"

"Simple." She looked at his hands, at his chest. "We get a lot of oil guys in here. But oil guys in Wyoming are different."

She nodded at a customer a couple of bar stools down, held her finger up to new guy.

He shot down his tequila and winced, looped his finger as she got back to him. "You realize you'd be laughed out of the Lone Star State with your tequila selection."

"Maybe, but that means I'm right about the Texas part though."

He rocked his head from side to side. "Perhaps."

"Ball cap is a dead giveaway." She floated her head sideways to indicate the packed bar. "Wyoming boys wear them backward, trying to look cool, or what they think is cool. Texas boys are already confident, wear their caps like grown men should." She was flirting, but he was a safe sort. The kind just passing through on their way somewhere else. Not like he'd be interested in her anyways. Since the courtroom visit—her sweet and salty explosion of junk food continued, ending last night with an entire key lime pie. Instinctively, she glanced down the counter to Angela. But here new guy sat, had sat. She knew better than to read anything into that.

After three shots, he slowed down, nursing his beer, staring so intently at the coaster, there had to be something unpleasant and deep going on. There was no way one night on her barstool would touch his problems. No matter how many shots he did.

But in an instant, his buzzed ass stared at her with blue eyes, glacier blue, burning straight to her insides. She liked to think she could hold her own looking someone in the eye, but she was the first to look away. She didn't need anyone trying to analyze her lengthy list of problems.

"Do you have family here?" she asked, trying again. She'd never worked so hard for a conversation. Two nights off diminished her let-me-into-your-world vibes.

"Huh?"

"Mom, brother, sister? What you Texas boys may call kinfolk?"

She didn't miss the flinch when she said brother. She also didn't miss his eyes lighting up and the bite at his lip when mentioning a sister. Within ten short seconds he pulled out a photo of not only his sister, but two adorable nephews, in full cowboy attire.

He put his credit card on the bar and returned the pictures to their sleeves. After he signed the receipt, he hitched his hip and jammed his wallet into the back pocket of well-worn, faded-to-soft jeans.

He tipped his cap, looking over the crowd for a minute, and turned his hat around backward, making her laugh. "Does that make me blend better?"

"Maybe. You'll have to tone down the swagger when you leave."

"Alrighty then. Mara, is it?"

She nodded, kind of shocked he'd remembered anything. He looked like he could be lulled into sleep in about thirty seconds.

"Very pretty name," he said. "Luke. Luke Whitten." He thrust his hand forward, making her wonder if she kept him from walking out the door, if he might welcome her listening skills into his pain. She could definitely listen to that voice all night. She snapped herself out of her thoughts and giggled.

And he had a name now.

"I was so right. Even your name reeks of Texas."

Chapter Three

Half of Luke's body hung off the bed when he woke. He rolled onto his back and stared at the yellowing ceiling of his room. A sliver of light peeked through the blackout curtains, the wind now nonexistent. After his swaying, stumbling trek across the parking lot last night, he wasn't drunk enough to insulate himself into thinking Wyoming was anything other than fucking freezing.

His head lolled to the side, and he managed a blurry glance at his wrist. Once his watch transitioned from hazy to focused, he was shocked to see it was after nine. His internal military time clock usually rousted him long before dawn. Fortunately, he'd never been one to experience extreme hangovers, even with the excessive tequila and beer chasers last night. With his destination unknown today, it was probably a good thing.

A month ago, his second stint in the Marines had ended and he'd decided not to go for round three. Two weeks ago, he'd stood at the massive wrought iron barrier of his ancestral home in San Angelo, Texas, hoping his ties to the big W at the tippy top would not just taunt, but grant him entrance.

Hope was a strange word though. Building up your heart, then crushing your dreams into little more than a fairy-tale mirage.

The shiny metal speaker box stood proud on a pole next to the gate. Inanimate, but still mocking those, like himself, who didn't know the digits.

When the gates had rattled open, his father's massive diesel truck idled, then he exited.

Time supposedly healed all things, but when he'd stood in front of his father outside the gates, he wasn't sure time passing was the case. Would ever be the case.

Once his hero, now just another damaged, faulty father.

After a brief shuffle of reintroductions, an argument about respecting their city and not being a delinquent, his unanswered request of whether he could stay at the house for a few nights lay between them. Unanswered because his stepmother returned. With a mocking look and a knowing smile, she'd kept driving.

"I think you know I can't let you," his father said. His eyes downcast as he dug his cowboy booted toe through the dirt.

Luke hated when he did that. The old hung-head shuffle he used to call the tap out. He wanted to shout at him to be a man, be a father.

"Can't or won't?" he had spat.

Stubborn maybe, but hurt mostly, he'd put himself back into the saddle of one of Claire's horses and headed back down the road to his sister's house.

After a healthy dose of nephew nighttime snuggles, he'd taken the coward's way out and disappeared himself while his sister was at work, leaving a tented note next to her coffee pot.

I can't breathe here anymore.

Somewhere in New Mexico, creating distance laid the groundwork for his beaten and battered soul. Accusations and tangled up lies from his dad and stepmom weren't what he wanted out of life any longer.

He touched the classic watch with the outdated metal band his father had given him at fourteen. The timepiece may last forever. The relationship? Not so much.

He'd made a hard right in Albuquerque, and well into week two of his road trip, he took a little time to play tourist in Durango then hit the road again, heading north, ending up in Wyoming. Yesterday, sleet began leaking from the clouds, sending his beat-up truck skating and circling across a deserted highway. After hydroplaning to a heart-attack inducing stop on what he hoped was the road's shoulder, he picked his way to the first exit he came across. The run-down motel advertised a vacancy with hissing neon letters. Across the parking lot of whistling wind and icy drifts sat a shack of a bar.

Luke rolled onto his back and smiled at the ceiling, remembering the aging door of the nondescript bar. Although the "O" wheezed in and out, most of the gaudy letters were in place. As a huge movie buff, the ramshackle bar called The Rock seemed like a sign.

Eighties and nineties movies were his thing. Yippee-ki-yay could be spouted from his mouth at any given time. For any reason.

This morning his stomach began protesting. Bar thoughts, and signs of his destiny, would have to wait. The steady roar of diesel engines was enough evidence the road was in motion again.

An old trucker smoking a cigarette outside his room said there was a diner four exits down, but the guy seemed in the throes of a heavy-duty hangover, so it might be thirty.

Turned out it was two.

The location pin on his phone showed he was in

Rock Springs, Wyoming. He smirked. Kind of made sense now, the bar name. The phone faded to black, waiting for him to punch in an address, something.

A horn honked in front of him, and the driver left the driveway with a wave to someone.

He glanced around. "Not too shabby for a hick town."

A chipper, informative voice on his phone began spouting off a dissertation about hick towns in general and a song of the same name.

"Shut up."

The phone went quiet.

Those new beginning adventures reemerged today. After last night, every shot of tequila loosened his pitiful tongue. What could he say? He felt like wallowing, and the bartender girl was a good wallower listener.

He looked at his phone again. "Go west, young man."

Making a hard right, he went west.

Ten minutes down Interstate 80, the highway became a traffic jam of semis. His little pickup, overshadowed by diesel mammoths. It gave him a chance to look around at the beauty of the mountains, their whitecap tips touching the sky. Last night, nothing had been beautiful, but in the heated cab of his truck, Wyoming was quite gorgeous. All white and green. Mountains, not hills. When things began moving again, the highway patrol motioned drivers off the road and into a rest stop.

The bright sunshine made the cold tolerable. The expensive lightweight jacket he picked up mid trip in Durango did its job, keeping him warm and comfortable.

He walked the on-ramp from the rest stop to the

highway, curious to see what the problem was. There were several truck drivers on the side of the road, arms crossed over their down vests.

"Any clue what's going on?" he asked an older man in a beanie, making a note he needed to pony up for a beanie to go with his fancy warm jacket.

The man pointed down the highway. "Hell of a storm. I'm going to miss my delivery in Salt Lake."

"They should have rerouted you if the dispatchers had any sense," one of the other men said.

They all laughed about the stupid-ass dispatchers, safe in their terminals somewhere.

"Might as well get some sleep. Going to be awhile," the older man said, nodding at Luke. "Only seen this happen once before, and that was a helluva long time ago. We're going nowhere fast today."

Luke thanked him and walked farther down the ramp, feeling fortunate there was nowhere to be anytime soon. He kicked at a sheet of ice on the road and maneuvered to the dead grass, so he didn't slide on his ass and make a fool of himself. He peered in the direction the other gentlemen had looked, holding his hand over his eyes as the sun blasted up and over a mountain top.

He said it to the bartender last night, to himself plenty of times in the last couple of weeks, but in the valley before him, his new reality stared him in the face.

Rushing, as if it had somewhere to be in a hurry instead of considering all the people inconvenienced, the Green River raced up and over the asphalt of the interstate in the distance.

The End of the Road.

Luke pivoted on the dirt, taking in the white mountains, the pine trees snaking up the incline into the bluest, widest sky he'd ever seen. All the air a man could hope to breathe.

Rock Springs would be a tough town if bartender girl were any sign. A tough town built with tough people who weathered tough times with grit and tenacity.

He cocked his head and smiled. He'd fit right in.

Chapter Four

Mara found herself fascinated with new guy's words. Greater than his preacher-worthy sermon about the end of the road, she wanted to breathe real air again.

Texas Luke wasn't a bad point to muse either, but his drunken ramblings were appealing in a way men just weren't these days.

Mara couldn't imagine the thought of leaving everything behind. He had sat at her stool until they were getting ready for the last call, rattling on the drunker he became, spilling tidbits of a story. A family who didn't want him—that too was in some ways appealing. Hers wanted too much of her. More than anything, she craved a fresh start with her daughter, a fresh start at a career she loved instead of the survival-of-the-fittest job. No, she didn't have the luxury of hitting the road, leaving her mom, her ex, walking away from her nothing job that paid her nothing bills. Her real was a beautiful little girl. Enough real to make her want to step up and make life work again.

She needed an abrupt change, needed to put on her big girl panties and thrust herself into the life she wanted.

Punching the elevator button to Rachel's floor in the three-story government building, she breathed deeply, then made her way through the aisles of eight-by-eight cubicles. This was not going to be a pleasant visit, but they needed a plan, and she needed to be mature, bite her tongue until it bled if necessary.

Earlier this morning, Mara stood in front of the mirror, sucking in her gut in preparation for this meeting. She was dressed in her best pants, her best blouse, her best—okay—her only blazer. And honest to God, even a little makeup. Clothes and mascara didn't matter for this meeting, but fake it until you make it, right?

"Give me a list, and I'll start plowing through," she said as she sat.

Rachel looked at her, dropped her pen onto the yellow legal pad in front of her, and sighed. "This isn't 'a list' "—she made air quotes at that—"sort of thing, Mara. Everything we have been working on, down the drain with your outburst. I told you they don't want to hear what a piece of scum Chase is."

"But he won't—" Mara interrupted.

"Cutting you off because you're doing it again," Rachel said, casting her hands upward. "We're not going to worry about what Chase is doing, what his mother is doing, what your mother is doing."

Mara leaned forward, opened her mouth, and Rachel held her finger up. Rachel had been one of her best friends long before she needed an ally in the social worker's department. She was not only amazing at her job, but she was also beyond loyal. Though sometimes a good thing, sometimes a bad thing, Rachel could always be counted on to pinpoint where you screwed up. More times than not, right.

"My job is to get you Charlie back. Your job is to do everything I tell you so next time in court, you're more than empty words. I get the fact that this is unfair, but let's not give the court any reason to deny visitation the next time. The faster we get started, the faster a judge will give you what you want." Rachel took her hand and squeezed it. "This is for Charlie; this is for you."

The tears welled, but Mara refused to feel sorry for herself. She embodied a whole host of emotions in the wake of Rachel's honesty. Annoyed, grateful, stressed. The list went on.

The end of the road must be something like a rock bottom. She and Texas had something in common after all.

She wasn't sure she wanted an end to this hellacious road, maybe just a bend. A last turn into a cute cottage-style home, with her daughter playing happily in the front yard. She wanted to be happy too.

"Alright. Where do we start?"

"First, get yourself enrolled in school and finish that nursing degree."

Mara sighed. "I need money to do that."

Rachel slid a scrap of paper across the desk, her nauseatingly neat writing glaring in lime green ink. "This is the financial aid director. She's expecting you. You'll be in debt when you're done, but worth it. You and I both know how much you love to take care of people. Your grades in high school and college are your ticket back in. You were made to be a nurse. Maybe volunteer at the hospital and see how the process works if you have some spare moments. They will love to have the help, and I think you would enjoy it too."

"But my mom relies on me in my spare time."

"Unfortunately, everything from this point forward will come at a cost." Rachel speared her with a gaze so intense, Mara's skin erupted into goose bumps. "Charlie. Mara. That is your mantra for everything right now. Okay?"

Mara looked into her lap. She didn't know what life looked like without taking care of the world. Her dad when he fell ill. Chase, because he could do nothing for himself. Chase brought in the mother-in-law. When she was younger, she had always been that kid taking care of the sick animals, the sick kids—a primary reason why she had been drawn to nursing. A perfect fit. Just a petrifying fit. But she had loved nursing school, even through the numbing, sleepless, studying nights.

"Charlie. Mara," she whispered.

"Exactly."

"I've emailed you some job prospects. You've got to get out of the bar."

Mara closed her eyes, nodded. The all-star cable package would have to go. The eating out would have to go. Hell, her mother's occasional bingo night would have to go. No doubt Chase would have a full-on fit. She always had a little extra cash to hand him when he claimed Charlie needed something.

She could do this.

"And then you get to the doctor." Rachel pointed right, left, up, and then down. "It's not about looks, being heavy or not heavy. It's about health. Not just physical, but mental. We need a good, solid doctor's report. We need to go in there in sixty days and say bam, bam, bam, we did this. And bam, my health is solid, I work out like a bad ass, and I've lost ten pounds in the process. Bam!"

She didn't know anything else to say but okay.

She could do this.

Charlie, Mara. Charlie, Mara.

****

Pulling her beat-up old sedan into the driveway, Mara turned off the ignition and slumped, wanting to melt into the seat. She released her hair, scratching and clawing her head as her hair fell, hoping to relieve the tension. She spun the elastic between her fingers, realizing the full impact of the judge's and Rachel's words.

The house before her, the same one she grew up in. When she left Chase, there were a slew of excuses she fed herself about the logic of moving back home. Who lives with their parents at twenty-six years old? Then the answer to her non prayers, the bar job. She'd rented a cozy little house in the wrong part of town, but it was hers. And back then, Charlie's. Every other week that is. In the wake of the divorce, her mother offered up her old room. She had been teased by the deal on the rent but embraced the freedom of shaking off Chase and moved into the house she still resided in now.

After leaving Rachel's office today, she responded to one of the job prospect emails, had an interview an hour ago. Not surprising, the pay was just a smidge over minimum wage, but she'd repeated her mantra, refocused, and here she sat.

Mara dropped her head onto the steering wheel, left it there.

The judge said she had choices. She wanted to laugh at that forty-eight hours ago. Now, her heart sped up and calmed. Choices, decisions. Both were in her hands.

Mara grabbed her bag and girded up. She'd avoided her mom's calls in the last week, so she prepared for her mother and her thousand questions.

"How'd court go?" The screen hadn't even closed behind her.

"Rachel and I worked together a new plan after, you know, I did the run-my-mouth thing in court."

Her mom groaned and smiled at the same time. "God, I wished I'd been there."

"No, you don't. Not one of my better days. Chase and Vivian… I took the bait."

"Did they remove the supervised part at least?"

"Nope. Told me to quit whining and get my life together. A few statements about bad choices, my weight, education, my job." Mara sighed. "Yep, strip me down, toss me aside."

Her mother chewed on her lip. Like she always did when she was disappointed. "But you have a job."

"I do. A job in a bar is another stellar choice of mine," Mara said.

Her mom sighed. "At least you work."

Mara smiled at the support her mother always gave in overwhelming heaps, whether she was aware of what she did, or not.

"Rachel's plan?"

Mara crossed the room and picked up a photo of her mom and dad at their twenty-fifth high school reunion. Side by side with a yellowing prom picture from a lifetime ago. There was the comparison. There was where she fell far short of a lifetime with the love of her life. Her father passed not long after that reunion, crippling them both.

She'd handled her divorce as well as could be expected. Chase balked about paying child support, didn't feel he should have to because it was a joint custody arrangement. Roadblock after roadblock had been tackled behind the scenes, and surprisingly, Charlie's life remained seamless. End goal complete.

Until that day.

Chase let her sit in jail following the DUI.

"Shows you can't handle life on your own, doesn't it?" He'd let out a long-winded sigh. "Come back. We'll be a family again."

"I'll only get help if I stand by my man?" she had responded.

His silence, the answer.

That particular price had been too high.

She returned the pictures to their side-by-side positions, turning to find her mom waiting her out.

"Do you think I could rent my old room from you? I can offer two fifty a month." She hoped her math skills were on target with a minimum wage job, child support, one dinky credit card bill.

"Hmph." Her mom leaned back into the cushions, crinkling up an eye that showed every laugh line she'd ever been awarded. "It's a small room. I'll have to take that into consideration. I'll counter at a hundred."

Mara fell into her mom's open arms, letting them wrap her up. Comforting in one way, disheartening that she couldn't handle life on her own, in another.

"We'll work that plan. We'll get that little girl home where she belongs."

Chapter Five

Never having entertained the idea of returning to the classroom, Mara did little happy dances in her head when she enrolled in nursing school for the spring semester. There'd be a mountain of debt, but fortunately, she'd been so close to graduation when she quit previously, it would be more like a hill than a mountain. Excitement loomed large and intimidating at the thought of learning everything about being on the front lines of health care. Every morning, she looked forward to facing the day instead of dreading what the unknown may deliver.

Passing round one, she made the second round of interviews as an intake and insurance processing clerk at the hospital. The same—well, only hospital in Rock Springs, where her end goal included wearing a name tag with those two little letters—R and N. Two weeks later, a phone call asking when she could start. She quit the bar that weekend.

The excitement welled when she shared a day visit with her daughter. The aimless chatter, and her daughter could definitely talk, left her smiling from ear to ear. They shared peanut butter and jelly sandwiches at the picnic table in the backyard of Chase's family home. Even that didn't dampen her spirits. And she was rewarded when her daughter leaned across the table and whispered loudly enough for the neighbors to hear, "Bestest day, Momma. Gramma doesn't let me talk when we eat. She says it's not po-polite."

Mara wanted to whisk her away. Together, they were going to have way more "bestest days."

She said nothing to Chase's mom as she left. She was not going to elaborate about anything going on behind the scenes, what drama their next court appearance would deliver. Complying, not complying, Mara couldn't care less what they thought.

The dreaded doctor's visit, court imposed physical, freaked her out more than any classroom or instructor ever could. In hindsight, the rest seemed simple. Today, someone would weigh her, something she didn't even do herself anymore. Normally, she ran a truth-or-dare game in her head to force herself to stop in front of a mirror. How she felt, every pound being lugged around like an extra appendage, in the reflection. She could still walk for good distances. Climbing stairs would set her panting, but who didn't, right? Internally, her knees were taking a beating, some nights necessitating more than a couple of ibuprofens. Her very unhealthy fast-food diet was not doing her heart any favors either. Or her cholesterol, or her blood pressure.

She was all about good news these days. So, the good news: at the end of this day, she'd have a starting point. Whatever fate, numbers on the scale didn't scare her anymore. Much.

Enough, she admonished herself.

"If you can step on the scale, sweetie," the same nurse who had said it her entire life instructed.

"Do I have to?" she whispered, glaring at the machine while holding her breath.

Mara sucked in everything and readied herself.

The nurse cocked her head. "Two seconds. It only

hurts for two seconds."

"That sounds like something you should be saying to a five-year-old coming to get their kindergarten shots," Mara mumbled.

"Oh, I've said it plenty of times to them too."

Of course, the damn thing sat smack dab in the hallway connecting all the rooms. She toed off her tennis shoes, dropping her bag on the chair beside the scale.

"And with an all-time high…" Staring at the scale, she could almost hear the announcers voice in her head. Holding her breath, she willed the stupid contraption into submission.

The scale didn't listen of course. At least the nurse said nothing as she motioned Mara to exam room four.

As she waited on the doctor, she tucked the gown around her thighs. When she left Chase a year and a half ago, she knew what she weighed because he made her get on the scale every Friday and log it into a small, spiral notebook. Berating her, yelling sometimes, sometimes not. Apparently, it didn't make any difference because she closed her ears, knowing she felt fine, knowing she could still fit in her jeans, sort of. She'd been so sure when she left him, her weight would drop without his incessant pressure. And it had.

Then "that night" happened.

Pounding her fist into her stomach, she realized she had to get this under control. Since she'd been a teenager, her weight had been a lifetime of the continuous up-and-down game. Never really about how she looked, always about how she felt. And she hadn't felt good in a really long time. Now that her mom was on board with all these changes, she'd said they could work through the changes together. Get healthy together, end the cycle, together.

A slight rap sounded at the door, and she straightened her back, sitting as tall as she could on the table, her thighs and pretty much everything else straining the gown for the world to see.

Gird up, Mara reminded herself.

"Mara, where in the world have you been hiding yourself? I'm glad we're getting you all checked out." The doctor looked at the file. "Good Lord, you haven't visited me in three years. I'm offended."

Mara looked away, hating she had let herself go in all the drama of her marriage and divorce.

"Never mind, never mind. You're here now. That's all that counts. You look good. Anything I should know about? Any concerns?"

"I feel okay, really, I do. But I'll be honest, I'm here because…I know I'm overweight and I need to do something about it. And I'm starting school again, finishing becoming a nurse, and this…" Mara's fingers pointed up and down her body. "I don't want to be the fat nurse."

The doctor had the good sense to just nod. "Well, then, we can deal with diet and exercise later. I want to make sure your insides are ticking the way they should be. Lie on your back for me, okay?"

Mara lay back and let her push and prod. A nudge to her upper belly left her gulping in a breath of air. The doctor looked up from her stomach to catch Mara's eyes.

The doctor smiled and returned to touching tender areas. After an intrusive minute, she called a nurse in to do the dreaded PAP smear.

"Breathe deep for me."

Mara sucked in, the intrusion of the cold instrument going where nothing had gone in quite a while.

More notes were scribbled, and Mara was helped to a sitting position.

"So, the good news: I'm not seeing anything major. We'll know more when your labs come back though. Your blood pressure is on the high side for your age, but that can be attributed to the extra weight. With that being said, I'm guessing your cholesterol is high also. I can put you on medication, but if you're serious about getting some weight off, we can try that route first. A lot of times eating better, taking a walk a few times a week, may do the trick."

"I'd rather do that. I'm kind of in that getting-myself-together phase of life, and this could get me in some good routines for when I get my daughter back."

"I'm going to stop you right now. Don't do this for your daughter. Do this for you. You may think it's a selfless, noble act, but things don't work that way. Not permanent things. It never sticks when you're doing a weight-loss program for others. The emphasis needs to be on you, how you feel. Then, we can get to what's real. It's not in any way, shape, or form about how you look. It's about how you feel."

The doctor was right. You can't carry anyone else on the journey, including the cutest kid going, if your life is a mess and you're not happy with yourself in the first place. She'd learned that in one of her post-divorce counseling sessions, forgotten the therapist's words by the time she got to her car and buckled herself in.

Mara heaved a sigh of relief; this was not going to be as bad as she thought. The number on the scale wasn't her issue. How she stood, how she walked when she was her best self, her strong self, those were the hurdles she wanted to tackle. When your knees hurt and your feet swelled, you resorted to shoe shopping. You get two or three chins, so you start wearing V-neck T-shirts. Then you wear leggings and sweats to have a degree of comfort as your ass spreads. She looked down at herself and didn't see the fat girl, the almost fat nurse, any longer. She saw a work in progress.

"How about activity? Is there something physical that puts you in a good frame of mind? Something as simple as a walk around the neighborhood." The doctor glanced up from her notes.

Mara reflected on the kickboxing classes she'd taken post Chase. They made her feel skilled, confident, strong on the inside as well as the outside. They did more for the head and self-imposed stress than any candy bar could.

She remembered coming out of those classes sweaty, bone tired, but standing taller. Simple self-esteem did strange things to people.

Some people are truly happy at whatever size. She admired that. That girl was not her. She was done being a whipping post. Done being physically, emotionally, and yes, mentally damaged.

Leaving the office, she imagined she'd be down, feeding herself all kinds of guilt-ridden talk, but it wasn't like that. There was still a long way to go, but the farther she got into this journey, the more empowered she felt.

Next up—work this damn plan, stand truly on her own two feet, and get her own little house for herself and the talkative little blessing she'd given birth to.

Chapter Six

The holidays hadn't been easy, but Luke managed to come out the other side. He'd even finagled a Christmas dinner invitation from one of his new friends and their vast extended family.

Within a day of arriving and roaming Rock Springs, Luke landed a job. The first place he walked into made an offer. He accepted the position on the spot, making for a quick and easy start in his new home. Experienced oil field workers, even semi experienced ones, were hired with only a few questions asked. A few summers in college worth of experience had been enough of a ticket. At the most basic level, he'd been exposed to the all-encompassing oil industry early on, always shadowing his father and the ranch hands.

Wyatt Oilfield Services was a contractor for Silverwood Oil, a big Texas outfit. Everyone in oil, whether or not from Texas, was aware of Silverwood. Technically, Luke would be employed by Silverwood, but the job was Wyoming based, the guys he worked alongside, Wyatt employees. A safety manager of sorts to start since he knew a little about that too.

Wyatt also offered a bed and three hot meals a day in their housing camp, but Luke didn't want that way of life anymore. He found a small little bungalow-style house in what he heard was a decent part of town. There didn't seem to be any wrong side of the tracks here. Rock

Springs was a blue-collar sort of city with one working class neighborhood blending into another. What Luke loved most was the Whitten name meant nothing in Wyoming. All the realtor cared about was whether there was enough in his account for the deposit and his first month's rent. The years in the Marines had been good in more ways than one. He had been able to stash almost everything he made for years on end. His old pickup sat proud in the driveway, mudded up, and looking more weathered nighttime sky than its original navy. The first night, he slept in a sleeping bag in the small living room. Since then, he'd hit garage sales and thrift stores for furniture. A trip to a local discount store rounded out his kitchen and linen essentials.

Life since running into the Green River had transformed into excitement at each new day. All he'd ever desired was to work hard and drop dead at the end of the day with a smile of contentment on his face.

Homesickness skirted the edges of his heart today, leaving him moody and melancholy. Countless missed calls tallied up from his sister in his phone log. The voice mail count stood at twelve. The last, a week ago.

Claire picked up on the first ring. "I should hate you."

He coughed to cover up the emotion her voice evoked. He allowed himself a moment to miss and embrace all he had left behind.

"But I can't," she said. Even the comforting sound of her coffee maker in motion made his heart skip. "I was hoping you'd be back by now."

He picked up his beer, made his way to the tiny deck off the kitchen. His blood had thickened. January in Wyoming brought snow last night, sunny skies today.

Outside, he shrugged into his jacket. Inconvenient to have to suit up every time you stepped outside, however, the view of bare aspens against an endless sky justified pretty much anything. "I had hoped so too. I'm not so sure anymore. Not right now anyways."

A sharp intake of breath escaped her.

"I wish I could be there today though. With you."

"I've been doing the anniversary of mom's death by myself for a long time now."

There was nothing to say. Good intentions meant nothing if there was no follow through.

"You're stronger than I am," he whispered.

"Pfft, I'm just more of a glutton for punishment."

Cancer stole their mom from them before they had a chance to seek any significant treatment. Their lives torn into thin little strips of barely hanging on. The family followed, fading in grief's wake.

Claire was the peacemaker. Prancing around the big gaping cracks in their family, skirting hairline fractures. They hadn't spent the anniversary together with their dad for too many years to count.

"I wish you were here. I don't want to visit her grave by myself."

Luke rubbed his neck, threading his hand into his hair and squeezing his head. He'd visited the hill of green before he'd pointed his truck westward, risking disappointing his dead mother once again. It had been a perfect fall day with the wind in his ears. The birds chirping away, ignorant of the mess the Whitten family had made of things. "I wish I had the strength to go with you. I'm doing a lot better, but sometimes, I don't think any of us will be alright ever again."

"Mom would hate this. We were her world."

"And yet, here we are."

"Best memory," Claire's happy, not maudlin, voice returned. "You first."

He laughed. "Easy. Sixth grade. When she stomped into the principal's office with me and not only cussed him out for suspending me, but her fingers and hands were all flying around like she would lift off any minute in a little spaceship or something."

"Well, you did tell old Mr. Colson to fuck off."

"Deservedly."

"Oh, I'm aware." She giggled. "Little Luke could do no wrong."

He sobered for a second. Little Luke could do everything wrong. "You go. Best memory. And it better not have the word horse or pony anywhere in there."

"Ouch! Give me a second." She took a loud slurp of her coffee. "Remember the year mom and I hiked up the hill through the snow on Christmas? The one in back of the house? We sat and soaked in the sunset, butts freezing while we drank a thermos of hot chocolate. So simple. She told me all about when she was a little girl and how much she loved…those words I cannot say in this moment, among other things."

"Love you, Claire," he blurted. "I don't know how I'd have lasted without you in my corner all this time."

"Happy thoughts, dude. How is it there? Wait, where is there?"

He huffed. "Let's just say I found my end of the road in the beauty of Wyoming."

"No shit? Damn, Mitch and I were kind of hoping California. You know, sunshine, zero humidity, amusement parks. Shall I go on?"

"You could, but you'd have to find another brother

to make…" He bit his tongue.

Claire ignored his slip. "I'm glad you're feeling settled. Job? Friends?"

He looked at his watch. "Both, thank you very much. As a matter of fact, meeting the guys in a little bit, so I need to get myself in gear."

"Dumping me for a new crew, huh?"

"Never." The job was a job. Friends—that was his superpower. Whether they were the ones he'd known his entire childhood or the few he dragged into his mess of a life in the military. Here, he'd settled in just as easily. Basic men, the majority with families, kids, and eating dinner with their in-laws on Sunday afternoons. Over the short time he'd been here, they had become comfortable with him, and like Christmas, he was soon being invited to Sunday dinners at one home or another. He was fast becoming a crowd favorite because he was always eager to babysit so they could take their wives out.

"You take care of you."

He smiled at her words. Always their goodbye, even if it was just a trip down the street.

"You take care of you." He put his own hand to his heart, lifting his fingers to the airwaves in the sky.

He pushed himself from the back step. Earlier today, when the crew said they were heading to the other side of town to a bar called The Rock, his smile broke loose immediately.

The bar looked different in the daylight, but altogether the same. Still a dive, with several greasy, mud-ridden trucks in the gravel parking lot, but thank God, no ice whipping around his ankles. He was now comfortable in long-sleeve shirts, thermals. As he strode in and spotted the guys at a table on the far side of the room, he glanced toward the bar. The place was a whole lot cleaner, and the help didn't look like they were running ragged.

Defiantly, he turned his ball cap around backward. The only trace of Texas he wanted was the twang his buddies said made their own girls' ears perk up.

As he sat, they were already bashing the other new guy who'd just been hired. The one who thought he was better than all of them combined because he had worked in the sand fields of Alberta.

"And where are you now, dude?" one of the crew said. "Sluffing with the rest of us. You would think he'd understand, in Canada, the jobs go first to the Canadians. He thought because of his experience, he shouldn't have been let go."

"Take note Whitten, your Texas ass could be booted from our crew. We're allowing you into our little circle tonight. Congrats."

They all laughed.

They turned when the waitress sidled up to their table, tossing coasters at each of them. Luke recognized her from his first night, the big boobed one. She tossed her hip out, asking them what they wanted. They forced their eyes upward.

Rowdy, the senior driller, circled his finger in the air. "Couple of pitchers. And not that Lite shit."

Luke raised his eyebrows, nodding at Rowdy's gut playfully. "Sure?"

"Fuck you, Whitt."

Luke held his hands up in surrender. "Just trying to help."

"Hey, what they say when you reported the pressure line deviation?" his friend Brad asked him.

"Handed me a stack of forms and told me to write it up. Wiggins thought the fluctuation might be an equipment failure. I imagine they'll get maintenance involved. And not Wyoming maintenance, but Texas maintenance," Luke said, grabbing the pitcher and pouring.

"You saying our maintenance isn't as good?" three of them said at once.

"Whoa, whoa, I'm just saying this would be on Silverwood's equipment. Their property, so their responsibility. We're just the labor, remember?"

Brad looked at him. "You think the infraction will get reported?"

"Above my pay grade, man. But I think they have to—legally, I mean. No one wants a lawsuit, so I would guess yes."

"We've only been working on this rig six months or so. Shouldn't be anything wrong. Drill down, hard left, drill horizontal." Rowdy thrust forward a diving hand and then a horizontal plane in front of them.

"Shit, I'm not saying there's anything wrong. Just doing my job." Luke dropped his head back. "Thought we were out for a brew, not to talk shop."

"You got that right." Brad plopped his head into his hand. "My old lady is driving me nuts with all the stupid baby shit. I plan on being the last one out of here since she let up for a day."

"Just remember with all her 'stupid baby shit' drivel, you're the one who sent your little guy swimming in the first place," Rowdy reminded him.

"We've been chatting here, Whit. We have questions," Brad said. "Dave here works in the office. Onboarding, whatever the hell that means. We're not trying to pry, but he said when he ran your packet, you came from oil land. We all know you're from Texas, but you're from oil and cattle baron Texas."

There was no question posed, lying there just the same.

Luke glanced at the TV over the bar. A baseball game was in progress. He didn't like the prying, but he assumed they were just normal curious. Fully enjoying his new present, he hadn't really had a conversation about his past. Rock Springs had maybe been a simple end of the road, but it was as good of a place as any to lay his head for however long the good times lasted. The job may not be his life's calling, but it paid the bills and gave him a purpose.

For the first time, a sense of healing left a calmness. Not the angsty, my dad's done me wrong. Maybe because he was making his own way, maybe because he'd just talked to his sister.

"I come from a massive spread in west Texas," he said, using his index finger to spin the coaster. "Grew up running the land, trailing the oil guys, training horses. Fully operating ranch, land rights for oil, leasing rights for natural gas. The imposing figure at the helm, my dad." He shrugged, thinking of his father. A perfect personification of a Texas cattle and oil baron. "The land's been in my family for generations."

The men leaned forward. Whoever said only women craved gossip? Roughnecks and drillers were just as proprietary of the underrated skill.

"And you left?" Rowdy raised his eyebrows. "Dude, you're a fool."

"I want to make my own mark. Have my own..." Luke thrust out his hands. "Something."

"Be your own man," someone said.

He nodded. Four words described what he was after. You always want what you don't have, and to him, they all had it. Grass is greener scenario. He hoped to find the same someday. Maybe here. Maybe even a little overexaggerated moaning about his old lady driving him nuts with all the stupid baby shit talk.

As the night wore on, and he reflected more on the four words, he glanced toward the bar. Remembering something the bartender said his first night in Wyoming too.

Grabbing the empties, he headed for the bar, juggling the glasses while trying to pull out a decent tip.

Luke set the glasses down. His efforts not quite as nimble as the server, but they landed on the bar and clattered to a standstill. Boobs tossed a giggle over her shoulder, heading his direction. She really was cute, but really cute in the way where she flaunted how cute she was. He'd had enough of that shit in college.

No more relationship games he had decided in those endless miles getting here. Female or otherwise.

"What can I get you, cowboy?"

Feeling a hint of a dimple in his smile, he raised an eyebrow. "Another pitcher," he said, passing the empty her direction.

As she filled, he leaned across the counter so she could hear him over the loud chatter. "I was in here a couple months ago, the night of the bad storm?"

She glanced up as the pitcher hit the halfway point. "Those storms pack us in for the night." She set the pitcher down, grabbed some fresh glasses.

"I was passing through then. Now I've settled here, working with those idiots." He pointed back at his table.

"There was another bartender here. I think her name was Mara, maybe Marla? Like you said, the bar was crammed and loud."

"No, you're right, it was Mara."

"Is she working tonight?"

"She quit. Not long after that night if I remember correctly."

"Oh." He didn't know where his unanswered questions went from there.

"I thought she was a lifer like me, but she had to get a different job."

"Oh." He stammered, not knowing what else to say.

But the woman kept feeding him information. "We're both single moms, the money's good here, but the optics of a bar job aren't the best. And…"

Luke leaned in but she didn't continue. "Well, I just wanted to thank her. She was a great listener, and I got shit faced and rambled forever. Not one of my finer moments. I hope she's doing well."

The waitress set six shot glasses on the bar and filled them with whiskey. She slid them across the lacquered surface to the man sitting in the stool next to where he stood. The man and his friends lifted in unison, grabbed their pitchers, and wove through the bar to an empty table.

"Mara is queen in the listening department. You can think it's for the tips, which yeah, we're all trying to pay our bills, but she's a good person. I'm jealous she got out of here, but proud of her too."

Luke nodded, thinking about his first night. He hadn't been so drunk he didn't remember how in tune she was to everything and everyone, not just him.

"The bar job had to go, though. She's trying to get

custody of her daughter back. And she's got her moron of an ex. Doesn't help."

Once again, all Luke had was an "Oh." He wanted to ask why, stuck on the mother losing custody thing, but it wasn't exactly any of his business.

He carried the pitcher back to the table and topped everyone off as they all stared. "What?" he said, glancing around the table.

"You going to hit that," Brad nodded at the bar. "You're the only single one here. She looked willing. The rack was able."

His cheeks heated, and he pasted on an "aw shucks" cover-up face.

"See, I told you." Rowdy pounded his fist on the table. "Good for you, Whitt, good for you."

The conversation wound around the pipeline again. The older two rattled on about accidents, one experience after another. They didn't shut the bar down; the wives and girlfriends won out. When texts started, the phones vibrating, they all started bitching and complaining, and as if on autopilot, began sliding from stools and heading toward the parking lot.

Chapter Seven

Mara found being back in the classroom much like a drug. The energy to spend hours every day in class, in labs, in clinicals, then to head to the hospital for the night shift only to rinse, repeat the next day. Forward momentum propelled by happiness, pride in herself, and most of all, the desire to be a better mother for a little girl. As it stood, this semester would be a lock on a close-to-perfect GPA. If she could repeat again in summer, she'd be a nurse by the time the leaves turned and fell.

The afternoon of her last final required the most precise timing. Charlie didn't care for her dance, tap, jazz class, reiterating the only thing good about the lengthy class was the pink tutu. It didn't mean she didn't expect everyone to attend her recital and sit in the front row. Mara had made the promise weeks ago, long before the schedule for finals was determined. Dance and school times butted up against a very slim line tonight. Like every-light-better-be-green to be doable.

The teacher flew into the room, twenty minutes late, amid a flurry of excuses. The instructor was no nonsense. Mara had seen that each day in the classroom and again when her request to take the exam early had been denied. Mara tapped her pencil trying to speed up the passing out of booklets, while trying to figure out if she could answer a hundred questions in forty-five minutes. Fifty, if she ran to the parking lot and snuck into the back row of the auditorium. Charlie would put on her mad little pout face, but Mara knew she would be forgiven.

Clinical theory hadn't given her any problems over the semester. This exam was like a loud grandfather clock ticking away in an empty house though. Nerves taut, she forced herself to slow down and pace herself. More important than rushing, answering correctly. She fast calculated she could still pull out a B in the class if she answered sixty percent of the questions. As long as sixty percent were all answered accurately. It would drag down her GPA, but she could still keep her daughter happy, still finishing her classes with just one semester remaining.

Ten minutes before she needed to be three blocks over and maneuver herself into the dance building, she began jamming things in her purse and walking to the front. She'd answered sixty-five questions, confident they were all correct, leaving a small reserve for an incorrect one here or there. Hopefully the back row would be dark and vacant.

"I have somewhere to be." She handed her packet over.

"We all do," the instructor said, leafing through the booklet. "I'm surprised by you. Isn't this important to you?"

"I have a four-year-old who's important too."

She hit the hall and ran full out, sliding through corners, wishing she had a remote starter as she huffed her way across the parking lot. Luckily, she'd shown up early enough to get a third-row parking spot. The music blasted to life from her speakers, and she was out of the spot with the clock only having ticked away four of her minutes. One red light messed up a clean front row slide in, but with darkness encasing the auditorium, she was able to slip through the doors before they closed. Amid a couple of apologies, she slid past an older couple and a bored teen playing a game on his phone.

Ten pink tutus strutted onto the stage, springing and scissoring to the left, back to the right. Her eyes watered at how confident and adorable Charlie took her dance steps. Of course, outdoing every other girl out there. Twenty legs sashayed to a little jazzy dance, crisscrossing their knees and hands, getting a little tangled up and grinning themselves out of their scrambled-up limbs. Scuffing to the side, five of the bodies, including Charlie, disappeared. Mara strained her neck, wondering why only five of the girls were doing another ballet number. When the music ran down, Charlie and four others tapped their way onto the stage in leotards, an array of rubber ears fastened to their headbands. Each girl portraying a different animal. Charlie, playing the tiger, roaring aggressively, making everyone laugh. Her little pink cheeks with streaks of eye liner or mascara for the whiskers were beyond adorable. Charlie told Mara and pretty much anyone who would listen about her second favorite costume, a leopard print body suit, and black tights. Loving the crowd and the stage, her diva innards hammed it up.

Three songs later they were all taking bows and curtseys. Short and sweet. Priceless.

When Charlie spotted her, she waved excitedly. Mara clutched her heart and threw a million kisses from her lips, her hands fanning outward toward the stage. Charlie flailed with little spirit fingers, grabbing the bulk of them back to herself.

A quiet hum of chatter began, and Charlie folded her

arms and glared at the front row. "You were wrong, Grammy V. I told you my mom would be here."

People began staring at Vivian, who ducked into Chase, filled with shock. Mara was never so glad she'd blown off a test. Whatever the outcome, whatever the price she had to pay for pissing off a teacher who controlled her future, it was worth it.

Mara rushed to the stage, held her arms out, and Charlie jumped. Her heart was so full, she missed the talk around her, the social stigma Vivian had set in play prior to this moment.

"You were gorgeous, baby," she whispered into her ear.

"I know."

Chase maneuvered himself from behind and put a possessive arm around Charlie, pulling her away from the embrace. "You need to apologize to your gram."

"She lied." Charlie shoved him. "She said Mommy had better things to do and wouldn't be here."

"She wasn't in the front row, like you wanted." Chase held her face. "That's what Gram meant."

"You're wrong, Daddy." Charlie grabbed his cheeks after he bent down. "But I understand." She patted his hand, pulling some kind of kid-style role reversal.

Mara wasn't sure she herself understood, but as long as her daughter did, she could live with it. Talk resumed around them. People drifted back to their own families, their own drama.

"And there she is." A bouquet of roses pushed their way toward Charlie, the dance teacher following. "Our little star."

Vivian touched her hair and preened, taking a quick glance around.

Charlie took a sniff. "Mommy, did you get me flowers?"

Mara clutched her heart, wishing she had thought of the kind gesture. "I'm sorry, baby. I didn't. The flowers were very nice of Ms. Everett."

"Miss, actually," the teacher said, batting come-hither eyes at Chase.

Charlie started into a monologue about how flowers were pollinated, but Chase and the teacher were eating each other up with their eyes. She'd guess teacher was after a tumble with her ex, probably a second one. They were familiar enough they flirted openly, but Ms. Everett was still in the impress-the-daughter phase.

"How about we say thank you to Ms. Everett," Mara said pointedly. "Then I believe we were going out for ice cream, right?"

Vivian glared. "Charlotte, your mother has to get back to class. School always takes precedence over little girls and ice cream."

"Grammy V, you're silly." Charlie pirouetted, her hair lifting and settling again after she twirled. "I want chocolate, with rainbow sprinkles. No, strawberry and chocolate both and…"

A high scream rose from the other side of the room, and everything lapsed into silence.

"Richard, talk to me. Oh, my God."

Everyone turned toward the commotion. Whispers about someone collapsing or fainting floated around in hushed murmurs.

A woman screamed. "Call 911!"

Mara maneuvered her way through the circle of a dozen or so people surrounding an elderly man. He had both his hands at his chest and gasped for air. In the harsh fluorescent light, his forehead was damp with perspiration.

There were at least four phones in different people's ears. A million thoughts raced through Mara's head. Every single one of them at odds. Fear and anxiety. Confidence and a cool calm. She not only was in her final semester of nursing school, but she'd been the one to demand Chase and his mother go with her to get CPR certified right after Charlie was born.

The closest fire station with an EMS unit was ten minutes away. She forced people out of her way until she got to the center. She collapsed to her knees at the man's side and checked for a pulse. His heart rate raced. "I know CPR, can anyone help me?" She looked around, and everyone shook their heads. Someone hollered an ambulance was on the way.

"You can't do this, Mara." Vivian tried to yank her away from the man. "He may die. If that happens, you will be at fault."

She wrangled herself free. "I have to help. Chase, can you help me?"

"Don't you dare," Vivian growled.

They were wasting precious time. She checked his airway and began chest compressions. Counting in her head and switching to deliver rescue breaths. Maneuvering a human was more difficult with a real live person rather than a practice dummy, but essentially the same. She repeated the rotation three more times. A ruckus erupted at the auditorium doors behind her. Readying to switch again, a gurney stopped beside her, and a paramedic tapped her on the shoulder and took over the chest compressions. His counterpart put a mask over the man's nose, and they counted to three and lifted him to the gurney.

"Great job." The paramedic winked at her and rolled away his charge. The man's wife following as they exited the building.

Everyone thanked her. The adrenaline ebbed, but the sense of accomplishment didn't. She didn't lose her cool. She didn't falter under pressure.

One of the little girls hugged her knees. "Thank you for saving my papa."

Mara squatted and hugged her, looking around for her own little girl. There was no Charlie, no Vivian, no Chase. She ran outside and caught them turning the corner, Charlie high atop Chase's shoulders. She sprinted to catch up.

Vivian glared at her as she caught up. "You can't be doing that. What will people say?"

"Thank you?"

"And if your rescue attempt had gone bad? If he died?" Vivian planted her hands on her hips. "What would you tell your little girl then?"

Mara counted in her head, attempting to calm her racing heart. Just a moment ago she'd been proud, felt good about herself for the first time in a long time. It was one thing to be trained to act, quite another to plunge in and do it. The best awkward, real world, initiation.

"I'm becoming a nurse, Vivian, whether you agree with the choice or not. I was trained to help. I helped. I don't know what you want from me," she said. "Let's just go get some ice cream."

Charlie scrambled to get down.

"You were not invited," Vivian snapped. "If you're going to be divorced, be divorced. You don't get to be a parent when you want, not be a parent when you feel like doing your own thing."

"What are you frigging talking about?" Mara yelled. "This is between me and your son. It has nothing to do with you. I came to the recital to see my daughter. As far as I know, that's what parents do. Divorced or not."

"You just can't keep coming in here and upsetting…"

Charlie sobbed and hugged the nearby parking meter. "Stop fighting. I don't know why everyone can't stop fighting."

Mara's heart broke. She'd have to go away tonight. Without ice cream. Without a little girl's endless chatter. Vivian would die on her "I'm right" hill before she'd walk away.

"Baby." She squatted and wrapped herself around Charlie's tulle waist. The leotard was so soft. Her daughter needed a little soft before she conquered the mishappen world she'd been born into. "You go have ice cream with daddy, okay? We'll celebrate another time. Just me and you."

The sniffles stopped; the tears abated. "So, I get two celebrations?"

"You do." Mara hugged her. "You're one lucky little girl to have so many people who love you to the moon and back."

"To the sun and back." Charlie giggled.

"You're entirely right. The sun is way better than the moon."

Charlie held her hand out. "You've got yourself a deal."

Chapter Eight

"Isn't this place perfect?" Mara spun in tiny circles in the middle of what she hoped would be her new living room.

Rachel looked out the huge picture window facing the street. "Fenced front and back yards."

"You donned your social worker hat at a new warp speed," Mara said.

Just five minutes ago, Rachel and she were like stupid teens talking about their first real apartment. With Charlie at stake, the kitchen needed to be scrutinized for functionality. The bedroom for ample room. The bath, for cleanliness.

Unsupervised visits were granted earlier in the year. The judge impressed with all she had accomplished in a short period of time. Determined to blow the judge's socks off at the next round in court for weekend visitation, she had hoarded her pennies for months now, preparing to move into her own place again. She still had to finish up the summer semester, but the interim night job at the hospital had given her stability on a financial front and also downtime for studying.

"Is the fridge included? Or the washer and dryer?" Rachel asked as she opened the fridge for whatever reason. It wasn't like they were going to stock the shelves for potential renters.

"The fridge, yes." Mara slid past Rachel in the

galley kitchen and opened the slatted doors at the end. "The connections are in here for a stackable washer dryer unit, but they're not included."

"You can rent those for about thirty dollars a month," the realtor offered.

Mara asked her a few other questions about the normal cost of utilities, knowing how thin her budget would be stretched with this house. Once she drew a nurse's salary, everything looked promising. She wanted this house; it already felt like a home. Her home.

"There will be yardwork." Rachel walked down the hall to the two small bedrooms, took a peek at the one bathroom.

Mara nodded, thinking about the lawn mower at her mom's house. These days, her mom had a gardener, but Mara had mowed the yard enough times, she imagined she could handle the small front and back yard.

"This room could be Charlie's. It's a pretty color. Kind of between butter and a banana," Rachel said from one of the bedrooms and returned to the main room.

"No doubt she'll want to splash some purple around." Mara flung a make-believe paint brush at the walls.

"You can't paint, but you could do purple curtains and a comforter."

"Gaudy, but yes, I can sell all things purple."

They walked back into the living room, and Rachel tapped a loose baseboard into place with her sneaker. "From the court's point of view, this area's a great family neighborhood. Close to work, close to your mom for your backup system. Charlie's daycare is only a couple miles out of the way, and bonus points for falling in budget."

"Besides being my best friend and all, your court's point of view is my final approval. Thank you for that."

Things were definitely moving now in every facet. She filled out the rental application, signed with a huge grin and a whole lot of flourish. Laying down the deposit, she crossed her fingers and toes the owners would pick her to be their new tenant.

****

Charlie's hand clasped tight in her own, Mara stood on the outskirts of the park. Her daughter was jumping out of her jewel-incrusted sandals, staring wide eyed at the mayhem before them. Mara had been included in the hospital's annual picnic honoring healthcare workers. Every kind of playland fantasy for a four-year-old lay before them. The smell of funnel cakes drenched in grease drifted her way, but the old jean shorts she slid on earlier today felt so good, she might be able to resist.

"Mommy, can I get face painted?" Charlie and her sandals scanned the field. "And a balloon animal, and oh, look, a fishing thing. Can I get a goldfish? I want a puppy or a kitty so bad, and Daddy says Grammy's 'lergic, so I can't. Maybe a fishy would be okay." Charlie began dancing on her toes in unrepentant excitement. Mara and her mom, who came also, each grabbed a hand and waded in.

"Yep, fishy too." Mara shot a quick look at her mom, who rolled her eyes. If nothing else, the fish could stay at her new place—once she moved in that is.

A clown greeted them as they ventured forward. Charlie pulled hard in one direction, then the other, unable to focus on one thing at a time.

Mara knelt and held her cheeks. "Baby, we can do everything. We're here all day, so let's just take one thing at a time, okay."

"But daddy said I could only stay until lunchtime. I want to do…" She spread her arms wide and spun.

Mara cursed Chase for putting a timeline in Charlie's little head. She had told him the picnic was an all-day affair. Especially since she had been recruited to play on the admin's team for the baseball showdown. It was, without a doubt, why her mother insisted on coming. Her words were saying she could keep Charlie entertained. Mara personally thought her mom wanted to have humorous stories to share. Whatever the case, she thumbed a quick one-handed text to Chase and read it aloud so Charlie would know they were clear.

"Let's make a plan." Charlie stood in the center of the game area, her finger in her mouth. After a brief moment, she pointed at the fish booth. "Start here. Then go here, here, here, here." She pointed from one to the next until Mara and her mom nodded.

"Good plan, but how about we save fishy booth until last? That way, if you do win one, we don't have to carry Mr. Gold the whole time."

"You're silly." Charlie threw her hands up. "But okay." She walked toward a face-painting chair. "But I'm not calling him Mr. Gold. I'm calling him Mr. Wiggles."

Mara's mom laughed. "What will we do if it's a Mrs. Wiggles?"

Mara nodded at her mom's shoes. "I told you to wear tennis shoes. We're going to have a hard time keeping up."

"There's nothing better than running after an excited little girl. I know that from firsthand experience. So, you just try to keep up."

Mara laughed and got her own face painted. Then her mom opted for the same. Charlie had them all in her "silly" category before they pulled themselves from the first booth, painted up in purple butterflies and pink unicorns.

Three booths in they realized Charlie's loot would overwhelm them at some point.

"I have a tote bag in the car. I'll be right back," Mara said as her mom and Charlie made their way to the beanbag toss.

Midway across the field, she saw her boss dressed in geometric patterned capri leggings, with a lime green tunic hanging to mid-thigh. Seeing everyone in street wear was weird, out of context. At the hospital, her boss's hair would be in an efficient little bun. Today, there was a wild and curly vibe.

The woman hugged her. "I'm glad to see you were able to come today. Especially since we need warm bodies on the team."

"Well, I'm a warm body, but that's about all I'm going to be good for." Mara pointed out her mother and Charlie. "Thank you for the invite. My daughter is having a blast. I think my mom is having more fun than Charlie and I combined, and we just got here."

"We're just happy to get as many people out as we can. We make the event an all-day affair. Staffing the hospital at the same time gets a little dicey. You're one of the lucky ones with today as your regular day off."

Another woman walked up to them, and her boss introduced her and slipped away.

"Mara, I hope you don't feel overwhelmed because our haphazard, but carefully orchestrated introduction came off flawlessly."

"Oh." Mara's stomach flipped, knowing this woman was the head of nursing. "Is there something wrong?"

"Not at all. I wanted to talk to you outside of the hospital. I have heard so many great things about you, and I want to make sure when you finish school, you'll consider our little hospital first. You'll have opportunities in larger hospitals, but we do really value you already. You're a hard worker and Elaine says you're a quick learner. On the academic side, I'll admit I have friends at the college in teaching positions, and I know your grades are outstanding."

Mara's heart sped up. She fought the urge to touch it. She was so excited. She should be saying something but didn't have a clue what that should be. Professional? Witty? She settled on grateful.

"I really appreciate your kind words. I hadn't considered relocating. I'm a single mom, and my daughter's father is here. Right now, staying in Rock Springs makes the most sense for my family." Mara halted, not wanting to go overboard with too much personal data. "I was hoping my break from school didn't affect my employability. And..."

The woman cocked her head.

Mara lowered hers and kicked at the grass. "I have a DUI. A misdemeanor, but still."

"You leave that part to me. Okay? I love underdog stories. I raised three kids on my own. A single parent is a whole level of difficulty most people don't understand. The DUI throws a little more of a wrinkle in things of course, but we've all been through rough times. Admitting mistakes are the easy part. Reassessing and getting back to having a good life takes a lot of hard work. Your grades and work ethic more than make up for your indiscretions."

"Thank you. I'll be in contact once I finish."

The woman smiled, and with a brief wave, she sailed off to a couple of doctors who were motioning her over.

Mara held herself back from skipping to her car.

****

Tapping her foot on the little white square, Mara grinned wide. Amazingly, she hit the ball. It flew past the oncologist at third base and swept far into the outfield. Not only did she get herself on base, but her teammate had huffed his way to third. They were still down by ten runs, but who was counting?

When Charlie's little voice echoed through her plastic bullhorn, Mara fought herself from not to bursting into ugly, happy tears. "Whoop, whoop. That's my mommy," the tinny voice squeaked out, making everyone laugh. Then Charlie stood on the bleacher seat and did a little happy dance.

Their team never closed the gap in the score, but the game itself was a lot of fun. At the end, the doctor's team took bragging rights for the year. Same story, different year.

Chatting with a few of the other admins, the head of nursing gave a quick wave. Mara turned to locate Charlie and found her mom holding a baseball on the pitcher's mound and a man showing Charlie how to hold a bat. The man was all kinds of tall and lanky, gorgeous with longer beachy hair. Endearing Mara further, he was beyond patient with her lefty daughter. As he instructed her how to hold a bat, then swing a bat miles too big for her, the awkward try caused a well of laughter to bubble up and erupt.

"Mommy, Mommy, I'm going to play baseball. I'm

going to learn to hit, then catch, then, I already know how to run, really fast. Mr. Max says I can be a good player if I practice lots." Charlie jumped up and down and faced her grandma pitcher. The man shimmied her sideways, and she straddled the plate. "Watch this. Nana, let it rip."

Her mom did a long, drawn-out windup. Mr. Max put his hands on top of Charlie's and choreographed the hit perfectly. The ball did a three-bounce skip toward Mara. She grabbed it up and tossed it to Mr. Max as Charlie spun her little legs wildly, racing toward first.

Max laughed and with arms flying outward yelled that the runner was safe.

When Mara made her way to home plate, the man stood tall, and damn he was good looking the closer she got. He had to be six or seven inches taller than her, with hazel eyes she could drown in if given the chance.

"That is one adorable little girl you've got," he said.

"Thank you. She is pretty special."

"She's got some great energy. She would be a good athlete. I coach a soccer team for four- and five-year-olds. I'd love to have her if she's interested."

Charlie danced around them both. "Please, Mommy, please. I would be the greatest player ever, I know it."

"I'll check with your dad and see what he thinks."

Charlie crossed her arms over her chest. "He'll say no because Grammy V says girls can't play sports with boys, because they're too rough. Grammy V is just stupid. Boys aren't too rough. I'm just as tough, and I can run faster than any boy at school. See, I'll show you." Charlie headed for the fences.

Max grinned with raised eyebrows. His own arms, popping with muscles, crossed over his chest. "Wow! Poor Grammy V."

"I suppose I should have a talk with her about the respect thing." Mara smirked. "Truth be told, kind of agree when it comes to my ex-mother-in-law."

"My lips are sealed. My ex-wife hates all sports and without a doubt would get along great with Grammy V." He dropped his arms and thrust his hand forward. "Max Kaufmann. I'm a physical therapist at the hospital."

"Mara Sawyer, intake. Thanks for working with her."

"Think about signing her up. If you can get Grandma or the ex on board, that is." He handed her a card.

Charlie barreled back to them, huffing and puffing, bringing herself to an abrupt stop. "See, Mommy, I'm really good at running."

"Yes, you are." Mara spotted Chase making his way toward them. "Thank you again, Max."

Max high-fived Charlie and she ran for her dad.

As they walked toward Charlie and Chase, her mom popped in at her side and nudged her shoulder. "You realize he was flirting with you, right? He's pretty good looking too."

Mara knew she was not the type of girl men normally flirted with, but with the confidence of the day radiating, she was coming to the conclusion she was more than just an overweight bartender. Flirting was what that man was doing, just as she herself was. Dropping the "ex" part into the conversation and noticing that he managed to do the same. But all she had to do was lay eyes on her daughter, and the thought slipped away.

"I know, Mom. It's not on the agenda for the near future." She nodded at Charlie rambling away at Chase.

He squatted down and listened with every serious bone in his body, making Mara painfully aware he may be an ass to her, but he was a pretty good dad.

"I want the shorter part of that duo. That's more important in this moment."

"I get it," her mom said. "I'll take Charlie to the playground so you two can talk."

"Thanks, Mom. I'm glad you were with us today. Such a great day."

"Kept up with both of you and everything." Her mom smiled, bumped her from the side. "Munchkin, let's go swing for a bit."

Charlie started jumping again, clapping her hands and running any number of words and sentences together at once.

"Lordy, child, do you ever take time to breathe?" Mara's mom said as she grasped the little hand.

"Grammy V says she's going to take my batteries out, but that's just silly. I don't have batteries…" It was all Mara heard as they walked away, words trailing after them.

Charlie and her mom walked away hand in hand.

"Your mom looks more like her old self. How's the chemo going?"

"Well, she's been in remission for a year now, so I'd say her treatment went pretty well. Quit looking for things to go wrong in my life," she blurted.

"You don't have to get snippy, sheesh."

Mara looked at her feet. She didn't want to fight. The high from today was already grinding to a halt now that she had to turn her daughter back into his hands. Their daughter, she reminded herself. The situation sucked, all of it. Even the end game, because all she could ever hope to gain was shared custody.

Chase blew out a deep breath. "In any case, I'm glad she's doing better."

Mara nodded and made a valiant effort to calm down. "Charlie wants to play soccer. Can we do that for her?"

"She wants to ride unicorns bareback too. You don't always get everything you want in life."

Mara groaned and murmured something at the same time. Even she wasn't sure what it was.

"Can you think about it? I can help get her to practices and games. At some point the custody arrangement is going to get modified, and I'd like to see her involved in something other than dance, which, for the record, she hates."

"My mom thinks it's good for her coordination."

"What do you think?" Mara looked hard at him. "You're the dad. You get more than a passing say."

Chase ignored her, looking across the field as it was being cleaned up. "I think you should focus some of your attention on things other than custody battles. Get a life."

Mara did a quick shake of her head, wondering what he meant, or if he was just spitting out cruel words.

"Soccer is hardly the same as unicorn riding, but let's table this conversation for another day."

He nodded and yelled for Charlie. She flew from the swing, the wood chips jumping with the impact. She skipped across the grass in their direction.

Mara grabbed her up as she threw herself into Mara's arms. "I'm going to miss you, baby. You be good for Daddy."

Charlie rolled her eyes until only the white's showed. "I'm always good, Mommy," she said, smooshing Mara's cheeks together. "Say I'm going to miss you again with fishy face."

Mara did as she was told. Charlie giggled, and Chase took her from Mara's arms and lifted her onto his shoulders.

"Bye, Momma. Bye, Nana." She twisted her little body around and blew a hundred or so kisses as Chase strode toward his truck.

"That girl is the best of all of us."

That she is, Mara thought. *Adorable, quirky, fun, caring, sweet, energetic. A thousand other things, all good.*

"A good day. In fact, a really good day." Mara took her mom's hand.

And she had resisted the funnel cake urge with all kinds of positive vibes. Powdered sugar pastries became inconsequential without her even noticing.

Chapter Nine

The normally quiet emergency room was in chaos when Mara arrived. When rigs exploded in an oil town, all hands-on deck didn't begin to describe the fallout. Not to mention a great initiation for her first week as an official RN.

Men she knew, men she attended school with, arrived in a stream of ambulances. She hustled to do everything she could to keep up. Doctors rushed everywhere, and the nurse supervisor shouted at pretty much everyone as the men were loaded into rooms. The more critical rushed off to the operating rooms in the other wing. A rumor floated around the nurse's station that a man died en route, but Mara didn't recognize the name. A boy she dated for a short amount of time in her junior year of high school had been rushed into a room, and they were working on him. She sat with his wife and parents in the waiting room for a minute, but then she was called back to help with a man screaming as they set his broken leg. She held his hand as he squeezed until her fingers crunched. Shaking it off, she winced for a second, flexing her hands together and proceeded to her next patient.

"Mara, can you go with this man up to surgery?" the supervisor asked, tapping a gurney. "I know you don't have a whole lot of real-world experience, but this is training day. Times a hundred."

She rushed down the hall following the gurney, taking a hard right into operating room number six. The man's face was bruised and bloodied beyond recognition. She began setting tools on the tray as the doctor shouted.

"Goddamn oil companies," was all he could get out before he started trying to cut off the patient's shirt, quickly assessing and preparing to repair a deep laceration in the stomach. "This guy's lucky to be alive. One inch to the left and the spleen would've split."

The patient twitched and jerked. Mara looked at the patient's face; he was in oblivion.

The doctor yelled something at the attending, jolting her from her thoughts.

"You know him?" the doctor asked as he scraped at the burned skin, applying ointment, puncturing oozing blisters.

"Hard to tell," she said, trying to pay attention to how he treated the skin, running through the differences in first, second, and third degree burns as he worked. The burns weren't the brunt of this man's injuries—or maybe they were. He was too much of a mess to know for sure.

The attending flipped through a stack of paper on a clipboard. "EMTs said this guy rushed into the fire, trying to rescue the man who died. Explains the burns. He was thrown into the scaffolding from the blast." He stepped back. "Crazy stupid shit, who does that?"

"Let me see that." The doctor motioned at a rag hanging over the sink. Mara handed it to him, and he brushed his patient's chest, up to his shoulder. "This is why." The doctor wiped the blood clear from one side of the chest, revealing a mangled tattoo of an eagle's body, the head turned into the man's shoulder. The doctor touched a scroll beneath the expanse of the wing that spread across his chest, halfway down his torso.

"Semper Fi," the doctor whispered. "To rescue a brother. He's military."

The attending rolled his eyes. The doctor looked ready to cry for a minute and then regrouped.

"Semper Fi buddy, we'll get you fixed up."

"Will he be okay?" Mara asked, transfixed by the doctor's emotion.

The doctor nodded. "Long recovery, but not a death sentence. Not sure what these oil companies are thinking. What is he, twenty-five, six, maybe?"

"The money's too good. And guys this age? They never think about life and death. They think they're invincible," the attending answered.

Mara looked at the attending. He might be thirty. He had no room to talk. People did what they had to do to survive. She knew that firsthand.

She brushed the patient's hair from his brow. Taking the cloth, she wiped his eyes. He never stirred as she removed the blood and grime, picking bits of glass from his cheeks and forehead. The doctor butterflied one of the gashes, sewed up another on his cheek. They rolled him over and began assessing the burns on his back.

"He's going to need some grafts. Let's get these burns treated for the moment and get him into recovery. We can look at them better in a few days."

"Shouldn't the burns be dealt with now?" the attending asked, echoing her own thoughts.

The doctor ran his hand over the wounds. "It'll be better to see what happens naturally as the body fights to repair itself. He's young, in good shape. His own system can do a better job at this initially." He finished dressing the burns and rolled him back over. "Besides, there's more men out there. We've got to move on."

"Log him in." The doctor nodded at the counter and left the room. "Wallet is in his jacket pocket. See if there's someone to notify."

Mara pulled up the form on the tablet and dug the wallet out.

When she opened the man's well-worn billfold, she turned back to the gurney as two orderlies rolled him out the door. "Hold up."

She looked at the ID and then to the bruised and battered man. Apparently, his end had been Rock Springs. But she'd never forget the Texas-ridden name, though he now sported a fresh Wyoming driver's license. Brushing at the wad of hair on his forehead, she finger combed the strands out of his face.

What the hell, Luke Whitten.

The men rolled him away, and she searched the waiting room for a representative from the company. His wallet was empty except for a credit card, debit card, and the pictures she'd seen at the bar a lifetime ago. There was no information of who to notify in case of an emergency. In the waiting room, she called for anyone there for Luke Whitten. One of the company's management team stood up.

The man was already talking before he reached her. "He doesn't have family here. I'm not sure he's been here a year yet. I think I have an emergency contact at the office though. I can have my assistant look up his emergency info."

He'd been here since that night? Rock Springs, his Jerusalem? More like Sodom and Gomorrah.

"He's stabilized for the moment, but we'd like to

Kathryn Beck

notify his family. They're welcome to come and visit or call the doctor for updates. Does he have something on file authorizing us to talk to anyone about his condition?"

"Yes, we require an emergency contact before we hire." The man typed out a text to his assistant. "Do you want me to call?"

Mara nodded. "Yes, since you have the authorization, it would have to be on your company."

"Can you stand by in case they have any questions?" He held up the phone. "I've got a name and phone number."

"Sure. For a second. I need to get back to your other men though."

He held up a finger and thumbed the speaker button, moving to a private corner of the room as the phone was answered.

"Ward Whitten please?"

There was a long hesitation.

"Can I ask what this is regarding?"

"Um…" The man stumbled. "It's regarding his son. I'm afraid it's important."

"This is Mrs. Whitten, his wife. I'm afraid Luke and my husband are estranged, so I'm not sure he's available. Perhaps I can get him a message?"

Mara froze at the iciness of the voice and remembered again the drunken ramblings.

"Ma'am, there's been an accident." Mara leaned into the phone to speak, glancing at Luke's supervisor. When he nodded, she continued. "I can't tell you any more than that because of HIPAA laws, but he has signed a consent to notify his father if anything incapacitates him." Surely that was enough to get her moving. Then again, she wouldn't know as much as she did if she

70

hadn't listened to him ramble that night so long ago.

"An accident?" There was a long pause. "Is he dead?"

Mara and the supervisor both jerked back from the phone. The phone sat in the supervisor's palm, suspended, dangling, reeling with the unsaid. The supervisor raised his eyebrows, not knowing how to answer either.

"We can't give out that information," he finally said. "If you can give Mr. Whitten this number? I'm at the hospital with my men, but I can get a doctor if he wants an update. Otherwise, you can call St. Francis hospital in Rock Springs, Wyoming and ask after him. I'm sure they can get your husband to the right person."

"Wyoming? Good Lord, what has that boy done now?" she hissed. "I'll pass along your message. Thank you for calling."

The line dropped off and died.

Mara stared out at the parking lot full of cars, full of wives and moms and dads all here to be at the sides of their loved ones. People who cared. Luke had no one. Nothing. Just as he said.

"I'm going to guess that message goes nowhere," the Wyatt manager said. "Luke hasn't said anything about his past. Nothing. No wonder he landed here with no ties, no family."

"He had a sister."

The man looked at her and cocked his head.

"I met him when he first came to town. Seems like forever ago, I didn't know he had stayed. Can you see if the sister was on the emergency contact card?"

The whoosh of a text flew out, and an answer pinged back in just as fast.

"Nothing. Just the dad. I can't try to run her down, can I?" he asked.

"No."

"God, no wonder he left Texas," he said as he plopped into a chair.

Mara touched his hand. "Maybc he'll call," she said, trying to make the man feel better. Drunk or not, Luke Whitten had not been exaggerating about anything.

She shot a look down the hall where the world went crazy once again. The head nurse was frantically motioning to her.

Mara touched the overwrought man on the shoulder, his face slumped into his hands.

"I'm sorry, I really have to go. I'm sure he'll call. Let us know if we can help with the conversation."

Chapter Ten

Luke's hand wobbled as he raised his arm to massage his throbbing head. Feeling only gauze and cloth, he worked hard at opening his eyes. After four attempts, the light crashed through to his eyeballs, causing a radiating pain deep in his skull, far greater than the mass of pulsing tension already there.

A machine at his side beeped away.

Hospital. Accident. Reality came at him in waves.

The release of gas, the sudden, unexpected flow into the well bore, the subsequent fire. And then, himself, flying off the top of the rig and landing hard on the scaffolding as he raced to get men off the platform. The searing pain ripped into his back as he crashed. Rowdy's body was thrown into the sky with the explosion. Fire snaked high into the mid-afternoon sun. Then he must've passed out, remembering nothing more.

His head lolled to the side, where a few arrangements of flowers and plants sat. Little cards peeking out from the greenery made him wonder how long he'd been here. His mouth felt like he'd shoved a handful of dry and grainy whole wheat crackers in there at once.

Nothing came out when he attempted to speak.

An efficient-looking nurse rushed in. "Well, welcome back, Mr. Whitten." She held his hand, placing it at his side when he grasped at his mouth. "Let me get a doctor in here, and we'll see if we can remove that tube. You gave us quite a scare with the chemicals you inhaled in the accident."

He attempted to speak again, but she touched her finger to his lips, changing out an IV bag. He fell back into dreamland.

A metal tray hitting the linoleum jarred him awake again. The room was dark. Another nurse on duty, checking the tube feeding into his mouth. He grabbed at her hand, pleading with his eyes to get it out. Then his gaze was drawn to the bandages covering his hand and forearm. He looked at his other arm, seeing plaster from wrist to bicep.

Raising his head, he took stock of his lower body, wiggled his toes to make sure he could.

The nurse giggled. "You haven't lost anything down there, if that's what you're checking on. Let me see if I can get the doctor and he can remove the tube. Think you can stay awake for me?"

Nodding emphatically, he willed his eyes to remain open. He felt like he'd been slammed by a truck, and not a wimpy pickup like his either. More like full-on diesel. He fought the meds kicking in, needing to find out what happened to everyone. All he kept seeing was the flames shooting into the sky, himself flying before he could clamber to the top of the rig. Nothing afterward. Not how he got to the hospital, who the flower things were from, or who else may have been hurt.

A doctor took his pulse, shined a pin prick flashlight in his eyes, and checked his heart. After his eyes were checked, the doctor set to pinching and prodding around his shoulders and neck, down his arms. At the bottom of the bed, he poked at Luke's thigh, checking for feeling in multiple spots. Luke nodded at each. When he raised his bandaged hand and pointed at his tube, the doctor nodded.

His throat was scratchy and raw when the tube slid out of him, ripped out of him. Trying to clear his airway, he coughed hard, throwing himself into a coughing fit. The coarseness of his throat was like nothing he'd ever imagined.

"You'll be a little hoarse for a while, so don't be yelling at any of my nurses until you heal some. You're going to be okay." The doctor patted his hand.

"My friend? Rowdy Finch?" he gutted out. The voice didn't sound like his own. His voice had always been the hickish and smokey sort, much like his father's cowboy rasp.

"Oh, Mr. Whitten. I'm so sorry. He passed on the scene." The doctor stopped in the doorway. "The investigators are going to want to talk to you. I'm going to hold them off until you're stronger."

A tear fell onto the sheets as he stared out the window.

The nurse, who looked and sounded like his mother, arrived with a needle of something an hour later. Her hair cut at her shoulders with just a little flip. Classic, his mom always said. Even her nose turned up right at the tip.

"I'm going off duty now. You'll get the new girl for the midnight shift. Try and be nice." She patted his hand.

"Thank you for taking care of me," he coughed out, trying to smile through the sewn-up cuts and scrapes. He could feel the pressure on his cheeks and chin, lips that were parched and chapped.

"Aw, you're very welcome, Tex."

Luke closed his eyes. His mom always called him Tex too. There was no one he wanted more than his mom right now. Another tear crept down his cheek.

When he woke up again, the new-girl nurse backed into his room, a machine on wheels following her in. She ducked and squatted beside the bed, and whatever it was hummed.

Checking out the machine, she tapped it a few times. A steady white noise filled the room.

Luke attempted to raise himself up, tensing up as pain in his shoulders and back assaulted instead.

The bar girl. It looked like the bar girl. She looked different, but very much the same. Or perhaps, his mind was playing tricks on him.

Luke tried again to maneuver himself sitting.

"Whoa, big guy." She settled him and took his hand, cocking her head with the most beautiful smile he'd ever seen. "Well, if it isn't Texas Luke, back among the living."

The touch was so whisper soft; it was barely there. But it was there. A heart-stopping combination of feelings. Or maybe drugs. Who knew at this point?

Luke tried to speak. The sear on his windpipe squeaked out something that wasn't really anything. He concentrated hard and tried again. "Mara." His gaze dropped to her name tag, confirming. She wore sky blue scrubs with little orange suns on them. At her shoulders, her hair hung in short waves. The straight, serviceable bar tender ponytail was no longer.

"Not bartender."

Her eyes lit up from inside, turning brown, then amber, back to brown. "Please don't tell me Rock Springs was the end of the road."

She handed him a glass of ice water. The coolness felt good going down, easing the ache and soothing the burn.

"Turns out it was…You're a nurse now."

"They're pretty hard up for help these days." She fumbled with some tubes and checked his wrist where the IV was plugged into him. "I graduated a day after your accident. Don't be afraid, though. I can do surgery with the best of them."

Luke scanned her once again. Her fingers rested on his wrist, taking his pulse, her touch strong and sure now.

Something both external and internal had changed. She radiated, glowed. And her smile was so bright. A sunrise, not a sunset.

"You have…" Luke doubled over as a scalding pain ripped through his gut.

She settled him back into the bed.

"You look great," he mumbled. The pain killers hit, and he drifted off.

Chapter Eleven

Before going off the clock, Mara checked in and found him staring out the window. She wondered if he had slept at all. Earlier, awake and aware, he left her with an excess of nervous energy, checking all sorts of things that didn't need to be checked. He was eighteen shades of purple and orange, but still one good-looking man. Solid and soft at the same time, with hollowed out eyes, but full. Beaten down, but still bright. A mass of contradictions and adjectives.

"How's my favorite patient?" she said, walking in with a cheery smile.

He wiped his eyes with the sleeve of the hospital gown. There was nothing more breathtaking than a big man, a solid and tough man, letting their mushy side show. Kind of gave the world a little glimpse of hope and goodness.

On him, it was downright gorgeous.

"I'm sorry. My friend died in the accident."

Every sensitive thing she could think of saying got caught in her throat. Masculine, manly men, definitely big, bad Texas boys didn't share their thoughts and feelings. They clammed up, gave in to those bundle-it-up-inside rituals. The word desperado came to mind.

She got entangled in so many emotions about stereotypes of men and women—where the ideals of each initiated, where they ended. Why they never changed. There was indeed hope for the world if Luke Whitten were as real as the tears that dried into his cheeks.

"I'm so sorry," was all she could come up with. She'd heard all the placating words when her father died. Most times, they meant nothing in the thick of enduring grief.

The motor began humming as he maneuvered himself upright.

She grabbed a pillow and gently prompted him forward, placing the sterile, white casing behind him. "Let me help."

He scrunched up his un-purple eye. "So, a nurse, huh?"

She nodded and smiled. "I also needed my own road ending. Thank you for that."

In an instant, he pivoted away from his emotional display, mock tipped a hat. "My pleasure, ma'am. But if I'm remembering correctly, I was pretty plastered. I'm not sure I was giving any sage advice."

"You were pretty…shall we call it what it is? Plain, old drunk. But leaving your home and family, hitting the road wherever the asphalt took you? I wanted that freedom, so…here we are."

"Here we are," he said with a nod. "I returned to the bar a couple months later. I don't know why, maybe just to tell you my road ended." He laughed a deep and guttural belching laugh. "Quite literally."

"I'm glad things worked. Not sure Rock Springs is the promised land, but you do seem more, shall we say, settled? Calm."

"Until this." He flung a still bandaged hand at the room. "But honestly, I wanted to apologize. I was very selfish that night. You were hurting too. But I was so wrapped up in my own issues, I never asked. I just yacked and yacked. I'm sorry for that."

She stilled for a second, fumbling with equipment while she wondered what he had seen. How desperate had she come across? "I was the bartender; listener was in my job description."

He pivoted once again and skipped right over her uncertainty. "I guess you take your job description to heart. In all seriousness though, talking and listening is a two-way street. Even at a job like that. I am glad you got out though. Not judging, but in a town of roughnecks, it's no life."

Spellbound, Mara opened her mouth and couldn't think of what to say. To know he noticed, recognized her pain. Recognizing her messed up life without her saying a word.

Recovering, she crossed her arms over her chest. "Your kind is not so rough when you know how to handle yourself. The money was good. I've had to adjust for sure."

"Yes, I seem to remember a headlock on a graying trucker somewhere in there." He laughed and looped a finger at the whole of her. "You look different. I didn't recognize you at first. I'm not…"

Mara held her hand up. "My road wasn't so much a definitive place with an end, but a full-on U-turn. I needed to change everything. My health was just the tip of the iceberg. Still have quite a way to go, but…" She wanted to spin in little circles, waving her arms over her head in an exaggerated dance. The kickboxing classes were indeed helping her confidence. "I'm looking and, more importantly, feeling pretty darn good these days."

She stopped her want-to-be carefree dance. Everything in his gaze front and center, the constant contradictions were mesmerizing. His cheekbones, soft; his jaw, angular; his nose and ears, small; but his eyes, heavy and lidded, almost like he was half asleep while being fully awake. They were bruised, a weird shade of bluish yellow, but animated and fun.

She had to get gone. Her choices in the male species thus far hadn't panned out so well.

And she wasn't risking anything with Charlie hanging in the balance.

"I'm sorry, got a little carried away." She fiddled with his machines, topped off his water.

"Carried away looks good on you."

"Yeah, well, you're on drugs, so not sure your opinions hold much weight."

He wrapped his hands up in the sheets. "My boss said you were there when he made the phone call to my father."

"Is he dead?" The words from the same night of the accident caused an instinctive jerk in her. She'd never heard anything so painful, and she'd heard a lot.

"I'm sorry." She wasn't sure why she was sorry, but he deserved to know someone understood the pain of words. There didn't seem to be anyone else in his corner. She may have to live with Chase's words, but she also had her steadfast mom standing staunchly behind her.

He shrugged, pasted on a fake smile that did a reasonable job at covering up a mountain of hurt. The bed began rumbling back down.

"Get some rest," she said. "I'll be back with something to help you sleep."

Hesitating in the doorway, she couldn't help but cast

one last glance and found a now steely gaze on her retreating back. Like he was exploring and analyzing her from the inside out. Searching within for the origin of her pain filled past.

Absently, she wrapped her fingers around her waist to touch her lower back. Where the tattoo encapsulating the whole of her insides sat. Understanding with just the little she learned about her newest patient, he would understand the complexity of needs and freedoms.

A moment ago, Texas Luke's caring for his coworker became borderline painful to watch. Refreshing at the same time. The small lines fanning from scrunched together eyes, marked natural, and genuine hurt. Tears leaking like they held one of Wyoming's tallest peaks worth of heartache. He would be one who wept when he couldn't hold on to any more agony. Men didn't show obvious vulnerability. They bottled up their insides, letting them explode when the bottle got too full. Even her hero of a father buried pain where no one could see.

"Is he dead?" His stepmother's words slayed her.

She did alone, she did alone well. He was just beginning his alone journey. His vulnerabilities made him a dangerous game that no one could win.

Dangerous didn't work. Dangerous never worked.

Not when custody arrangements were involved.

Chapter Twelve

The detectives had made an appearance earlier today, leaving Luke feeling more than a little uneasy. They asked their questions in an accusatory manner, leaving the logical side of his brain going all sorts of directions. When the doctor redressed the burns on his back, they were very intent in their perusal of his injuries, asking more questions of the doctor than he himself had. He wished he could call his dad and ask his advice, wondering what the investigation team was after. When his boss told him yesterday about giving the "Whitten residence" lady the message, he looked at Luke with such a look of pity. The same one he'd seen on the bartender turned nurse last night, although she'd covered up her reaction with more compassion than pity. And she looked a whole lot better in general than his boss, so there was that.

After Mara left his room last night, he'd called his sister, needing to erase the pity looks, needing her calm voice in his ear. The moment she answered, he could tell she'd been crying. Her wavering voice split him in two. Especially when she explained the latest battle with Evelyn, their stepmom. Claire always tried to make everyone happy, hoping for an extended family she didn't have. He may not like what his family was, but he was a realist. Claire liked to dance around issues. When she rattled on about how her vacation plans with Mitch and the kids were interrupting a charity event Evelyn had been chairing, all his thoughts of sharing about the accident and his hospital stay flew out the window. It wasn't like he expected her to jump on a plane to be at his side. As he listened, he knew it was his turn to stand in her corner. Claire had done enough of it for him.

The accident had made the national news, and when she'd wound down, she asked about it. He brushed it off, said he worked that rig, but that was the extent. They'd signed off soon after. He'd tell her one of these days.

A few more guys on his crew showed up bearing some decent food. Wasn't the same as family, but beggars couldn't be choosers. Having company, even if it was just for a few hours, brought normalcy.

Mara pushed through the door just past midnight. "Alright, Whitten. Round two."

A smile crept onto his face. "Die, Sawyer. Just roll over and die. You suck at cards." He said it out loud, but the truth was, she was pretty decent. She was not easy to read, in poker or life. But she was here, the bright spot in a not-so-golden day.

She rolled a chair across the floor to his bed, glancing at her watch. "I've got a couple hours of downtime before I have to check charts." She dealt the cards, moving hers around in her hand.

"How were your days off?" he asked, laying down a card.

"Good. Were you a good little boy for the other nurses?"

"You know us Texas boys, primo in the manners department."

"Nurse gossip says a couple detectives visited today."

"Yeah." He went quiet, thinking of his next steps and wondering what they were really after. "I've got to go to headquarters in Texas when I'm cleared. Trying not to read too much into the request."

"How can they lay blame when a gas line busts? Isn't it just an unfortunate accident?"

Luke couldn't come up with a logical answer to her question. "Is there anything on the news? I can't bear to watch honestly."

"They just keep saying your friend's death is under investigation and they can't comment."

"I don't know what they're after. The only thing I can come up with is a 'who's at fault' sort of thing. Big oil, or the contractor I work for?" The jitters set in. He could lose his job, or maybe they were trying to lay blame at his feet. He smiled and shook his head at himself. He had always been the kid coming up with conspiracy theories.

"I've got a little time before they come back. The doctor wants these burns on my back to heal more, try some sort of skin grafts surgery. Not sure I want to go down that road. I might just see how my skin heals. It's itchier than shit right now."

"A lot of times you have to do the grafts. If it's just cosmetic, then they'll leave the decision to you."

"Does the procedure hurt?" he asked without thinking.

"Come on, Whitten, big strong guy like you? Are you turning away a chance to prove your machismo?"

He smiled, laid down a card. "Just seems unnecessary. I come from a family of klutzes; I've already got enough war wounds. Maybe this would add to my machismo?"

"I assisted the doctor the night you were brought in. I saw a few of those war wounds. Care to elaborate?"

The card he'd been about to play hung in his fingers, wondering which of the wounds she had seen. The shrapnel from a car bomb in Fallujah that was removed from his thigh? Maybe the stray bullet that had swept through his shoulder in a brief clash in Iraq? Or maybe the poorly sewn stitches from a wicked fall on a piece of glass when he was ten. That one was right down his forearm. There was quite the selection of wounds from a life spent on a ranch, in sports, in the military.

"Lean forward, let me peek," Mara said. "Sometimes it depends on how big of an area the burns cover."

With a still fuzzy, not a hundred percent head, he took a minute to remember she was talking the skin graft question.

She gently removed the bandage, and he winced.

"Sorry." She placed her fingertips on his back. They were cool and comforting. "This area is pretty damaged. Those were third degree ones. The ones on your arm are second. They'll heal better. You should just need them here." The sides of her hands outlined the affected area. "The ones on your arm and shoulder are probably going to scar."

"Not sure anyone would notice anything out of the ordinary there."

She replaced the bandage, the contact like a breath of air. He wondered how she did that. His hands were large and clunky, calloused with callouses. His father would call them workingman's hands. He shook the thought away; he didn't want to know what his father thought.

"Enough about me." He stacked up the cards. "Tell me about your daughter."

He laughed at the look on her face. "See, I can listen and be a drunk fool at the same time."

She walked around the bed, tucking sheets, propping pillows, tapping on a machine or two. "I should get back to the desk." She turned and smiled.

He cocked his head, recognizing clam-up time. "You said you had a couple hours. Last time I checked, there were sixty minutes in an hour. I'm not the greatest at math, but thirty minutes is barely a portion of one of those hours."

"Yeah, well. I try not to blab to my patients. This isn't the bar anymore. I take care of you. That's the deal with this job."

She shuffled from one foot to the other, stuffing her hands in her pockets, then played with the stethoscope hanging at her neck, finally landing with a death grip on the rail of his bed. Amazing how tightly she sucked herself in. What mom didn't want to talk about her kid?

He put his finger to his lips and crossed his heart. "I won't tell. I promise. Seriously, entertain me. Isn't that part of the job description too?"

She looked into the hall, no doubt contemplating a hasty and awkward escape.

"How about we start easy. Name, rank, serial number?" He nodded his head back and forth. "Maybe age would be useful too. For perspective, I mean."

He covered her hand gripping his rail, and she said nothing, staring at his hand atop hers.

"Please. Sit." He nodded at the chair and tried again. "My brain needs an escape from all the uncertainty of this shit."

Her gaze shifted to the chair she had rolled away from him with that same blank stare.

He gave up and pointed the remote at the TV. "At least watch a movie with me. Oh, shit, tonight's a '90s movie marathon."

"So?" she asked blankly.

"Sawyer, Sawyer, Sawyer, tell me you're not one of those?"

"One of what?"

He smiled, watching her relax and pull the chair back to his side.

"Oh, one of those morons that thinks our age has cornered the market for the best movies. The greatest movies of all time are '80s and '90s stuff. How could you not be a fan?"

Her smile curved into a grin. "Tell me you're not one of those ones who thinks the one with the Yippee-ki-yay dude is a Christmas movie."

Now, he was dumbstruck. And impressed. "Of course it is. One and two are set on Christmas Eve. That makes them Christmas movies."

"He protests too much." She plopped into the chair. "You're hopeless."

"A hopeless fan. Yes, yes, I am. I think you should go find some popcorn and settle in. I can recite this from beginning to end. You're not going to want to miss any of it."

She rolled her eyes and was gone.

He stared after her. "Wait, are you coming back?"

She waved. "Popcorn, remember."

Chapter Thirteen

Escorted into the opulent conference room, Luke was met with true, dressed-for-success (especially for Texas) businessmen. They smelled and breathed of money. Oil money. When he finished his last surgery, a courier arrived with a plane ticket, hotel reservations at one of Dallas' finest, and was told a limo would meet him in baggage claim. He wasn't sure what all the fuss meant and called his boss in Wyoming. Technically, though, he was an employee of Silverwood Oil, so there were no answers on what awaited.

He was way out of his element in this architectural behemoth of an office structure. Contemporary design inside and out, with decades-old art and décor pieces strategically placed in the lobby.

He had opted for business casual, a pair of good jeans and a blazer since the meeting would take place at the mirrored-into-the-sky corporate office. Facing four men, in, no lie, three-piece suits, he was rethinking the tie now. His chair, the only one on his side of the table. The meeting, more like a one-sided inquisition.

"Mr. Whitten." A middle-aged man with a receding hairline walked in and shut the door. Even the graying, receding temples looked elegant. "I trust you had a good flight."

"Yes, thank you. I'm sorry, I don't know who you are." Luke panned the table. "Who any of you are. I'm not sure why I'm here, although I assume we need to discuss the accident."

"Of course, where's our manners? I like a man who gets right to the point." The man did his best to look pleasant. The finger and thumb tapping told another story. "I'm Gray Lansing, CEO of Silverwood. These two gentlemen are our corporate lawyers, and Todd at the end is our CFO."

Luke noted he didn't introduce the lawyers. Trying to calm his breathing, he waited until he could speak with a degree of confidence. "Should I have retained my own lawyer?"

"Oh, no, son. They're just here to keep notes. The family of the dead man is filing a lawsuit against us and Wyatt both. Frivolous, but we want to get everything tied up nice and legal."

Luke blinked a number of times. He wasn't aware of any lawsuits pending, unsure why Rowdy's family would pursue something that would only lead to a time-consuming migraine. Oil companies were known for tying up lawsuits for years.

"I didn't know," Luke said. "I told the Rock Springs detectives everything. You didn't have to do all this. I'm sure you can get the files."

"Are you intending on filing a suit?" one of the lawyers leaned forward and asked.

Luke squinted his eyes together. Maybe he did need a lawyer.

"I hadn't contemplated doing that, but again, I'm really confused at all this. The last I heard Wyatt was paying out the life insurance. I wasn't aware there was any legal action being taken. Was there something at fault in the equipment?"

"We ask the questions," the other lawyer snapped.

Luke jerked back and crossed his arms. "And I'll be happy to answer them, but not blindly."

"Please, Luke. I apologize for my lawyers. Mr. Finch's family is alleging the equipment was faulty, that the gas leak and fire were caused by negligence on both Wyatt and Silverwood's part. Also adding, you and your crew didn't follow protocols for reporting the incident. I've assured my men here"—he nodded at the three piecers—"that you were not at fault. We just want to see how all the pieces fit. Since you're our resident Texan up there, I wanted the lawyers to get a feel for what you have to say."

Luke's head swarmed as he reasoned everything out, coming back to the petrifying realization he'd been an ignorant, naive fool.

"I would assume the two companies would run the same defense," Luke said, tapping the pen they'd given him on the table, distancing himself and hoping they'd give up a little more information.

"Technically you work for us. You were maintenance, our eyes and ears."

Luke wondered how heavy of a hand Silverwood had in his initial hiring.

Gray plastered a smile on his face. "Just spitballing, but how about we transfer you closer to home? We can place you in Midland where we'll fast track you to a driller, at a significant pay raise of course. We'll pay your moving expenses, and we have a home-buying assistance package we offer to our new recruits, so you will have access to that as well." He slid an envelope across the table. "And a little bonus."

The manila envelope was sealed, but thick.

"With you in close proximity, we'll prep for trial. Testifying can be quite intimidating."

Luke continued to stare at the envelope, lifting his eyes to one lawyer, then the next. Something was not right here. Vulnerability sat in his gut at not being lawyer smart.

He leaned into the flats of his fingers as he rose. "I left Texas for a reason. I have no desire to come back. And I'm uncomfortable accepting anything until I figure out what's going on. I'd like to think about this for a day or two."

"You have forty-eight hours."

Oh, yeah, something was definitely wrong with this picture.

When he arrived back at the hotel, he set to packing up. He didn't want to spend another night on their dime.

He rebooked his flight to Rock Springs and was in a shuttle on his way to the airport when his sister called with more bad news. While his father had been picking up groceries, he'd had a heart attack and was in the ICU ward at the hospital.

Instructing the driver to drop him at baggage claim instead of departures, he shuffled from one foot to the next as he waited for a bus to take him to the car rental center. He went to the first clerk with a "rentals available" sign on the counter and was on his way west within an hour.

"Claire, I'm on my way," he whispered, cranking up the music to take his mind off lawsuits and culpability, whether his father was dying or recovering, whether rushing to his father's side was even worth the trip.

The last visit home stung, but the one a decade prior—worse. Twenty-one years old, and his family turned him away for the Thanksgiving holiday. Ironic, since the holiday was made for families. That visit had plummeted a knife deep inside where the blade would remain encased, like the mythical sword. Removal, a fantasy.

He rolled the window down and let the musings escape into the sunny skies. Wyoming, his new friends, and the psychological fallout from the accident left him hoping he'd made enough of himself now to shove the past aside and simply be the son who loved his father, helping him through a rough time. Letting go of the rejections that bred a pain deeper than any death could.

Arriving a little after eight, he sat in the hospital parking lot with no less than a thousand questions swirling. Visiting hours would be over, and he was quite sure Evelyn would have him on some kind of you're-not-allowed list. Roaming the empty parking lot, he looked for her luxury car, killing time, waiting for his sister to text him back.

"To hell with it." He shoved his phone in his back pocket, heading toward the entrance.

Visiting hours were indeed over, but the Whitten name granted him access to check in with the fifth floor.

San Angelo was not a small town in relation to Rock Springs, but he'd never been so grateful his hometown remained smallish. One of the nurses at the fifth-floor desk was a girl he used to date. If her social media was up to date, he needed to navigate cautiously. Divorce number two was on the court dockets.

"Luke Whitten," Alicia's voice whined. Not feminine whiney, but whiney whiney. "What brings your sexy ass to our neck of the woods?"

The other nurse nudged her.

"Oh, I'm sorry, Luke. You're home to see your daddy."

He nodded at them both. "Good to see you, Alicia. I hoped to get an update."

The other girl looked through the charts. "We don't have authorization to give information on his condition to you."

"Oh, for God's sake. His stepmom is a witch. Of course we can. I've been locking lips with Luke since we were thirteen. His father would want him to know."

They bantered back and forth, and he didn't interrupt. Hopefully, Alicia would win the argument. Then again…his sister was finally calling.

"Never mind." Luke wagged his phone at them. "It's Claire. Sorry to trouble you."

They argued a little more as he walked down the hall and sat in a waiting room.

Claire explained how lucky their father was, with the EMTs arriving quickly on the scene. While Luke was caught up in his own hospital woes, his father was scheduled for bypass surgery in a couple of weeks.

"Where are you?" Claire asked.

"Here, at the hospital." He sat in the empty waiting room. "They won't tell me anything. I'm not on whatever list they've got going."

"What do you mean you're not on the list?"

"C'mon, Claire."

There was a long silence. "I'm sorry. I thought because… Shit, doesn't matter what I thought."

The hall was empty as he set off toward his dad's room. Standing before the glass, his father's peaceful, ashen face sank deep into the pillow. The wrinkles deep in his skin, evidence time always marched on. He leaned his face against the glass listening to Claire in an argument with her five-year-old over whether he really needed yet another glass of water. All sorts of tubes, bags, and machines surrounded his dad. The respirator hissed away, giving him the first smile of his day.

"Luke, I am your father." His dad loved the line out of one of his and his father's favorite movies back in the day. Luke physically hurt at all the time now bundled in the back-in-the-day category.

"Come on by. We'll drink and talk." Claire shooed his nephew away. Bottles rattled. "Damn, stop and get some beer though. I'm out."

"Naw, get some sleep. I've got a hotel, and I'm whooped."

"Yeah, well, too bad. I want to have a beer with my brother."

Luke turned from the feeble, vulnerable sight of his father. He didn't want to, but he missed them, missed every single one of them. Every single piece of his broken-down, broken-up family.

One beer turned to three. He told her about the accident. The real story about the accident. She cried, yelled at him, and elicited his promise to change his emergency contacts in the future. Her husband, Mitch, wandered out to the kitchen at one point. Seeing the turmoil, he nodded at Luke, kissed the top of Claire's head, and disappeared again. When the crying ended, the laughing started. He took off at midnight when he deemed himself safe to drive again.

In the morning, Luke rolled over to stare at flimsy curtains, giving a shadowy glimpse of a downpour outside. In the harsh light of a dreary Texas day, and away from his sister's kitchen, he wanted to go home. He did not want to be here. He missed his friends; he missed being in the hospital playing cards with Mara. The cards, the stupid '70s television shows they poked fun at, the gentle touch of her helping him… He needed to visit his feelings for her outside of the hospital confines one of these days.

He rolled onto his back and studied the ceiling. Damn. At some point, they'd become more friends than nurse and patient, with their conversations about nothing, and sometimes everything. He wouldn't say he had breached the fortress of Mara, but he'd made progress. Charlie stories, at least. It really wasn't any of his business why she lost custody of her daughter, but feeling nosy one night, he broached the conversation. After she stared and fidgeted, testing every pillow under his head, the most he got out of her was, "Mistakes happen."

What did that even mean?

He did miss her though. Missed laughing. There was nothing to laugh about in Dallas, or now in the dregs of San Angelo.

Looking at the date on his phone, he knew her court date was tomorrow. She had been nervous and twitchy the last few days before he left, and he assumed the looming custody hearing was the reason behind her dour mood. At one point, she slipped and mentioned something to another nurse about an upcoming decision about weekend visitations. Swapping over to a search engine, he found a flower shop in Rock Springs, ordered a simple bouquet to wish her luck. At least she would know someone believed in her, even if the someone knew nothing about her.

Chapter Fourteen

Luke joined a couple of old friends for breakfast, trying to put off the inevitable. In the bright sunshine, even pancakes around a packed table at his favorite diner didn't fill the void. Jealousy gripped instead. He loved time spent with his buddies, but they had all found what they were looking for. Some going away to college and returning, some never leaving in the first place. He was the first to leave and stay the hell gone.

Was he back? Was he staying? Would his father need him? Would that make any difference? This morning, he wanted out of here as fast as a rental car and airplane could get him home. In the cold light of day, he was still assessing. And he refused to admit, whether he stayed in San Angelo really depended on his father. Would he stand up to the woman he'd been unable to for a decade or more? Would Evelyn know she couldn't handle everything and ask for his help? Luke wanted to make her beg, but that was a little man. He wanted to be the bigger man his father used to be.

A text buzzed in from his sister that their father was awake. Evelyn walked out the hospital door he'd been watching from a parking lot. When she didn't turn around and head back inside, Claire perfectly choreographed the time for him to visit.

Claire pecked him on the cheek outside the room. Cole, her youngest, flailed from her arms, already readying for a toss into the air. He lifted the two-year-old high above him to little-boy giggles and shrieks of delight. A few people looked down the hall at the noise and smiled.

"Cole, you're in trouble…" Luke drew out, holding a finger to his lips.

Cole put his fat little hands on Luke's cheeks and smooshed them together. "You in trouble, Uke."

"Oh, my God, let me have him," Claire said. "You two are a match made in troublemaking, adorable heaven."

Luke pressed his forehead to Cole's and did a giggly stare down. "We're adorable, Cole. You heard your mother." Luke's heart skipped at the happy sounds and rolls of squirminess from his nephew.

Through the window, his father talked to the nurse. She checked on the IVs and propped pillows, reminding him of another nurse. He was quite sure that particular career path was God's gift to mankind. Their tenderness and caring were beyond beautiful in this messed-up world.

"How long's she gone for?" he asked Claire.

"Not long. She can't stomach hospital coffee. She likes that new specialty coffee place downtown."

He sidled through the door. The nurse stopped in her tracks as a tender look swept over his father's face. A lump got stuck in his throat.

"Well, you must be blood," the nurse said, tossing a remote into his father's lap. "No missing those emotional eyes. I'll leave you two alone."

The nurse swept out the door.

"You're back," Ward whispered.

His father's gaze softened to the point of glistening.

His own cheeks ached with the effort of holding in tears.

"Of course." Luke sat at the bedside, picked up his father's hand. "You gave us all a scare."

"It's hell getting old." He looked toward the window. "Stress, I imagine. Getting too old to hold my own."

"I doubt that. Look how long Grandpa held in there. He was barking orders until we lowered him into the ground."

A tear slid down his dad's leathery cheek. He smiled and looked at the ceiling. "I miss him. Every day I miss him."

Luke didn't know what to do. His father had never been the emotional sort, really, ever. An IV trailed into the frail, crepe-y arm, making Luke wonder if the drugs were too strong.

"Did I ever tell you about the trip we took?" his father asked. "One of my best memories. Outside of his time overseas in the military, he had never crossed state lines. He wanted to go to Washington. Do you remember how much he loved history?"

Luke nodded, speechless, hanging on every word. Two, maybe three sentences. Calm sentences. Words strung together that were heartbreaking and happy and a whole host of emotions he hadn't felt in so long.

"Then there was the trip to Duane's, that old chain of diners. It was the very first time I can remember he let me buy him a meal. Not to mention his first venture into a Duane's. I don't remember what town that was…" He trailed off.

Luke leaned forward, waiting for more, wanting more. Not just stories of his grandfather, but of his father. Maybe this heart attack would force him to re-evaluate his life. Luke choked up and didn't realize a tear had slid out until his father stopped and looked at him.

Luke lifted his shoulder, letting his T-shirt absorb the tear. "I miss you, Dad."

His dad squeezed his hand, the intimate gesture surprising Luke.

They launched into conversation about the upcoming auctions. His father seemed to be assuming he was staying. He didn't know if that was his case, but he let him rattle on. Wyoming was calling, but thirty minutes with his father made him question where he wanted to be. His phone vibrated in his pocket.

—*Thank you, they're gorgeous and much appreciated. Sick judge so hearing postponed—*

And right behind it.

—*Take care of those lawyers. And yourself of course, haha—*

His father studied him. "Everything okay, son?"

Luke smiled for the second time today in his father's presence. Not at the question, but at being claimed verbally.

"I'm good. How long are they keeping you here?" He blackened the screen of his phone.

"I'm having bypass surgery tomorrow to repair my ticker." He settled his hands on his stomach. "This could have been a lot worse."

His father's gaze riveted on the door where Evelyn stood. Claire mouthed a sorry his direction.

"You need to leave," Evelyn said, moving to pick up his dad's hand. "I heard you were gone for good. Injured or something. Now you're trying to come home and take advantage of your father when he's not in the best of health?"

The look his father shot in his direction let him know the accident message had never been relayed.

"Did you even tell him I was in the hospital?" Luke accused. He lifted his shirt where the burns were still evident. "For weeks."

"He hasn't been in the best of health." She flung her hand. "I protected him from your exploits across the country. Besides, obviously you're fine now."

His father's gaze ping-ponged back and forth as they argued.

Luke bit his lip, trying to be the bigger man. "I'm allowed to visit my father."

"No, no, you're not. You're adding to his stress. He needs to get healthy and get back to our home and heal."

"Luke's going to help run the ranch while I'm down. I can't do everything right now. That's pretty obvious."

Luke swung his gaze, gauging the seriousness of his father's assumption.

Evelyn shook her head. "My nephew Justin will be here in the morning. He's been working at the Longman Ranch down on the border. Your 'son' here—" She did air quotes at that, looking like a moron. "Your son deserted you when you needed him."

"His 'son' "—Luke did his own stupid air quotes—"was told to leave. Told he wasn't wanted."

"And he's still not. If you're going to raise your voice, I'll buzz for security." Her finger hovered on the button. "Let's all face reality. You run. It's what you do best. You ran after your father paid your college tuition. You left your brother when he needed you. You had all the friends, he had you, and you left. So, keep running. Head on back to South Dakota or wherever you were hiding until you pounced on an opening to take the ranch from us."

"What?" Luke scrunched up his face. "I left because you told me to. I have no interest in being where I'm not wanted. He was the one, not an hour ago, who was happy to see me. We were just shooting the shit, there was no job mentioned, but I would stay if my father wanted me to."

He looked at his dad. His dad looked away, and Evelyn smirked.

"And don't even dare talk about my leaving Bo. He was twelve. Of course, he stayed when you refused to let me come home. He died. Died on your watch. Don't be attacking me with your 'poor me' agenda." Tears loomed just mentioning his brother. His voice was high and pitchy, but maybe this confrontation deserved to have some light shed on it.

Evelyn's cheeks turned a bright red, the color sinking into her throat. Looking like a deep red rose against her crisp white blouse. The Evelyn rose was strewn with very jagged thorns though.

"You should have been there, keeping an eye on him," she screamed. "This is on you. You would think you'd have figured that out by now."

"Me?" Luke laughed. "Dad, you understand this blame is not even rational, right? I was eight thousand miles away, serving my country. Even if I was here, what were the chances I would have been swimming at the lake in the middle of the day instead of working?"

None of them knew whether Bo's drowning was an accident or intentional. Lake Nasworthy hiding secrets from them all.

"Dad?" He sounded like a little boy, but he couldn't help himself. Just once he wanted his father to choose him over his wife.

The hum of the monitors filled the room in silence. Distant voices from down the hall floated and drifted away again.

"You left because you were ashamed he wasn't a big, bad, Texas boy," Evelyn cried, dabbing at her eyes. "You think you own that title? He didn't fit. Admit it."

The fire lit deep in his stomach at the accusation. The story may be what they wanted to tell their friends, but the truth was, there was no truth.

"Oh, that one again. I left because I thought he was gay? You'll have to do better than slinging accusations because I've got proof. Wanna see?" He held up his phone. "I can scroll for days through his emails."

Evelyn lunged in his direction and began clawing at his face. Luke grabbed her hands, forcing them to her sides, and she kept wiggling free. An orderly, or maybe the security guy she'd called to cart him out, grabbed her up in a massive hug-type thing from behind, lifting her to the other side of the room.

She straightened herself. The security guy let her go, and she set to propping pillows, cooing to his father.

"Luke, you need to go." His father garbled out, plummeting into the pillows as Evelyn raised the bed.

He tried one last time. "Dad. I will stay if you need me. But if I leave…" He pointed at the door. "I won't be back."

Claire hiccupped back a sob. Cole sucked on his fingers in her arms, looking at them all in wide-eyed wonder. "You in trouble gin, Uke?" Cole asked innocently. "Grandpa, Uke in trouble?"

They all looked to his father. Nothing but silence.

"I think you have your answer." Evelyn crossed her

arms.

The bile rose. His morning pancakes now turning to acid. He hovered in the doorway and held Cole's little face in his hands, stroking his cheeks. "Yeah, Cole. Uke in trouble."

Cole giggled and smiled the most perfect of smiles.

"You take care of your mama, okay?" With one hand on Cole's face, the other weaved into Claire's hair, he tipped her head and kissed her hairline. "I'm sorry. I'm really sorry," he whispered. "I love you."

He didn't turn again, walking a straight path to the elevator, ramming the G button so hard, he was surprised elevator didn't slam to a standstill when he landed on the ground floor.

Chapter Fifteen

Mara fiddled with the card in her pocket, willing good thoughts into her tattered nerves. Yesterday, a bouquet of flowers was delivered to the nurse's station. More shocking, they were for her. To see they were from he who occupied her attention since the day he left her charge, made her heart do some pretty phenomenal flip-flops. She loved her patients, but who was she kidding? None of them were him.

The hearing had been rescheduled again. Of course, he wouldn't be aware of the date change. She assumed he was still in Texas with the corporate bigwigs. She didn't want to hope, but gave more than a passing consideration to whether he planned on coming back. Probably some high school sweetheart back in the Lone Star State, and his sister. The man lived and breathed for his sister. Sweet, yes. But bittersweet if the sentiment kept him down south.

"All rise," the bailiff called.

Mara folded her hands together in front of her, sweeping Texas out of her mind. Today she was more nervous than she could ever remember. Everything the judge had asked, she had done. And then some. But this one was important. This wasn't about a Saturday with her daughter without the evil eye in close proximity. This was about weekends, picnics and real-life slumber parties, baking cookies and playing at the park. Then hopefully, someday, real life. Day to day, shared custody.

She bit her lip, hard, not wanting to get ahead of herself. Her lawyer reminded her again how well the last hearing concluded because she kept her mouth shut.

"You can be seated." The judge leafed through some paper. "Ms. Sawyer, you're looking for weekend visitations with your daughter, Charlotte, correct?"

"Yes, ma'am," she squeaked out.

"How are the unsupervised visits going?"

"Good. We've had some nice outings, and she chatters up a storm. She's a very happy little girl."

"I must say you've made substantial progress in a short period of time. How about you tell me why I should grant visitation? I know you finished your schooling and changed jobs, so what does your schedule look like? How does Charlotte fit into your new life?"

She stood and clutched her hands together in front of her, forcing herself to talk with her mouth, not her hands. "I finished the RN program while working at the hospital at night. Soon, I'll have more flexibility with my schedule. I've already talked to my supervisor about days off. She doesn't anticipate a problem making my schedule work with a custody arrangement. My coworkers and supervisor have supplied letters to my work ethic."

"Yes, I've read them. You've made huge strides recently. How about personally? Friends, family, boyfriends? What does your time off look like these days? Where are you living?"

"My schedule right now is jam-packed with work, and I take kickboxing classes. Any time off besides my workout schedule is usually spent with my mom."

Her mother-in-law sighed heavily. Loudly enough everyone turned in her direction. Then she rolled her eyes.

"I'm not sure what your problem is, but let's get it out there." The judge flung her hand at Vivian.

"The problem is…" Vivian leaned forward, pointing at Mara's table. "She does a few months of good deeds, and you're ready to buy her lies? Chase, tell the judge what you saw."

Surprised Ms. Cool and Confident broke courtroom protocol, Mara racked her brain for anything detrimental Vivian could conjure up.

Chase stood and buttoned his suit jacket. "One of my friends recognized her at the bar she used to work at, flirting with the truckers. One morning, a different friend saw my wife coming out of one of the oilfield company's trailers. Very early in the morning if you get my drift. They have barracks on-site."

Rachel touched Mara's shoulder. She grabbed her friend's fingers as she fought the urge to remind him of the fact that she was the ex-wife, not the wife. She bit her tongue hard, forcing herself to swallow as the taste of blood hit her taste buds.

Her lawyer was on his feet. The judge held up her hand, and he sat down.

"Any truth to these rumors, Ms. Sawyer?"

"No, Your Honor." Mara's breath caught as she kept her words to a minimum, her replies simple.

"Are you calling my son a liar?" Vivian said harshly. Even the judge raised her eyebrows. "You think you're better than him now that you're a nurse? How dare you!"

The room quieted as the judge began beating her

gavel on the podium. Mara sat strong and erect, calming herself as the accusations flew. She kept her hands clasped in front of her and didn't say a word. Rachel smiled so broadly; Mara wanted to bust up laughing.

"I will have order. One more outburst and you will be held in contempt." She air hammered her gavel in Vivian's direction.

Vivian slumped back in her seat, crossed her arms, and glared.

"Now, Mr. Owens, any problem throughout all this getting child support from Ms. Sawyer?"

Chase shot a quick look at his mother. Mara smiled, knowing the judge's question was rhetorical. The receipts of transfers were, no doubt, right in front of her.

"No, ma'am. Every month on the first of the month."

"And are you working?"

Vivian stood. "He's out on disability. Our family has money to support our granddaughter."

"From what I can see, he's very able-bodied. And it is a matter of concern if he's not pulling his own weight and paying half of Charlotte's expenses. He needs to be involved financially."

The judge's retort shut her up. It didn't stop her mouth from opening, but the scathing look from the judge must have been enough to make her think twice about what she planned to say.

"Very well, then, Ms. Sawyer. Where are we at with living conditions? Do you have adequate space for your daughter for a couple nights at a time?"

"Yes. I'm still living at my mother's, but I signed a lease for my own place close to the hospital. There are two bedrooms. It'll be available for me to move in next month."

The judge nodded, shuffled some paper around. "Is Ms. Cartwright here?"

Rachel stood.

"Can we get an in-home inspection scheduled at the mother's house before this weekend?"

"Of course."

"Alright, Ms. Sawyer. Assuming everything is fine on the inspection, you will have your daughter every other weekend. Friday night to Sunday afternoon, Charlotte will be surrendered to Ms. Sawyer without incident. We will revisit the issue in three months and see if we can return to the original joint custody agreement."

Mara's heart slammed to a standstill, thrusting her forward where she collapsed onto the table. A huge smile, face planted into the wood. Chase and his mom hurried toward the exit and whooshed out the heavy double doors.

Once outside, Mara held her hands to the sky, gripped empty air. Life now had the beginnings of restoring itself.

Now she too, felt ready to breathe again.

When she hugged her supervisor who came in support, she saw the one who taught her to seek breathing. Luke leaned against a bench, arms folded across his chest, his gaze locked on her. She lifted her fingers in a half wave; he smiled in acknowledgment.

When she was before him, she looked to his tired and worn eyes. Like everything with him, they changed in an instant.

"Looks like there's reason to celebrate." He nodded at her circle of supporters in the distance. "I'm thrilled for you."

"Thanks. Today is such an exciting step. The flowers...I know I have people in my corner, but I felt people in my corner. There's a difference."

He flinched for a second, dropping the veil, then his eyes closed, and he regrouped by the time they opened again. "Yes. There's very much a difference."

There were gashes down one of his cheeks, reminding her of when she attempted to bathe her cat when she was twelve.

She pointed at them. "Bad dream? Get into it with a vegetable peeler?"

His eyes clouded over as he smoothed his finger through the gash. "Do you remember the old fairy tale about evil stepmoms?" He huffed with a smile. "Turns out some of those old story books should be housed on the nonfiction shelf."

She nodded, sensing he didn't want to go there. "Outside of wayward fingernails, how was Texas? Did your sister talk you into moving back? I need a new patient to make fun of stupid shows with."

He smirked. "You don't need a patient to do that. I don't have to be patient Whitten anymore, or barstool warmer, Whitten. I can be a friend, Whitten."

She looked down, letting the silence hang while she garnered some strength. "My lawyer's taking a few of us out for a drink to celebrate. Do you want to come?"

He looked away. "No, but thanks. I've had my fill of lawyers this week. No offense to him. I just wanted to make sure everything worked out okay."

He studied his feet, looked up at her, and smiled a crooked smile with one dimple.

They called her name, and she spun and waved,

holding up a finger. "I've got to go. You take care of yourself, Whitten." As she walked toward the crowd, Rachel lifted her eyebrows in question.

"Mara?"

When she turned, he walked toward her, stopping when he drew close to tuck a wayward strand of hair behind her ear. His touch was so gentle, her nerves escalated, and her head began spinning. She looked to his chest, to the smile playing on his lips. "I don't want to jeopardize anything with your daughter, but I would like to take you out sometime. I missed your silly ass while I was gone."

When had the stars ever aligned so perfectly in her favor? Could this day get any better?

"Huh, I might have missed you too. I'd like that, Whitten. Let me make sure…outings, have no impact on my little girl."

"Of course." He took her hand, his touch again sending all sorts of sensors haywire. "I'll call you tomorrow."

Chapter Sixteen

Luke spent three weeks trying to make plans with Mara. As he waited in the hospital's parking lot, he tried to tap down those first date jitters. Mara requested low-key, no fanfare, wanting to keep the date word out of the mix.

In the spirit of "low-key," he planned a little Texas intervention to her Wyoming world.

When she exited the hospital and headed toward his truck, the only word coming to mind was *wow*. Her beauty was simple, tan but not too tanned. Mysterious eyes, drawing you in, not pushing you away. A small nose and a flawless complexion outside of a simple mole on her left cheek. She waved at a coworker, and in her pivot he could tell she not only had lost more weight but had built up some impressive muscles since his hospital days.

As she slid into the passenger seat, he reminded himself he needed to go slow if he wanted this to go anywhere. She wasn't the sort to give her heart or emotions to just anyone. He would venture to guess she was heart first, body second, in the sexual realm. He didn't mind this. Actually, he preferred a little naivety.

"Hi."

Luke grinned. "Those are some incredibly underrated conversational skills you have."

She looked him over after sliding into the passenger

seat. "You definitely do the low-key thing well."

"Yes, ma'am. Admittedly though, jeans and ball caps are my normal everyday attire, so I'm quite the low-key expert."

Mara glanced over her shoulder. "Do I see a cooler in the bed of the truck?"

"Again, yes, ma'am. I fancy myself quite the planner in the date…whoops, the adventure department. I hope you enjoy tonight, because I'm already enjoying just looking at you and knowing I have your undivided attention for the entire evening."

Her mouth opened, and nothing spilled out.

"Did I say that? Dammit, I was supposed to keep those thoughts to myself. Slap me if I start drooling." He picked up her hand. "You look great. Unfortunately, it'll probably get lost tonight."

He started the truck and exited the parking lot, heading out of town. The sun dropped dangerously close to escaping behind the mountains, and he hoped he remembered how to get to the track in the pitch darkness.

Rounding the corner, the blazing stadium lights came into view. She grinned, her smile spreading wide. "Wow, when you say no fuss, you take semantics to a new level. So, what is this? Like dogs following a little rabbit or something?"

He put the truck in reverse and grabbed his heart. "Slay me now! You've never been to a stock car race?"

"Um, no, can't say as I have."

"Then you're in for a treat. The best part of these backwoods ones is you back your truck up and can tailgate with a front-row seat. Thus, the cooler. No wine list, but I've got cerveza's. Complete with limes too, so there's that."

They met as he lowered the tailgate of his truck.

He spread a thick, red-and-white checked blanket on the metal. "Viola."

"This is...I don't know what it is, but it's great."

"Yeah, say that after a car drifts in front of you and you end up with a mouthful of dirt."

She wiggled her butt onto the tailgate. "Now I get why you said to wear jeans."

He took out their gourmet meal of sub sandwiches and jalapeno chips he knew from hospital days she loved. Besides, they also complimented his Texas Wyoming intervention. The cars began taking a parade route around the track. Lots of loud motors, Wyoming and Colorado flags billowing out passenger windows, idiotic plays on words scrawled across the sides in bright paint.

He pointed at his friend Carson's car, a bright neon blue '80s sedan, "Caroline" elegantly swept down the side.

Mara rolled her eyes. "Oh, Lord. A folksy rock fan, huh?"

Luke laughed. "Kind of, his mom is, and he's a mama's boy, so..."

"I get that more than you know. I can bust out in song to any of the greats. Complete with a vacuum cleaner. It was cleaning music when I was younger."

"Yikes."

A smile swept over her face, and she pulled her knees up and wrapped her arms around them. He swore he could watch her all night; she was so engrossed in everything. It did amazing things to her features. Simple girl, simple tastes—perfection in his book.

"They'll drop the flags now. Basically, they just try to bump one another off. This isn't an international

114

raceway or anything, mostly, just a bunch of guys driving their big boy toys around a loop. Did you play with cars and trucks when you were little?"

"I'm a girl. I did the doll thing."

"Yowza, fighting words for Claire." Luke thought of the car crash battles with his sister in the dirt mounds on the ranch, her hair sprouting wildly out of ponytails.

The racers rumbled to life and were off in a spray of gravel and dust, the dirt creating a cloud that leaked through the chain-link fence. Mara took her hand from his arm and shifted, putting her hands on the sides of her thighs, and leaning forward. Her excitement left him trying to explain how the cars would maneuver and jostle for position, but he wasn't sure she heard a word he said. Pulling her eyes from the track, she glanced at her empty bottle. Luke rammed some limes into another and placed a fresh bottle in her hand. She took a long swig, her gaze following Carson's car and then another as they jockeyed. A red car from Colorado skidded across the lanes and spun off into the middle of the loop. She grabbed his arm and clutched until it skidded to a safe stop. His hand covered hers, grasping it into his forearm. Her grasp was natural, organic, the warmth comforting. Sparks for sure, but sparks for how much she was enjoying his escapade, how easily she settled in.

After a time, the remaining racers took a break. Luke dumped their empties in a nearby trash can, settling himself closer on his return. Corny maneuver, but classic in that high school sort of way.

When she grabbed his hand and threaded her fingers with his, he thought life was pretty damn perfect.

"Tell me about your trip? Was it weird being home?" She squeezed his hand. "You get all clammed up about your family. Well, outside of the drunken stupor night."

He laughed. They both quieted, and their feet set to swinging in unison. The comment could be his lead in. He hated to think about an arrangement being a tit-for-tat thing, but hell, he really liked her, and was still genuinely curious about what makes a mother lose custody. The cost, high, with his father's latest rejection still stinging.

He sucked in the feeling of vulnerability and tried to release it. "I'll show you mine if you show me yours."

She smiled and looked into her lap. "You want to know how I lost my daughter." The wind blew her hair in front of her face, and she looped the wayward strands behind her ear. "It's not a pretty story, Luke."

He drew his breath in deeply when she said his name. Her voice was so soft and fluid, the first time she hadn't called him Whitten.

"I want to know everything about you. We all have our demons, but the way my name rolled out of you. It makes me want to go all He-Man and slay all those pesky demons. But…how about we start with the basics? My father and the associated history, in exchange for why you lost custody."

"Pretty heavy conversation for a first date."

"You said the date word." Luke wagged his finger at her.

Mara dropped her head back, snaked her hand into the cooler, and grabbed another beer. "Gentlemen first."

"I know we're not saying the date word, but this doesn't seem like a first date. I think we've done enough laughing as friends for forty not dates."

"True, but you're evading."

Nervous now, he opened his mouth to begin, and words escaped him.

"Maybe the beginning?" she prompted, taking a grimacing bite of lime before shoving it in the bottle. "Whatever caused your family to part ways?"

Parting ways. That was an interesting description. He wondered if giving her words a non-drunk voice would make the pain hurt any less. The pain was like cancer waiting to attack an organ other than his heart.

"I need to let you know, in guy land, I'm what you'd call a sensitive sort. I wear my heart on my sleeve. So just being upfront about that."

"I already knew that. I guess not knew, but you give those vibes."

Her concern unnerved him. He had to press on if he wanted this. And he definitely wanted this.

"When I was ten, my mom died. My dad collapsed. First there was a shadow of a presence, then there was silence, then he hid in his work. Claire and I didn't know how to cope. Our mom brought life to our world; she painted in the color. Then cancer made the world turn gray. A year goes by, and he begins drinking. A lot. The bottle turned into an endless parade of women. They all want to come in and play mommy to Ward's orphaned kids. It works for a while, but at some point, you know the effort is fake and self-serving. In the end, the stream of women morphed into a hard landing with Evelyn making the trip down the aisle."

"What was your mom like?"

Luke's heart skipped. Over time, images of his mom faded, yet, if he concentrated hard enough, his mom's sky-blue eyes and easy smile were there again. Beautiful, ageless. "She was always laughing. Always telling stupid jokes that would make our eyes roll. God, I'd give anything to roll my eyes at her just one more time." He floated his hand out, feeling foolish when he grabbed at the empty air. He sat for a second, hoping the tears would flow inward instead of outward.

When he regained some composure, the pending tears dissipated. "When Evelyn first entered our world, became part of our day to day, things were good. My dad became happy again. He became a dad again. We fished and hunted and took road trips to Dallas or San Antonio. I was his mini me, and proud to be so. A few years in, Evelyn got pregnant. A new person joining our crew sounded so exciting. I never dreamed that would be the beginning of the end.

"In high school, I was super popular in that small-town, big-fish, little-pond way. I played every sport, worked on the ranch during the summers, had any girl I wanted. But the best part: I was close with my dad. I never had to hide anything. I drank, but he trusted I would be safe. There was just one girlfriend, and in spite of how he grabbed hold of his wild side after my mom died, he bred a decent respect for women into me."

Luke hadn't allowed himself to go to this place in a long time. Everything he valued about himself was placed there by his father. When he thought about having kids, it was his own father he wanted to emulate. As he was, not as he is.

He shuddered, wanting to skip over this part and not draw out a perfectly depressing story.

"Bo was my little brother's name. A nice Texan name and Evelyn had big plans for him. She wanted him to have my father's attention, all his attention. I guess she started resenting me, because by this time my father was wrapped up in everything I was doing. My dad didn't ignore Bo, but even at that age, I could tell the attention wasn't the same for him."

"What about Claire?" Mara asked.

"Claire?" He drew his eyes together. "Claire was daddy's little girl; she had plenty of attention also. She was in a saddle from the second she could sit, and that was where you would find her, well, forever. She has kids of her own now, and a great husband, a high-profile job. But you watch her ride, and it's like an angel who has found her place in the clouds."

The cars were moving to the starting line again, the drivers chatting across the dirt. Laughing so hard, Luke could hear them from the opposite side of the track.

"When I went home for Thanksgiving my senior year in college, Evelyn forbid me from entering the property. She wanted Bo to have the attention I garnered whenever I was home. That was when my dad quit on me. It messed with my head. I went back to school, held things together until the semester break at Christmas. One day, I got up in the middle of class and walked away from it all. I guess I thought it would get my dad's attention, but…" Luke balled his hands into tight fists.

"So, I quit school and picked up a job as a roughneck in Midland. I was with friends one day, hitting some bars, and I saw a recruiting office. I walked in and asked them how fast they could get me the hell out of Texas."

Mara smiled at the two drivers who were out of their cars yelling at one another with arms flailing. "And your brother?"

"You realize that ventures beyond our contract for the night." She gave his hand a squeeze. "Bo is another long story. But in the years that followed, Bo became a depressed mess. When Bo died, somehow that was all on me."

"So, she got what she wanted? And you had to sacrifice the relationship with your dad?"

"No." Luke looked away, fighting the tears hard. "My dad sacrificed that relationship," he whispered finally.

The racetrack sank into a moment of calm and stillness while it anticipated the next race. The cars took off at the gunshot.

"Before my journey that we all now know landed in Wyoming, I returned home, hoping enough time had passed since Bo's funeral and things would change, but he still…" Luke shrugged.

"Maybe they needed time." She took his hand into her lap, making him realize how much he missed human contact.

"Well, nothing changed then or when I was just at home." He thought about the blowup at the hospital. "It's like she sucks the life out of him as soon as she walks in the door."

He paused and let her digest the slew of words.

"But that, that is the reason I ended up on your barstool. Perhaps I have the big and strong Texas thing going. But that badassedness?"

The cars careened around the loop.

"Luke?"

He wanted to melt all over again the way she said his name. All the disappointments he just revealed, disappearing into the Texas tumbleweeds.

"Badassedness takes on many forms." Mara let go of his hand and ran her thumbs over the last of his tears. "And on you? It's beautiful."

He had to smile at that.

In a cloud of dust, the winner was declared, and people started heading toward their cars.

"Alright, chickie, you're up."

"It's time to go. People are leaving." A couple of the massive megawatt lights started clicking off. Taillights began snaking through the hills and away from the track.

"What are you? Afraid of the dark? You don't strike me as the type to try and wiggle out of a deal."

She set her stare on the darkened track, took a long pull on her beer.

"When Chase and I split, things got nasty. Once they started going bad, they went really bad, really fast. In hindsight, I should have known sooner than I did, but I let the verbal abuse go on too long." She took a long breath. "Or emotional abuse. I guess they'd be one and the same. He was always talking about how much I ate, how I wasn't taking care of myself, how horrible it was to roll around in bed with…pick the daily descriptor. His degrading words usually had the opposite effect, though. The more he nagged, the more food became my drug. My way to shut him out. All his words did was make me want to shove six donuts down my throat. I was still in school and trying to do something worthwhile with my life, and he harped on how stupid I was. Telling me there was no way I could become a nurse when I couldn't even take care of him or our daughter properly. I'm not saying this to make you feel sorry for me. I don't need your pity."

Ramrod straight on the tailgate, her silhouette was strong, her body language in sharp contrast to the laid-back atmosphere of the track.

He held his hands up, knowing she needed to hear

something. "I have enough pity parties in my own life. I've got nothing to spare for you."

She laughed. "We're quite the damaged, excess-baggage pair."

"But…" Luke held his finger up. "We've both got sense enough to have a death grip on a life preserver someone tossed us when we needed a friend."

"You're right." She crossed her ankles, and they started swinging. "I crawled out of that hole one night… Damn, this is hard. One night he got this fire, a blackness. His eyes turned completely black. He was drunk, and I started in on him because I missed a class because he hadn't come home after work. I'm yelling. He's yelling. He's stumbling all over the place. Charlie was crying, screaming crying, and he swung around, raised his hand, and I don't know what stopped him, but something did. The blackness was there, dead center of his eyes."

Luke wanted to puke. Of course, he knew men beat on women, but he had never known anyone who did. You treated women with respect. You protected them, treasured them. They were not to be walked on; they were to be walked with.

"Of course, the next day he apologized all over the place, but I paid attention in all my psych classes. The belittling verbal slander was a prelude to something more serious. He showed me in that look that he was more than capable. I may have been fat, but I was not about to become a cliché. When he was at work the next day, I packed up Charlie and we crashed at my mom's. We stayed there until I found a new place."

"That's not normally the way those things go. I'm sure you learned that in psych too."

"I did. There was just something in his eyes that scared the living shit out of me. The fact that he could. I'll leave the demise of my marriage for another time. My contract does not require those explanations."

"Mara, there is nothing more I get than the pain of words and rejection. Besides, you don't want to break our contract because that gives me an excuse to continue the extended phase of this conversation into a second date."

She laughed. "Smooth, Whitten."

"I thought so. I will be asking though. But we still haven't got to fulfilling your contractual obligation, so…"

"Fine." She upended her beer and drank until only little bubbles were left on the bottom of the bottle. "Fast forward six months. We shared custody of Charlie. One Friday when it was his weekend, I dropped her off at daycare, and sometime that afternoon, I was having one of those pity parties. School was kicking my ass, I was working two part-time jobs, and it was the first weekend in a while that I had nothing going on. No work, no schoolwork, no Charlie. So, I was drinking wine, my mom was out of town, so I was hanging out at her house. Then the daycare center called because Chase didn't show up. I called every phone number I had, then I started trying to run down his mother.

"My mom was gone, and honestly, I've got no one else. All our…couples friends determined him to be the bigger prize. I knew I shouldn't drive, knew I wasn't one hundred percent, but I wasn't drunk. I kept thinking about my baby waiting on a father who wasn't coming. And I suppose I should mention that my dad forgot about me once at school. I know she was too young to know anything like that, but you just flash to those scenes, and you can't let go. I go back to that night, and I know all the right answers—taxi, ride share—but I couldn't get past that image of waiting on my dad. I convinced myself six miles were doable. What are the chances? Two miles away from the center…"

"One of those decisions that is the definition of life changing." Luke nodded, having had a few of those himself.

"And my screwup gave his mother what she was waiting for. An excuse to grab full custody."

"My dad always said to me it's not how you go down in a fight. It's how you get up."

Mara smiled. "I think I like your dad. Outside of not realizing how special his son is."

The silence hung for a second, and he knew, one tailgate dinner and a short conversation, and he was falling fast.

She touched his chest and kissed him, or he kissed her—it didn't really matter how the gentle kiss started. No tongue, no stroking his ego. Just a soft whisper of a kiss and it rocked his world.

He couldn't care less about DUIs, divorces, working in bars—whatever else lay under that unflinching exterior.

Everything paled in how she got up to go at life again.

Chapter Seventeen

The peeling wallpaper in the kitchen made Mara cringe, reminding her that she needed to either repair the damage, or strip the shit off the wall and paint before she moved. The wallpaper was dated and old, a dingy orange-and-yellow floral pattern, but filled the house with comforting memories. A sense of home she wanted her daughter to experience one of these days. She loved her weekends with Charlie, and with so little contact with both Chase and his mother, their new arrangement was working out well, launching into the scary, other-shoe-dropping category.

"How was pedis with the princess?" Her mom set tea in front of both of them.

"I forgot how much I love getting pampered. Paraffin soaks and hot rock massages are underrated."

"You know, she laid out a four-year-old business plan for my cookies."

Mara smiled. "She loves your cookies. How's it feel being able to one up ole Vivian in the grandma category?"

"You know I'm not petty like that."

"Ha, liar." Mara slapped at her, looking again at the wallpaper. "Next week, I need to get a few things done around here. I'll try and get them taken care of before I give you your house back."

"I can get the Collins' boy." Her mom bit her lip,

fiddling with the handle of the teacup. "You don't have to go, you know. I know staying here makes your financial situation more manageable. It's always nice to have a little extra to spend on pampering sort of things."

Mara took her mom's hand. "I do though, Mom. For me. It has nothing to do with custody; I just want to stand on my own two feet again."

Finances always made her twitchy, but she needed something all hers. Putting her wants and needs at the forefront had been a long time in coming.

"I'm proud of you, but I will miss you. I'm thinking about going back to work. I could use a distraction from all the empty hours of doing nothing."

"Liar again." Mara smirked. "You do more volunteer work than anyone I know. But I do understand. Did you talk to your doctor? Does she think you're ready? Is working advisable in remission? It won't make things worse, will it?"

"Whoa, hold up with the questions. I am an adult, you know. Able to make educated decisions and everything."

"I know. I just worry. I don't want the cancer to come back. You're doing so well. You have color and stamina. You didn't ever give up."

"Silly girl, working isn't going to make the cancer reoccur. And I know I leaned on you and fussed about all the changes, but the truth is, I'm just so damn proud of how you've rebounded lately. You're my hero, and I want to do my part, too."

"I think you might be rushing things," Mara interrupted.

"I think I get to decide that for myself."

"Touché." Mara tipped the fine bone china teacup in

her mom's direction. "Will you grant one wish for your loving daughter, though? Will you tell me if anything is wrong? Goes wrong? I want you to be honest with me. Always."

"I promise."

Charlie shuffled into the kitchen in her puppy dog slippers. "I think I may have 'somnia. I may need a glass of milk and one of Grandma's cookies. Peanut butter, please."

Mara's mom stifled a smile.

"Insomnia? Where did you learn that word?"

Charlie shrugged. "Here and there. You think I'm sick?" She sighed, thrusting her forehead forward for a temperature check.

"No." Mara lifted her into her lap and snuggled her lips into Charlie's neck until she giggled. "I think you need to go to bed. And milk and cookies don't cure insomnia. So, git. I'll be down in a minute to make sure you're snoring away."

Charlie scowled and stomped down the hall. Puppy dog heads bouncing with each step, mumbling how she didn't snore. Daddy snored.

"My Lord, her teenage years are going to be torture. You better find yourself a good man to help with that."

Mara smiled.

"Speaking of…" Her mom grinned. "I overheard your friend from the hospital asking you about a certain patient you've been seeing."

Mara swished the tea from side to side. "Still in the getting-to-know-you stage."

"And?"

"And it's good. Really good. But we've only had a couple dates. Our schedules are crazy, and with the insomniac." Mara stared down the hall. "I'm scared."

"Oh, honey, scared is the only way to go down."

"Spoken like the woman who married the first man she met."

"True, true. Tell me about him."

"Our first date was the goofiest thing you could have seen, and I pretty much melted on the spot. Second date, typical dinner and a movie. He kisses good enough to turn your ears bright red."

Mara quieted, thinking about the simple first kiss, and then whoa, the suck-the-life-out-of-you-in-a-good-way second kiss on the second date. An equal mixture of igniting and tempered, leaving her fully satisfied but still wanting more. And when the kiss left them both breathless, he dove into her neck, touching her breast through her thin T-shirt. Cupped it as if testing the weight, then caressing, stoking fires she forgot existed. Then he broke away, whispering in that husky breath, "Second date, second base. My buddies would be proud." With no words to describe anything, she only giggled at his comment. She never giggled. She laughed.

"You will be beyond beautiful to make love to," he'd said.

His touch made her want to crawl into the back seat and see if his whispers rang true. She wanted to be discovered, and he was aching to explore.

"But," he declared after pulling out of her mouth from another full-on make-out session. "I'm one of those old school cowboys. Your body may be saying yes, but your head and, more importantly, your heart aren't there yet. Don't worry, I'm a patient sort of guy."

Her face heated up at the memory. Her mom was silent while she recovered.

She looked away, then rattled on. "Mostly? We're having a lot of fun. We've done lunch a couple times at the hospital when he's in between classes. Navigating two busy schedules isn't the easiest. In fact, for our next date, I'm hoping he'll think toting boxes is somewhat romantic, and help me move. He is a hopeless romantic. Never imagined I'd like that. I always thought romance was sappy. But, well, here we are."

"Any truth to the rumors he's at fault? With the accident, I mean."

Mara shook her head. "There's a lawsuit pending, and he lost his job. But he's the one who ran back into the fire to save the man who died in the accident. His burns took weeks to heal. I hope the detectives get to the bottom of things. But, no, I can't see he was at fault. The good thing with being laid off, though, is he's hell bent on finishing school, and even thinking of law school."

"He makes you happy."

Mara looked up, and her mom smiled. She nodded. "He does."

"You look bright and healthy, a little glimpse of the old you. And I don't mean that in a bad way. You lost yourself somewhere in Chase. I'm glad you found that girl again."

"He's got a lot of baggage."

"We all have a lot of baggage. You've got forty pounds of luggage hopefully sleeping down the hall. Not to mention your seven-pound organ that is filled with scars and wounds. Everyone has baggage."

Mara took her mom's hand, not wanting her mom to go to places she herself didn't allow herself to dwell. "I know you have my best interest at heart, but please don't put your relationship with Dad up to the light as the shining example. I'm not sure people get that anymore. I'm glad you did. I'm glad I had parents who loved each other with everything in them. I'm just not sure the swoony, dedicated-for-life love exists anymore. I just want to ride this and see what develops."

Her mom smiled knowingly and nodded in response.

And as if he was connected to the always-listening puck contraption on the counter, her phone lit up with a goofy selfie they took at lunch the other day. The image of them, tucked together tight, made her smile.

"Go and talk to your man. I'll check on the insomniac." Her mom shooed her down the hall. "Let him know he has me to deal with if he hurts you. You've had enough of that for ten lifetimes."

Mara rolled her eyes. "Spoken like a true mom."

Chapter Eighteen

Mara flipped through the preschool's sign-in notebook.

"Oh, Ms. Sawyer. Your daughter didn't come today. Your mother-in-law said she was sick. I hope she's not getting one of those nasty spring colds."

Mara dialed Chase's number as she slammed through the door. The smoothness of everything settling into a nice, neat routine was now threatening to explode. The reassessment hearing neared, the one that decided shared custody, and she didn't want to overreact. She had again done everything to perfection, last weekend finishing the final step and moving into her new place. Rachel's "kid friendly" inspection was completed just this morning.

Chase answered as she slammed herself into her car. "Did you take her to the doctor?"

"What?"

"You know, since she's sick and all." She backed out of the space, the car picking up the Bluetooth mode of her phone. "Never mind, I'm on my way."

She hung up before he could respond. Ignoring his call back, she put all her energy into driving the speed limit, trying not to let her anger come into play. Around the corner from his house, she did a quick gut check before she made the final turn. Her stomach flip-flopped, proud of herself for holding back on calling Rachel and tattling. She breathed deeply and put the car in park.

The door opened, and she caught sight of the man who, at one point, had taken her breath away. His jeans were snug, his polo hanging untucked and loose, yet fitting perfectly at the same time. His all-business build a quick glimpse of the man who stole her heart. It would have been nice if that all-business look could've held down a job, but ambition slid out of him in the work world also.

"She's sick, Mara. And asleep. We'll swap for another weekend."

"You know I can't do that; my schedule gets set a month in advance. So, if you don't mind…" She tried to slip under his arm.

"I do mind. Let her get better."

"What did the doctor say?"

"You know it's just that petri bowl of a daycare. Colds and the flu runs rampant. The bug will work its way through her system, and she'll be good as new by Monday."

"You're in violation of the court order. Should I call the social worker?"

"Your buddy? Yeah, that ain't going to fly."

"Then I would suggest you let me take our daughter. I'm a nurse for God's sake."

"Oh, yeah, throw that in my face."

"I'm not throwing anything in your face. I can take care of her as well as you or your mother. We're going to court soon. I don't think you want to be in violation of anything."

"Are you fucking him?"

Mara blinked several times. The cruel words so assaulting they caused her to step back and fight the blitz attack in her stomach, wondering how he even knew. Luke had helped her move in last weekend, and that was their third date. Moving. They'd been surrounded by a few friends and their husbands. The moving excuse was more of a chance to get together than anything. She hardly had a moving truck full of stuff.

"Are you?" The sneer appeared instantly as he looked her up and down. "I mean, you look a ton better, but those thighs will only get you so far."

She didn't even know what to say to that. How to not explode. She fought to keep his words from being sucked inside, but she couldn't get the barricades in place fast enough.

"I'm not talking to you about this." She leaned in. "Charlie? Do you want to see your new room?" She fought to find bright and chipper, but she heard the crack in her voice. Knowing he did too.

"Ah, so, he won't do you either. That explains it."

Mara wondered what it explained, squinting at him as he continued blabbing.

"That nursing degree doesn't mean crap. You don't know how to take care of a man, or your daughter for that matter, and yet, you think you became a someone."

She wanted to pound fists into his mouth, stop the onslaught of words from slithering out.

As he shut the door behind him and stepped onto the porch with her, she speed-dialed Rachel at her side.

"Wait, are you following me?" she asked Chase, hoping Rachel would hear the conversation. Just in case. Just in case she murdered him on his own front porch.

"Yeah, right? Like you're worth that. You still can come home, you know. Let me enjoy that newfound, almost there body. Maybe some of that ice inside has thawed. I would take you back—just to give our daughter a real family, of course. I hear he's jobless right now, anyway. That's what you're crawling into bed with. Or not, as the case may be."

The inner battle welled, and she fought the good fight to keep the tremors inside, far away from the outside. Wanting desperately to point out that he had no room to talk in the job category.

She crossed her arms. "Are you going to get her or not? Should Rachel call the police and force you?" Tattling was now back on the agenda.

"She's sick, goddammit. What kind of mother wants to take their kid out of a perfectly good bed and into a second-hand one, with her mom and the Texas boy rolling and rutting in the other room? I won't put our daughter through that."

"Rachel?" She put the phone to her ear, raised her eyebrows at Chase. Calmness invaded, the explosion of his vile words fought off for the moment. "What do we do here?"

"Fuck Rachel. She doesn't get to decide what's best for our daughter." The wave of red crept north, from his neck to his face. "I decide. I decide where and when she goes. Not the bitch social worker. You may put on a good show for the court, but they don't know you. They know nothing about your bartender turned nurse playdate. Hell, any stupid trucker would be better than your desperado, stupid cowboy. Let him go find someone else's wife to fuck."

"Ex," she stated calmly. She thought it sounded calm.

A quick glance upward toward Charlie's room left her heaving a sigh of relief that the windows looked to be closed tight. As long as his words didn't invade her daughter, she could deal with this. She drew a deep breath in, releasing it in slow little puffs.

"What do I do?" she asked Rachel.

"I can get someone out there to make him comply, but…he just launched into a complete tirade. That is not going to play well if they try to stop joint custody."

Mara hung up. "Are you going to get her?"

"No. Did your hearing go wherever your few pounds disappeared to?"

Mara glanced around at the quiet, affluent neighborhood, scanning for busybodies. "Okay. I don't want to cause a scene. Just take care of her. Sick kids need to be cuddled. Maybe you could stay home for a night and do that for your daughter."

"Are you trying to tell me how to be a dad? Because last time I checked, I'm the one with full custody. I don't think I need lessons from the DUI mom," he screamed to her back.

She forced herself to hold her head high and walk to her car. The tremors inside crept their way to the surface, and she stumbled for a second but righted herself and walked on.

"Sheesh, maybe you're drunk now."

She held a select finger above her head as she slipped into the driver's seat. The anger had a five second delay before hitting full force. Yanking the steering wheel down the first street, she parked and collapsed into the steering wheel. To counteract the tremors, she began picking at her nails until they bled. When the red trails erupted, she knew he had won. The words now marinating.

She may have won the battle, but he won the war.

She opened the door and puked into the street.

****

He opened the door shirtless, a pair of basketball shorts hanging from his hips. From the porch, he shot Mara a quick wave. His eagle tattoo, all majestic and provocative, stopped her cold. For a moment, she wondered how she ended up here. She was tempted to go up, answer his beckoning hand, but venturing closer would solve nothing. The intense look he gave her made time stand still, like he could read every messed-up word that had been said tonight.

He cocked his head. When she continued to sit, he walked across the yard in bare feet. "I thought you were going to show Charlie the new place."

She faltered for a second, looking at him all bare chested and end-of-day mussed. She regrouped.

He squatted at her car door, bringing him eye level, and she wanted to cry. Just looking at him made her want. Want so many things she just couldn't have.

"Are you okay?"

"Did you tell him? Did you go see him and tell him?"

"What?" He scrunched his eyes together like a little boy. If she wasn't so lost and pathetic, it would be downright cute. "Who?"

"Never mind."

"Do you want to come in and talk?" His gaze landed on her scratched-up arm sitting on the windowsill.

Moving her arm, she tugged at her sleeves. Her car quit clicking and went silent, giving her a long minute to decide what the hell she wanted out of coming here. He couldn't fix her. Only she could fix her; she knew that now.

"What did you see when you sat on my barstool?" she blurted.

He scowled at her, and his eyes transferred from their emotional blue to their navy color. Her gnawed-up fingernails were calling, but she held herself in check.

"What did he say to you?"

The silence hung as the crickets chirped away in the darkness. The calmness, his quiet but firm words, caused a sad envy to take over, causing her to want to break and fall into his arms. But not now. Not tonight.

"I've never been a gorgeous girl with a great figure. I know that. But you could… Can you just answer the question? Why my barstool?"

He crossed his arms on her windowsill, cradling his head. A clump of hair fell into his eyes. "You mean before some bartender got me plastered?"

She smirked and looked out the front windshield.

Luke tossed his head. "The bar was warm. You might remember it was my first venture into everything frozen northland. But that night? Everything, everyone, was invisible. Just like I wanted to be. What did you see?"

Mara shrugged. There was no way in hell she would tell him what she saw. Maybe someday, but not when she was this low. "Why my barstool?"

"Because it was empty? Because I wanted a drink?" Luke did his own shrug. "I wanted to waste away into the woodwork, drown in my pitiful self. If you're asking if I noticed you as a woman, I'm going to be honest and say no. I didn't notice anyone. I was too caught up in hiding, running, being selfish, pick your verb."

She slumped a little at what he was saying, but the honesty, sincerity, spoke to exactly what she saw in him that first night. After the second and perhaps third glance at his coarse and turbulent looks, that is.

"I will say though, by the end of the evening, that wasn't the whole truth." Luke's gaze was riveted on her now. "By the end of the evening, even half lit, I saw a strong woman who could hold her own with a rambunctious crowd. A funny woman, a caring woman. A woman incredibly observant and knew her tequilas, always a plus. And she had some stellar listening skills. And I'm not just talking about me, because, you know, I got that Texas thing going, so who wouldn't want to listen to all this?" Luke crooked a finger down at himself. "You remember everything about people. You care. There're too few people in this world who care anymore."

"There were tips at stake."

"I think you lie. I think you genuinely care. You asked the guy next to me if his son won his baseball game. Wished a happy birthday to someone else. That's the woman sitting here right now. I know you're asking about the weight thing. Girls get all hung up on that; your stupid ex seems to be all hung up on that. But, Mara Sawyer, I didn't see that. I saw you."

The tears threatened. A smile crept onto her face, and the pressure of her unshed tears dissipated.

"The hospital, our reunion," Luke continued. "Different, but altogether the same story. I did see you lost weight, but losing however many pounds didn't create what I saw—there was a newfound confidence that wormed its way to the forefront. Not to mention the impressive girl muscles." Luke smiled as he nodded at her arms, laying his head there, looking so gentle, she had to look away.

"Confidence breeds more than beauty, babe. That's so much more appealing than having the perfect hair style, being the perfect size… Crap, I don't even know what a woman's size should be."

Luke covered her arm with his hands, his gaze never leaving her face. "I see you, Mara. You are beautiful inside and out, no matter what Chad or Chase, whatever the hell his name is, says."

The shaking rose from whatever reserves she had left. Her hands began trembling as she wrapped them in and around themselves. The silence hung, and he didn't stir. A car backfiring in the street jerked them both out of their heads. She didn't know what she expected to hear when she arrived here tonight, but this wasn't it. This was better. Raw. Especially from him who had more than a few damaging words of his own to deal with.

"Can I ask you another question?" She sat her chin on his folded arms, putting them nose to nose, making his little boy grin erupt.

"Anything."

The only thing left to lose at this point was Chase's words that continued to do their thing.

"If I were to come inside, would you have sex with me?"

Luke pushed back, almost falling on his ass with a laugh. "Whoa."

When he settled into his squat again, he glanced down at her breasts and took his time raising his gaze back to hers. She ran her hands up and down her pants.

"No."

She drew back and nodded to her insecure mess of a life. Tingling began in her fingertips at pushing too hard for approval, wishing she had fought to contain herself.

He was a thinker, an overthinker. She should have held back, but she was desperate to hear she was worth something. That physically, she was still a pretty awesome person. Desperate, yes, but it was as honest as she could get right now.

"Mara?" he whispered, smiling his big boy smile, the one where the turn of his lip was only on one side. The angles slipping from his cheeks to his chin and becoming depressed and harsh. Strong. Beautiful in a different way.

He cupped her face. "If you need to hear how I want to experience all your beautiful secrets. That you make my big old heart pound in excitement to explore your body, then my answer is a firm, hell, yes. But not tonight. There's someone else hanging between us. You haven't dealt with his words or figured out how to conquer them. I hope that won't always be the case. You're not seeing you right now; you're fighting his words. And with him in between us?" He shrugged. "There is no us. I don't play for second place. When you figure out how to see me, how to wrangle around those ridiculous judgments he planted, I will be happy to accommodate your request. But his words are not mine. I won't compete with that."

Now the damn tears welled in earnest. His unexpected tenderness and emotion meant more than whatever she hoped to hear.

"How do you battle that? The words?" She put two fingers on each side of her temple. "They invade. They fester. They control everything you do or say. How do you erase them, or at least beat them into submission?"

Luke shrugged. "Everyone has their own coping mechanism. Yours probably used to be food. Maybe now it's kickboxing." He kissed her softly and slowly and stepped back. "Go be where you're happiest, then put a fist into the beast. Find a way to vent."

"How do you vent?" she asked as he walked away.

"I run." He hopped up on his porch and turned back around with his one wad of hair that refused to stay out of his eyes. He tossed his head, and the disobedient strand flew back in place. "I do the lake on Saturdays. In case your bag punching doesn't work."

The door banged behind him. She smiled and started up her car.

Chapter Nineteen

The benches dotting the trails were desolate in the crisp, early morning. On one side of the lake, tall, snowy peaks reached toward the sky. A thick border of two- and three-story trees outlined the road and trails on the opposite side. Sitting on the outer edge of Rock Springs, high school was Mara's last memory of being here. One of those places you frequented for beer guzzling and great make-out sessions. At night, the lightning bugs would float through the trees, reflect on the water. Leaving behind a time-forgotten feel. By day, the bur oaks stood proud, plump at the top, drooping as they settled into thick trunks. As a child, they reminded her of giant ice cream cones.

The fog hugged the surface of the lake, topping the glassy water with puffs of white. Luke rounded the corner in the distance, his body all long muscles, protracting and extending from chest to ankle. The sweat leaked through his shirt straight down the center. The quiet so intense, she could hear his stride on the dirt. Little wisps of gravel scattered with each foot ambling forward. When Luke drew close, the music was loud enough to escape through his earbuds.

Only breathing moderately heavily, he halted in front of her. Removing one earbud, he tapped around on his phone, and the music died. He began stretching to the side, at his waist, sweat falling from his face in fat little plops. Straightening again, he pulled a towel from his waistband and wiped his face and neck.

"Does it work?" she asked. "Are you able to outrun the verbal assaults?"

He sat next to her as his breathing leveled. "For an hour or so. The music takes them away. You? Kickboxing work any better?"

Her head wagged back and forth. "Same. Takes them away as long as there's a hunk of black leather before me."

"You look tired. I'm guessing an all-night kick fest?"

"Not quite." Mara leaned forward. "A guy I know told me to go where I'm happiest. That worked better."

"Ahh, do tell."

When she exhausted herself at the twenty-four-hour gym, she was nowhere near tired. There was a force that burned when physically kicking the shit out of something for hours, propelling and energizing her. Mara was in the shower when she realized where happiness could be found when she couldn't be with her daughter. And she'd gone for another drive at two in the morning through desolate streets.

"I went to the hospital. I planned on roaming the halls, see if I could be of any use, but I never made it in the front door." The man sitting outside broke her heart as he smoked one cigarette after another. "One of my patient's husbands was there, crying one minute, yelling at God and the world the next. I held his hand. That's all I did. All I could do. It made me sad and mad at the same time…made me feel like I'd found my place in this messed up world."

Luke nudged her from the side. "I think that same

guy told you caring was your gift. You thought a warm-hearted soul was insignificant; turns out this boy was dead on."

"Oh, Lord." Mara rolled her eyes and kicked up a foot. "I came prepared. See? Can you teach me to run?"

"Everyone knows how to run."

"I don't want to run like a girl. I want to run like an athlete."

He raised his eyebrows and rose from the bench. "Let's see what you got."

She took off at what she thought was a pretty decent trot, trying to pump her arms like the tutorial video said she should.

"You're supposed to warm up first," he hollered.

"Warmups are for chumps." She laughed and set off down the trail.

He caught her on the first turn, spun around, and ran backward. Running a quick circle around her, he skipped at her side, matching her painstaking stride. This was way harder than he made it look. After maybe six minutes, she was already breathing heavily.

"Oh, my God, you're going to go all tricks and quirks on me on my rookie loop?" she panted out.

Taking another dancing circle around her, he laughed hard. "Nope, tricks are for chumps." Plugging his metal-induced music into his ears once again, he took off.

So much for teaching her the tricks of the trade. She would have to go down an online search rabbit hole if she wanted to do this right and hold her own. First, she needed to survive this little run and decide if this was something she really wanted to do. His chosen coping mechanism did nothing for her at the moment, making her wonder where the Zen part of the deal was.

At the backside of the lake, she found him sitting on a boulder, not even a hint of a heaving chest. She used the excuse to stop and give herself a chance to catch her breath.

"You didn't stop. That's pretty good for a beginner."

"Yeah, give me four hours to breathe normal again," she choked out.

"Water?" A bottle appeared from somewhere on him. "Catch your breath, and we'll walk the rest."

After taking a long swig, she handed his high-end reusable bottle back to him and lay back on the rock. The crisp air was in stark contrast to the bright sunshine. The sun made a steady ascent, and she wished she had remembered to bring her sunglasses. Pine lingered in the air, relaxing her body as her breathing settled into normalcy.

They rose in unison and walked the weaving and meandering trail. His stride was long, and he kept shuffling to slow down and match hers.

"Don't let me stop you." She flung her hand. "If you want to run, by all means."

"Naw, too pretty of a morning. I stopped so I could take a walk with my girl." He grabbed her hand. "Just have to figure out how to keep my legs from outpacing yours."

"Good luck with that." The night wore on her, not to mention a poor attempt at a run. She decided right then and there she'd stick to beating the leather bag.

When her boob began buzzing, she fished her phone out of her sports bra. Seeing the big EX displayed, Luke stopped and began massaging her knuckles while she contemplated whether to answer.

"Something might be wrong with Charlie," he said.

"I don't even want to hear his voice right now."

"I know." He continued to twist his fingers in and around her own. "Want me to answer? I'll give him the what for."

She couldn't help laughing. "Yes, you involved would really help matters."

When she connected, it wasn't Chase. "Mama?" Charlie's voice, all nasally, squeaked out, making Mara's breath hitch in her chest. "I sick."

Mara smiled. "I know, baby. Are you feeling better?"

"I did purple throw up."

Overhearing, Luke fought himself from laughing.

"Purple? Ewe. What in the world did you eat that gave you purple?"

"Daddy said it was the medicine, but there was other icky stuff in the throw-up bucket too," Charlie said, her throat lowering her little girl voice into a painful-sounding rasp. At least the sick part wasn't exaggerated.

"Good job getting to the bucket."

Charlie giggled. "I didn't the first time. Grammy V put it right next to me after I missed."

Charlie talked about how she got to stay in bed and watch all the movies she wanted yesterday. Mara listened to her rattle up and down each of the movies, her reviews complete with character and story lines, what she thought would make them better. Mara listened with rapt attention as Luke wandered off down the trail, waiting at the next bench.

"Mama, Daddy says I have to go take it easy again." Mara held back from laughing at Charlie's swooning drama voice.

"You feel better. I love you."

"Me too, Mumsy. Daddy wants to talk to you now."

Mara held her breath until he came on the line, walking toward Luke in case she needed fortification.

"Hey, any chance you're not working Monday?" The voice of her nightmares was calm today.

"I work Monday, but I'm on nights. What's up?"

"I told my mom I'd drive her to Billings to visit her sister tomorrow. We were going to take Charlie, but my aunt isn't in the best of health, so I don't think the smart choice is to have a sick kid around her. Not to mention Charlie's cold is still hanging on. I can be back on Monday. She's getting better, but I think we should keep her out of daycare for a day. Can I drop her off tomorrow morning on our way out of town and I'll pick her up Monday night?"

Luke stared at her as she listened and nodded her head. She reined in her petty self from pointing out if he had just let her take Charlie home last night, he could've avoided this little chat. She wanted to make him grovel, but that was narrow minded her. Not to mention the cutting-off-the-nose-to-spite-the-face thing. Besides the fact, his voice sounded pathetic and sweet today.

"I can pick her up now if you want," Mara offered.

"No. I'm good today. She's sleeping quite a bit."

"Okay, no problem. Drop her by tomorrow. If you can't get back on Monday night, let me know and I'll use a PTO day."

"Thank you. I should be fine." The line hummed in silence.

"Is that it?"

"Last night… I'm sorry."

Mara raised her eyebrows, unsure whether she had

ever heard those two words slide out of his mouth before. She looked out over the lake, waiting for more, but no more came.

"Text me when you're on your way in the morning," she said and hung up.

"Are you okay?" Luke asked, gathering her close.

"Yes." She shoved him. "You stink."

"So do you. We can be stinky together."

"Ha ha. After all his crap last night, he wants me to take Charlie in the morning, keep her though Monday."

"That's a good thing, right?"

"A great thing, actually."

"But?"

She shrugged. "He apologized. I can't remember him ever apologizing for anything at any point in time. Kind of made my roller coaster of emotions anticlimactic."

"Maybe. Maybe whatever he's dealing with has nothing to do with you. I'm not saying what he did or said is right, not by any stretch of the imagination. You just happen to be his black leather bag. Don't be the black leather bag."

"If it were only that easy."

They began walking the trail again. He matched her stride.

"So, plans today?" Luke said, pulling her still glistening self into his side as they walked. "Want to go get donuts? I'm feeling donuts."

She stopped. "You can't run and then go get donuts."

He stared at her like she had three heads. "Why?"

"Because…because you can't. Sugar and carbs cancel out the run."

He shook his head and scrunched up his forehead. "Again, why?"

"I don't know." Mara shrugged. "Just doesn't make sense to run hard out and throw it away by eating donuts."

"Makes perfect sense. I like donuts. I feel like donuts."

"Sheesh." In her brain, it made little sense. He acted like it was the most natural thing in the world. "In any case, I'm keeping my burned calorie count on the plus side of things, and I am tired. My all-night kick-and-slam fest has caught up. Maybe we can do something later?"

"I can't." He shook his head and then grabbed her wrist. "Wait, want to go to a baby shower, gender reveal thing with me? It's a couples one. I'm tired of being the ugly stepsister, third wheel. I want to have a plus one."

Sticking his lower lip out, he pouted. She couldn't help but laugh.

"They won't mind a tagalong?"

"Hell no. They'll hand you a beer and welcome you to the family."

This was like going public. They were already somewhat out there, but this was real. They would be a couple. She loved the thought; she was petrified by the thought. She wasn't good in crowds, but she imagined he had the lowest key friends around.

"Did you buy a gift?"

"Gift card," he answered as they exited the trail and headed toward the parking lot.

"Didn't they have a registry?"

"A what?"

"A registry. One of those things telling you what they want? Or need?"

"I don't know. It said something about a baby store on the invitation, so I bought a gift card for there."

Men were so dense.

"Is he a good friend of yours?"

"I guess. He's one of the first people I met when I got here. We hang out a lot."

"First baby?"

"Yes."

"You need a gift. Good friend, first kid, you need a gift. A somewhat personal gift. The store reference on the invite was, no doubt, the registry."

"Oh. Interesting."

She rolled her eyes. "Registries are interesting? Personal gifts are interesting?"

"Kind of, yeah. What's more interesting is when my sister got married, I bought her a five-hundred-dollar gift card. I thought I nailed the wedding gift thing. She acted like the thing had demon horns, telling me she was my sister, saying I could have done something a little more…"

Mara laughed and interrupted. "Personal?"

He smiled. "Yep. Told me she even gave me the roadmap of what to buy. I had no clue why she was talking about roadmaps. I didn't need a map to get to the damn wedding."

"Oh, my God, you're killing me. Men are so ignorant sometimes."

She beeped her car into releasing the locks, and he opened her door.

"Sure you don't want donuts?"

"No! I probably ran off four pounds. I'm going to take the win."

"Fine. I'll go to sugar heaven by myself."

Sliding into her car, she faltered for a second. Sugar always sounded good. She talked herself out of the momentary high just as quickly. "I'm going to take a nap. Pick me up an hour before we have to be there, and we'll go spend your gift card. Don't forget the invitation so we can look up the info."

"Demanding little bitch today," he mumbled, leaning in to kiss her at the same time.

"Feeling more myself, so, there you go."

He chuckled and slammed her door.

Chapter Twenty

Silverwood left Luke stranded in unemployment land. Wyatt and his friends there were instructed not to discuss anything about the case. They needed to stay employed—he understood. Silverwood had gazillions of dollars to throw at lawyers, tying fault and culpability up in court for three lifetimes. In some ways, he wished Rowdy's family would take the life insurance money and be placated. In other ways, if either of the companies were negligent, they should be dragged through the court system.

Out of the whole mess, though, the accident and resulting repercussions gave Luke direction. Things with Mara were plodding forward, and since the employment front remained a dead issue, he had finished up his degree in the interim. With a whole lot of research on oil law, negligence, culpability, relating to his own case, he'd thrown caution to the wind and applied to law school.

A car door slammed as he drained a beer.

Luke opened the door to her hand poised to knock, pecking him on the cheek as she walked by. "I already ordered a pizza. And bought a six-pack."

"I already had a case. You didn't have to stop."

"You buy the cheap shit. I like my premiums."

"Beer snob," he mumbled, grabbing a bag.

He watched her ass as she bent and maneuvered

stuff around in the fridge.

"I worked in a bar. I can be a beer snob."

"Basic Lite's never done me wrong yet."

"Says he who will argue until his ears turn green that Angelo brew, whatever in the holy hell that is, is the best beer going. And yes, I checked. It's not so cheap either."

He grumbled, "It's only expensive here. It's a Texas brand."

"Liar." She jammed her hand into her mountain of a purse. "I brought a movie too."

"I was going to pay-per-view something."

"I wanted to pick, so I grabbed one of my favorites." She fell into his arms and kissed him hard on the lips.

Yep, she could choose whatever she wanted tonight. Movie wise, beer wise, he was a goner with every day ticking past on the calendar.

"You don't play fair."

"Not tonight I don't. I felt all girly and…" She wagged a DVD box. "Sappy chick flick. Not sorry."

He looked at the cover and flipped the sleeve over.

He rolled his eyes at her choice.

"And they sing! The music is going to be amazing."

"Whatever." He was saved from further conversation as the doorbell rang and the pizza man wanted to be taken care of.

"Kind of surprised you haven't seen it, being the gorgeous sap king you are," she hollered at his back. "You're going to love it, Whitten. I promise. You can even ogle over the beautiful blond star of the movie. I won't be offended."

"Pass," he said, dropping the pizza on the table.

Even though they talked or facetimed almost every night, they both were gushing with conversation. He

Kathryn Beck

found himself wanting to tell her every little thing. Sometimes when they were together, the words and sentences were a rapid-fire explosion.

The pizza and its box cleaned up, she plugged the DVD into the machine, and he pointed the remote to start it rolling. They plopped onto the couch, her snooty beer in hand, snuggling into his outstretched arm.

"Give it a chance. You're going to love the movie." Mara patted his leg.

He wasn't sure "love" was the appropriate word, but he didn't hate it. Well into the movie, Mara clutched at his arm. The grasp needy. He'd never seen her cry, tears trailed on her cheek, the river cutting and building as they slid down her face.

The movie wasn't sad—well, not yet. But he got the feeling sappy was headed his direction.

Her hand clutched again. Something unexpected moved him. He didn't plan what was happening, but he couldn't ignore the pull.

"Dance with me." He beckoned with an open palm.

She wiped tears and snot across her face in a moment so pathetically romantic, he couldn't help but smile.

Tremors, one hiccup, as he whipped her into his arms. She calmed into a sway, with all their pieces fitting just right. Her hand at his chest; his heart was out of control. He waited for the beat to flatten out and calm. It did, and then it didn't. It was a different kind of calm. His physical reaction was anything but calm. He wanted to pull her tighter, but there was no space. She already there. He wanted to strip his shirt off, remove the layer standing between them and feel her hair, her skin. Clutch the rawness.

At the small of her back, right in the center, his hands hovered just above her butt. Her breath escaped in a fast draft. The sensitive spot got stored away while he ran a lone finger along her spine, up the center of her back and grasped her neck, intertwining his hands, tilting her head to make their lips flush and tight. He ran his tongue around her lips, in her mouth and explored at a slow pace, watching a swirling kaleidoscope of color, a beautiful burst of oranges and reds, the faintest tinge of purple. A cloudless sunrise with one low-hung contrasting cloud. Though they'd had some great make-out sessions, the passion and depth boring to his core couldn't touch this. When she sighed into his mouth, it rocked his little world, making him separate their lips and take a tiny nip of her earlobe, then her neck. Luke's world completely erupted, and he wanted nothing more than to sink into the journey. With a tiny shake of his head, he fought logic and reasoning, wanting the world to disappear.

The movie wandered into dialogue but became an incoherent murmur. He was lost in Mara's gaze and what she wanted. Hopefully him. Just him. He didn't want either one of them to compete with anyone tonight. Sliding her hands up his body, she smiled and drew him back into her mouth, backing toward the wall. When they slammed against it, his hands smoothed up her sides, his thumbs brushing over her breasts, down her arms to twitching fingertips. The strap of her tank top slipped off her shoulder, and he kissed all the way from her neck to her forearm. The catch in her breath caused him to suck in a lungful of air, longing to give her those catches of breath for an eternity. Her fingernails were up under his shirt, weaving his shirt into her fingers and away from his body. Soft lips whispered across his collarbone, causing his body to react so primally, a shuddering jerk released itself. He pinned her to the wall, hesitating and forcing her to open her eyes. The recognizable fire made him long to right every wrong in both their lives. He took her hand, led her down the hall, stopping at his bedroom door, searching her eyes for answers.

She swung the door wide. Her gaze scanning, stopping at the simple navy comforter, the pictures of Claire and him on the dresser.

Her fingers grazed the hem of his shirt. "Let me."

His arms plummeted to his sides. Once his shirt was removed, she ran her hands over his chest, over the lean stomach, to the biceps tensing and spasming as she stroked. She hit the inner arm near his elbow and trailed a finger over the tender juncture, down to his wrists. He struggled to hold himself in check. He was good at holding back, but her brush touched pieces of himself he didn't know existed. His eyes floated shut. She saw the more. The raw heart, the ripped-up soul.

In a heartbeat, he shifted from defense to offense. Mara's tank top trailed to the floor, revealing a simple bra, practical and white with tiny, embossed flowers he traced with his finger. He lowered the straps and followed the line of fabric across the top of her breasts. Cupping a handful of satiny breast with one hand, he released the clip holding her hair with another. Hair spilled over his hand. Soft and rounded, she was full of jagged, complicated edges. Edges he wanted to smooth out and fit against his own.

When she reached behind her, he lifted her hand to his lips. "Let me."

The bra fell to the floor. He kissed her lips, down to

her neck, his tongue circling one nipple, then the other. Sucking tenderly, then sucking with more intensity. When she wiggled herself tight against him, he fought everything inside, straining to hold off until he discovered all her delicious, secret pieces. He fumbled with the button on her jeans, and they joined the bra and tank top. She wrestled with his belt, and his shorts joined the other discarded clothing. When her hand slipped inside his boxer briefs and grabbed his butt, they slid down his legs, and he kicked out of them.

For someone who struggled with the awkwardness of things of the heart, she slid into the sheets like they were the finest silk, instead of the lowest thread count the linen department offered.

Her eyes were heavy with lust and passion, making him wonder if you could touch another's soul in their eyes.

****

Mara's body exploded from the inside out. Everything he kissed, everything he touched, aching for release. She wanted to float here forever, holding on to the soft brushes barely touching skin, at the same time igniting the deepest core. His body was like liquid fire, melting himself and her at every touch. The body heat was intense when she kissed his tattoo, following the silky and salty trail of an eagle's wing with her tongue. And when he looked at her, she didn't know looks could burn. The expanse of emotion in his eyes was the most intense connection she ever experienced, and they were still tasting, still simmering. His body was rock hard everywhere, yet soft in all the good places. She skimmed her baby finger down his side. His breath caught. When she kissed the juncture inside his elbow, he bit his lip.

She'd never felt so powerful and yet so vulnerable at the same time. Her stomach tightened at the same time as his softened.

When her fingertips scraped across his belly, he took her hand and kissed her palm, kissed the pads of each finger. Her heart pounded as his gaze devoured her, everything exposed, inside, outside. She hovered over him, letting her breasts float above his chest. His gaze so absolutely gorgeous, her nipples hardened without being touched. He dipped his head, taking one in his mouth as the other slid back and forth across his chest until the inner pressure radiated the most pleasured pain. Cupping her bottom and rolling her to her back, his eyes turned a navy blue, full of passion and need. Her legs separated in response, needing to feel the hardness of him inside, but he kept torturing with wisps of reverent touches. An enamor with all her body held. Her body. The same body that was flabby in all the wrong places. His eyes were ripped from inside, making her blink away tears, it was so beautiful.

His lips trailed tiny kisses down her stomach, but she missed the heat of him, the hardness of him against her. At the bottom of her gut, he stopped.

She dropped her hand, cupped his face, trying to bring him back up. "I've got a scar, don't."

"Mmm, a beautiful baby scar," he said, trailing a line of tender kisses the length of her caesarian wound. Back again with his tongue.

And she couldn't think. She just wanted him. Inside.

But he wasn't done exploring.

While he explored, she imploded.

His lips dropped and kissed the tender juncture of her thighs, kissing the inside of her thighs, the inside of her, while his fingertips trailed down to her knees and back up. Planting the tiniest kisses where no lips had gone before. It was so intimate, she thought she would be embarrassed. Instead, the embers kept building. She squeezed her legs together, wanting to hold on to everything washing over her, through her, in her.

Then he was at her lips, sinking into her mouth, dancing a slow definitive waltz with his tongue. The kiss was so thorough, raising her toward some kind of crescendo. The simpleness caused everything to blur into brightness and sparks of light. Firecrackers rising into a darkened sky, falling soundlessly to the ground.

"Look at me, Mara."

Her eyes fluttered open, and his were boring into her, reading her. He smiled and plunged back into her mouth. He squeezed her breast, shooting tremors as he entered her with such strength, she found herself melting. When he pulled out, her hips rose in a cry of their own. The inside of her ached to explode, but he moved so incredibly slow, all his movements building momentum, instead of allowing them to erupt. She grasped for his hips, tugging him back into her, wanting to feel all of him, creating an endless stream of tingles that refused to abate. She ground her nails into his butt, speeding him up, pulling him as deep as she could. Wanting the tension to end, at the same time, wanting it to continue. Forever. When every force in her short history of sexuality lay at the breaking point, he slowed his rhythm again, the timing taking her breath away. The tremors shot out of her stomach, her thighs, rising into her breasts and arms. Everything exploded at once, and her mouth opened, her breath heaving from her.

As she floated down, he rose, smiling as he licked

Kathryn Beck

the sweat from her lip and kissed her nose.

"I just died." He rolled to the side, gathering her into him.

Her body was still spasming. She couldn't catch her breath. The interlaced emotions of power and vulnerability were the headiest experience ever. She had climaxed before, but never with her partner inside.

"I don't even know what to say."

His chest rumbled in her ear. "You can start with those Texas boys sure know what they're doing."

She smiled and splayed her hand across his eagle's wings. One of these days she would have words again.

The sunlight was streaming in the window when she woke from her stupor. Face down on her stomach, she couldn't help but smile into the pillow.

Realizing the heat of him was gone, she flipped her head. By the bedside, he sat in a chair, studying her. She smiled in his direction, wondered how long he had been watching her sleep all tangled up in his sheets.

He nodded where the sheet met her skin, just above her butt crack. "You have a tattoo." He kissed the marking. The pad of his thumb ran across the design. "Didn't figure you for a tat girl."

"Freedom marker." She smiled in abandonment as she voiced her words from so long ago. She'd fallen down plenty of times since it had been placed there, but this was the first time she'd understood the grip of liberty and indulgence. The first time she felt like herself in a long time.

He studied the design. "A drunk thing? Why an anchor?"

"Not a drunk thing. Probably should have been. Those things hurt."

A seriousness came over him. "You're evading. Why the anchor?"

She fought the evasion defense mechanism again, meeting his gaze head-on. "Strength, security. A mooring in place. My dad had an anchor, an old school sort of thing. My mom's name was woven through his."

He kissed the skin where it sat. "Interesting concept."

His finger trailed across the anchor.

"Are you writing your name?" she asked, smashing her smiling face into the pillow.

"Maybe."

"Your turn." She rolled over and nodded at his eagle.

He smiled a lazy smile. "Same. Freedom marker."

"Do tell."

He looked down at his chest, kissed her nose. "Me and a couple friends did them when on leave in Shanghai. We have so many freedoms here, and so few people really understand privilege, taking so much for granted. So, we did a partial eagle, with…" He touched the head. "See how it tucks its neck. That was our way of saying all men are fallible—not ashamed or embarrassed, just fallible. One of my friends had an abusive father, the other had an alcoholic grandfather and mom, and I…I had a family who didn't want me. Fallible, all of us. Reminding us, we can't be completely free until we untangle the mess of our lives."

"Wow, yours is way more prophetic than mine."

Luke shivered as she traced the face of the eagle, now noticing how it looked down his arm.

"Or we were just stupid drunk."

She didn't buy that at all. A lot of logic went into

their tattoos, a lot of messiness and emotional baggage.

Their stomachs growled in unison, and they both laughed.

"You need to make me an omelet or something," she said.

He hovered over her, his eyes drooping until they were almost closed. Her legs separated, and he filled the gap.

"In a minute, this won't take long." He crushed her; her breath escaping in little puffs. The build began anew.

Chapter Twenty-One

Life settled into a blessed normalcy. A beautiful, peaceful time until the news from home jarred him back into reality. Luke always knew the day would come when his father would be no longer, but that wasn't this call. Though in good health, he always envisioned the moment his father would be gone as a massive heart attack, like earlier in the year. Like his grandfather. Collapsing in his breakfast, quick, not cruel. That was how he pictured his father going out.

All those speculations rattled around as Claire babbled away.

Evelyn was the one who was no longer. He should feel something, but he didn't. All he had was his insides freezing, the same way they always did when her name was launched into a conversation. He should be feeling sympathy for his father, but he couldn't. No sadness, no sympathy. Relief, but a bittersweet relief.

Evelyn, who salsa danced once a week, played tennis with the girls before they lunched at the club, always the epitome of health. A brain aneurysm, knocking her down and taking her out, all in the midst of Sunday brunch with friends. She hadn't even survived the ambulance ride to the hospital.

Mara stared at him from across the room. Claire continued, not seeming to need any response out of him. He couldn't breathe. There was a whole host of emotions running rampant, but sadly, he felt nothing for someone so evil.

Except she left his father alone.

"Luke, are you going to come? Dad really needs us," Claire asked.

He was already shaking his head. "To Texas? Why?"

"Because she died? To help with arrangements? I don't know."

"No." He walked to the window. "C'mon, Claire, even I'm not that hypocritical."

"But Dad needs you," she whispered. He knew by the tone and level of her voice she was fighting a losing battle with her own emotions.

"Dad hasn't needed me for a very long time. I'm sure he'll manage."

He leaned his head against the glass, watching the kids in the street playing a makeshift game of soccer. Her comment about his dad needing him made him even sadder. Not because it was or wasn't true, but because it wasn't his dad on the phone asking. The woman lying in the coffin severing the thread, the man who either needed or didn't need his son, working the scissors.

"I need you." She said it so softly, touching worn, intimate places.

His eyes fluttered shut. "Don't. Please, just don't."

There was a long silence. Claire understood, just like she always did.

"Okay. I'm going to let you go. I've got a lot of phone calls to make."

"I love you, Claire bear. Don't let him run roughshod over you."

Collapsing into the window seat, he held the phone

to his chest long after she hung up. Mara sat next to him. The heat of her left him searching for her hand, saying nothing for a long period of time.

"Want to tell me?" Mara said as her head hit his shoulder.

A callous quip about the wicked stepmom being dead sat on his tongue. Wasn't there a song somewhere about the wicked witch? He didn't even care if he was being disrespectful.

He shrugged. "My stepmom died. Massive aneurysm. It's not like I'm flooded with emotion here."

"Are you going to Texas?"

Why did everyone assume that? He squinted his eyes. "I had no relationship with her. I would say my emotions bordered on hate. She made my life a living hell. Why in the world would I want to go?"

"For your dad."

He shook his head, hating she asked, giving a voice to his vulnerabilities. Claire knew enough to assume— no, Claire just knew all his soft spots.

"If my dad needed me, don't you think it would've been him on the phone?"

"Maybe he's as stubborn as his son. Maybe he doesn't know how to ask."

Luke rose and paced, letting her logic fester. "Maybe now he'll learn how to live without following her commands. Maybe this is a good time to figure out where he went wrong."

"You don't mean that, Luke."

"Yeah, I kind of do." He headed toward the kitchen, pouring himself a shot of tequila and slinging it back. "And then, if he did need me…I can't go through this again. Being able to put blame on her gives me excuses to feed myself that he wasn't at fault in this. What if it really was? What if she wasn't pulling his strings at all? What if he was the one who didn't want me home? Don't you see? With her gone, I can't live any longer in the neverland of not knowing. What if he really, really is ashamed of me? What if..." His voice rose, then dropped, becoming low to the point of almost a whisper. "What if he truly doesn't love me?"

Mara wrapped herself around him as best she could. He couldn't hold her tight enough, get close enough to the heat of her to melt his ice.

"I don't know if I can handle knowing the truth."

"You don't believe that."

"But I don't know. There's a comfort in not knowing."

He put her ear to his heart and let the hammer slow into a rhythmic cadence. "He doesn't need me."

She held his face, stared hard, and read him from the inside out. "But your sister does."

Claire's voice rang in his ears.

"I don't want to," he said after a long silence.

She smiled, stroking his cheeks. "You sound like a little boy. Did you want to add, 'And you can't make me?' "

He drew a deep breath. He would've liked to say a cleansing breath, but it really wasn't. Claire's little girl voice penetrated his insides like nothing else.

Mara kissed his heart, ran her fingers up his arms, trailing her heat-infused touch.

"I don't want to leave you. Not…right now." Things were so good. She was recovering from her ex's words. He was recovering from his father's words. He was happy, truly happy, for the first time in a long time. He didn't want to risk changing the circumstances and jeopardize whatever future they may have together.

"Do you want me to go with you?"

A lifeline tossed his direction together with the question. A bonding lifeline, where they became strong together. Or where she would see his dark side, his family's dark side.

His heart hammered. The fact she understood he needed someone in his corner pierced him. He didn't want to fall wholeheartedly in love with her yet. Okay, maybe he did, but he wasn't ready to be irrational.

"You'd do that? What about work? What about Charlie?"

"I have time accrued. I can be back by Friday for Charlie. Quick trip, but…" She shrugged. "This isn't about your stepmom; this isn't even about your dad. This is about your sister."

Shuddering, all the fight went out of him.

Chapter Twenty-Two

Mara curled into his side on the airplane. The whirlwind of arrangements winding down and letting him sleep for the first time since getting the news. A whole host of people owed Mara favors, and she had no problem finding someone to cover her shifts. Finding plane tickets with a return date allowing her to pick up Charlie from school on Friday was no simple chore. Lastly, notifying Rachel, making sure there would be no issues with the shared custody hearing next week.

Luke was a strong man, but watching him the last twelve hours took her back to when he arrived in town, drunk, looking for a place to call home. The uncertainty of knowing he would have to stand in the same room with his father and talk to, or not be talked to. Words could rip you in two, but silence was just as deadly.

They checked into a hotel, showered, and changed. On the drive, he began talking nonstop, not about anything in particular, just rattling off a quick primer on life in San Angelo. The schools, the industries, pointing out parks and people's houses.

After emerging from the compact rental, one leg at a time, he began folding up the sleeves of his white button down, looking all gorgeous in his black and white. Texas casual. No ties necessary. Straightening his collar, she moved a lock of hair out of his eyes.

"You can do this."

"I can do this." He breathed deeply. "I can do this."

A man in a full suit welcomed them, handing them a folder and motioning to the left. The room was immaculate, but Texas homey. In the lobby, thick wood lined the ceiling and walls. Paintings of oil pumpers and historical landmarks framed in burnt gold, tastefully dotting the walls. The carpet, thick and soft at their feet, integrating voices and sounds into hushed whispers.

A woman in the center of the room broke from a conversation and burst into tears, collapsing into a man at her side.

When Luke stepped forward, Claire fell into him. And they both sobbed.

"Mitch. Good to see you." Luke shook the man's hand at Claire's side. "Mara, this is my sister, Claire, and her better half."

Claire's head flipped on Luke's chest. Her red-rimmed eyes cleared. The smudged mascara didn't.

"Way to make a girl look like a mess." Claire swiped at her face. "I finally get to meet the girl you've been gushing on, and I'm falling apart."

Mara hugged her. "I'm so glad to meet the other woman."

"When did you guys get in? How come you didn't come by the house? How'd you get out of class?"

Luke took Claire's hand. "About thirty minutes ago, because it was just thirty minutes ago, and sweet-talked my instructors. Anything else you want to know?"

"No." She leaned in and hugged him. "Thank you," she said to Mara.

Luke pulled Mara into him. "Yes, thank you."

"Make the rounds, okay?" Claire smiled at someone and nodded at the crowded room. "There's a lot of people here you know."

"Yes, ma'am." Luke maneuvered around the room, shaking hands and introducing Mara. When they got to a man who was Luke, a quarter of a century down the road, his hand tightened on her own. The man's stature took over the room. Filled out a little more than Luke, but by no means stocky or hefty. He was just a big man. Dressed as a big man in Texas does. Jeans, a plaid shirt with a blazer for the more formal occasions.

"This man would have to be your father, babe." She held out her hand, trying to be friendly and confident, but it was nerve-wracking to face the man who inflicted so much hurt. "I'm Mara."

Luke's dad was silent, taking a minute to gather himself. He was dialed in on Luke and missed she was even there. If Luke couldn't see the definition of longing, he was downright blind.

Luke's dad shook himself away from his stare off with Luke and took her hand in his massive ones. "Mara? What a beautiful name. I'm Ward." He turned away from her and gathered Luke into his chest. Mara shuffled from one foot to the other as they hugged it out. When they separated, she was so proud of Luke when he expressed his sympathies.

"You'll come to the house tonight of course. I can text Carla to ready the guest room."

"We have a hotel, thanks," Luke bit out.

She stroked Luke's hand, trying to calm a flurry of words that didn't need to be said this early in the visit. He smiled and squeezed her hand.

"Let's give it some time, okay?" Luke said to his father.

Ward nodded. "I look forward to it, son."

Luke's hand turned from secure and solid to pliant and spongy with just a few little words.

In the morning, they headed to Claire's for brunch before the wake at the ranch after the service.

Barely clearing the threshold of Claire and Mitch's house, a cherub of a little boy with a mass of pretty blond curls ran headlong into Luke's legs. "Uke, I been waiting forever for you." Luke lifted him high over his head and fake dropped him, causing adorable squeals of delight.

"Cole? Is that you, Cole?" Luke held him upside down and twisted and turned, looking blankly around the living room. "I guess I'll have to eat breakfast by myself. Cole doesn't want to see me."

"I here, I here." The giggles flying from the little boy were heart-warming.

Claire grabbed Mara's hand and tugged her into the kitchen. "Those two are adorable, but hopeless."

"It's nice they get along," Mara said, taking the cup of coffee Claire offered. "He's beautiful."

"My other son is five. We're going to give it another go and hope for a girl." Claire crossed her fingers and eyes. "Please God, don't leave me in this house full of men."

"Can you imagine all the testosterone when they're teenagers?"

"Bite your tongue. I can barely handle it now. Mitch grew up in a big family, and to be honest, it's just fun being around all those siblings and relatives. We're trying, as much as you can plan these things, to keep all the cousins in the same age range, growing up together. It keeps Thanksgiving Turkey bowl games nice and competitive."

Mara couldn't help but like and love Claire. Down

to earth and laid back, she didn't have all the angst wrapping around her like her brother.

"Luke says you have a daughter. I'm beyond jealous."

Claire's husband strode in and kissed her neck. "I keep telling you, we just keep trying until we hit pay dirt. Five? Six? What's the magic number?"

"No way. You're not the one who has to wrestle these monkeys into the car every morning. Let alone getting all pudgy and wobbly while said monkeys are launched into the world."

Mara laughed. "Sorry to tell you, but girls? I don't think any of the little people know how to stop moving at that age."

"See." Mitch flung his hands. "Boy, girl, it just doesn't matter. They're all a pain in the ass." He whipped the five-year-old out of his seat and away from his pancakes. "Right, JJ?" Mitch blew lip farts into JJ's stomach.

"Hungry, put me down," JJ demanded.

Mitch nodded his direction. "Not a morning kid. Claire, we need us a morning kid."

Claire rolled her eyes. Luke came into the room with Cole on his shoulders. After spotting the pancakes, Cole about dropped six feet to clamber to the table. He took up a place next to his brother as Mitch cut. Luke dropped a kiss on JJ's bed head hair. JJ grunted.

"Rude much." Luke put him in a mock headlock, which earned him an eye roll almost as good as his mother's.

After the kids scampered off, Claire loaded up the table with platters of eggs, bacon and sausage, more pancakes, biscuits and gravy. She blew out a deep breath.

"I'm off duty for ten minutes."

"Oh, babe, I can give you twelve." Mitch winked at Mara.

"I'll give you fifteen," Luke added.

"Kiss ass."

"I can own that."

Mara wondered how Luke survived without this interaction.

"Hey, Luke," Claire said. "I hate to spoil this beauteous family time, but we've got to talk to Dad. I know you don't want to be dragged into the business side of things, but I'd appreciate some backup. Evelyn's nephew, Justin, the one who came to run things while Dad recuperated from the heart attack, he and Evelyn…they were doing some funny financial stuff. I'm not trying to say intentionally, but poor management is going to drain Dad in the not-too-distant future."

"Huh? You're going to have to explain better than 'funny financial stuff,' " Luke mumbled through a piece of bacon.

"Evelyn's always done his books. I mean she is—well, was—great at it. Dad wants to transfer everything to our firm now, so he asked me to take a glance before we sign a contract." She turned and looked at Mara. "I'm a CPA." Claire turned back to Luke. "Justin's blowing through a lot of money. I'm not sure if he just doesn't have the skills to run a ranch, or he doesn't care. He's overpaying the workers for one. I think most of the ones he hired were friends from Fort Worth. You know he let Mike go?"

Luke's fork clanked against his plate. "Why would Dad allow that? Mike's always been a good worker. And crazy loyal."

"Exactly. Mike's been with Dad, what? Twenty years? His salary was around seventy-five a year when he was let go. A little high considering Dad let him have the house on the backside of the ranch too, but not outrageous considering time on the job and the crazy hours he worked. Justin started Mike's replacement at one twenty."

"What? That's insane."

"Dad always pays decent, but in the forty-a-year range, with housing. Justin's paying two and three times that, with housing. In any case, there's a lot of fishy things I don't want to come back on my company because we didn't say anything."

"I doubt he'll listen to me, but we can try."

****

Luke's father settled behind his large, overwhelming desk in his home office. The funeral yesterday had been unemotional. It felt normal to be here, his father treating him like in the old days. Later, he found himself outside, finding it reasonably easy to avoid melancholy thoughts.

Today, the pending conversation needed to take center stage. His attention needed to be focused if he was going to be of any help. Last night, he and Mara polished off a couple of bottles of wine with Claire and Mitch. It was pretty evident what the books were saying. Oil was in the tanker, but history said if you hung around long enough, it would come back around. But while the Whitten ranch waited out the oil market, it leaned on the livestock and cattle. Right now, in spite of a solid herd, financially they were barely holding on. He wasn't an accountant, but even his non-math brain knew you had to make more deposits than withdrawals.

Claire shook as she held the file folders on her lap. He touched her arm, gave it a squeeze when Justin walked in.

"Dad?" Claire squirmed in her seat. "I'm not trying to be rude, but…can we talk first and Justin can join us later?"

Justin smirked and sat anyway, took his hat off and set it in his lap. He dismissed Luke with a roll of the eyes and put all the syrup he could muster in his words. "Well, darlin', we're all family now, even with Auntie gone." He wiped his eyes. "God rest her soul."

Luke fought himself from sighing too heavily, wanting to smash Justin's face into the hardwood floors at their feet.

"He's right, Claire. I'm not sure why you want to meet, but Justin's been running this place while I've been healing and doing a damn fine job at it. It could help him, as much as myself, to know what issues there are."

Justin crossed his arms and raised his eyebrows at Claire.

Claire stumbled for a second. She may not be accustomed to being low man on the totem pole, but Luke had plenty of experience, so he decided to wade in. "Okay then. But let Claire get all this information out before we discuss it further. She's done what you've asked, looked over the books, but there's some issues."

"Just a second here. Auntie isn't in the grave twenty-four hours; I won't stand for you disrespecting her."

Claire straightened, recovering her all-business persona. "Actually, I'm not saying any such thing. Evelyn did an immaculate job with the books."

"The problem then?" their dad asked. "If the books are in good shape, I'm not understanding why the urgency."

"You're spending too much," Claire blurted.

Justin scrunched his eyes together while his father stayed silent, wrapping his brain around the outburst.

"You're doing remarkably well in cattle right now, but you're not even breaking even. You're spending more than you're bringing in. For the last couple months, you've dug into your equity line at the bank to meet your obligations. From what I can tell, you're staff heavy, payroll heavy, and you're paying too much for nonessentials. I know you offer housing and a cook for the men, but the expenses for the food have quadrupled in the last few months. And you've run up quite a tab at the liquor store. I don't know you've ever provided alcohol for your workers. You can't keep going like this if you don't want to end up in bankruptcy court."

"I think you need to go back to your day job and leave the ranch's finances in your father's hands." Justin shifted his weight to the edge of his seat.

"This is my day job." Claire looked defiantly across the desk, ignoring Justin. "If you weren't my father, just a client who walked into our offices in town, I'd say the same thing. You should be thriving right now, but you're not, because you're overspending."

"I'm not listening to this. Ward, these men work hard. You can't cut the bennies and still expect to get the work done."

"What about the liquor? If I'm not mistaken, that can be a lawsuit waiting to happen," Ward said, looking quickly at Claire, then Luke, back to Justin.

"I order a case or two a month for Friday nights. Sorry." He drew the word out. "Didn't know a Friday night brewski was such a no-no."

Luke was not going to allow Claire to take this alone. "It's not a no-no, but I've looked at it too, and it's not just a case or two a month. More like five or six a week. So, if you're going to beat around it, at least beat around it accurately. No one's accusing anyone of anything, but you've got to cut back. There's no need for steaks twice a week, there's no need for any liquor, and there's no need to be paying people double the going rate. If you're going to overpay men, then cut back on the number of employees. I'm not saying they're not earning it; I have no idea what's going on, but I do know this ranch has never lost money before. We've weathered tough times, but we've never gone in the hole month after month."

"Well, that's the first honest thing you've said. You have no idea. You go off and leave your poor pop to recuperate on his own, and then you think you're entitled to an opinion? I don't even know why you're sitting in this meeting."

Luke looked quickly to his father, willing him to stand up and take this seriously. For Claire if nothing else.

"Now, Luke, there's no need to get upset with Justin. He's done a fine job. Maybe you should step out for a bit." His father nodded at the door.

"What?" Luke's heart slammed to a standstill. He forced himself to take a moment for his sister's sake. "Dad, I'm sorry for raising my voice. And Justin, I'm fiercely protective of my sister. You hit a nerve. I'm sorry. But Dad, you trusted Claire to look at your books. I would assume you value her opinion. You need to listen."

His dad stood and pointed at Luke. "I do trust Claire,

and I am listening, but she's not correct. Evelyn and I discussed this. You're looking at just numbers, Claire. You're not looking at the whole picture. This ranch has always been about more than money—it's about the people, the people who work here and the people and businesses in town we support. If you can't understand the loyalty part of the equation, then…maybe you're not the right person to handle the ranch's finances. Maybe you can't be objective, and my account should be passed off to one of your coworkers."

"I tried," Claire said. The silence hung in the room as Justin huffed and straightened out his legs.

Then the feisty Claire roared back. Luke was so proud of her because he knew she was busted in half inside.

"You will have to find someone else, another firm, to handle your portfolio. We cannot in good conscious handle this for you." She laid the files on the edge of his desk.

"Look, I'll have him quit buying liquor," his father fumbled. For such an impressive man, he could be whittled down to nothing in a breath of time.

"Did you know he let Mikey go?" Luke rose as he asked. "That's the value you're placing on your loyal employees these days. Letting them go after twenty years of dedicated service."

Justin launched out of his seat. "Mike was a no-account drunk who didn't know the meaning of the word work."

"Just sit down, all of you!" Ward yelled.

The room calmed for a second.

"Yes," Ward said quietly. "Evelyn told me he was caught skimming money in town on my account and drinking on the job."

Luke looked skyward, unbelieving. "Holy shit. Will I ever learn? Trust yourself, Dad. Yourself. You know better."

"Sit down, Luke; your temper's showing. I thought you learned somewhere along the way that everything is not always about you."

"Oh, my God, you're unbelievable. I know, trust me, I know this is not about me. It hasn't been about me in a very long time. But you've never taken your resentment out on Claire. Trust Claire and trust yourself. You're better than this. You're better than running roughshod over a daughter who would do anything for you. You gave her those books because you trusted her. Trust her now."

On shaky legs, he managed to make it to the door. He thought of all the hope he had yesterday, all the hope he had for another visit in the near future. Claire tried without success not to cry. His father striking at the heart of everything she was.

"Claire, I'll call you when I get home. Do not, and I mean, do not, let any of his filthy words settle inside. They will destroy everything good and kind and turn your soul to blackness." Luke looked at his father. "Just like mine."

Chapter Twenty-Three

They hit the ground running when the plane landed. Capping off a horrible ending to the Texas trip, their flight was delayed, and delayed again. When the announcement echoed in the terminal, it was obvious they weren't going to make Rock Springs in time to pick up Charlie. Not wanting to give Chase any ammunition with shared custody in the balance, Mara called her mom to see if she could help. Not getting an answer unsettled her nerves further. At the layover in Denver, she texted back and forth with Rachel, with neither able to find her mother. As they boarded the second plane, she tried one last time, then smashed the phone into her leg as they sat, losing count of how many messages she'd rattled off.

So, they ran. They maneuvered in and around people on the escalator, didn't stop for luggage, continued running straight for Luke's truck. He whipped out of the parking lot and grabbed her hand at the same time. She stared blankly out the window, wondering, hoping nothing had happened. Charlie had been picked up by Chase or his mom at this point, and as much as she hated to admit it, she had to let thoughts of Charlie go for the night. None of her mom's friends knew where she would be. Rachel went to the house and peered in windows and talked to neighbors. Her friend across the street saw her drive off but couldn't recall the time she left.

Luke screeched to a stop in front of the house. Mara

ran to the door, shaking so badly, she dropped the keys twice before Luke took them and opened the door. Nothing was out of the ordinary as they ran from room to room. No mess, nothing out of place. Her bed looked like she'd laid down on top of the bedspread, but even that was normal. She often needed a little nap in the afternoons. The kitchen was neat and tidy. A plate with a scattering of crumbs sat in the sink. The car keys were gone from the hook, but duh, since the car was gone. Mara chewed on her lip, trying to think.

"Do you want me to call the police?" Luke burst through the back door, after checking the garage.

"She doesn't do this." Mara put her elbows on the counter, cradling her head in her hands, looking past the plate in the sink to the garbage disposal. "Where are you, Mom?"

"She's got messages." Luke pointed at the old school phone sitting on the ledge between the kitchen and dining room. A separate answering machine sat at its side. The red light blinked. Mara studied the flash cycle. Six rapid blinks, hesitation, six rapid blinks, hesitation. How many of those messages were her own?

Luke punched the button.

"You have six new messages," the robotic voice called out.

The speaker rattled off the initial two clipped messages of her harried self. The next from her mom's neighbor. Message number four was Rachel, then Mara's first message, a calmer her.

The last message. As soon as the voice spoke, it was the one. Her heart slammed to a standstill. She wanted to shut the voice off, not listen, but couldn't seem to transport herself the few steps to punch the button. The oncologist, softly and surely asking Mara's mom to call to discuss the results of her latest tests. "I'm sorry, the results are not good." A long beep and a bright and cheerful voice stating that there were no more messages.

"Oh, God." She collapsed into a ball as she slid to the floor.

Luke crouched and pulled her into his lap. Cradling her head into his chest as he rocked her. "I'm so sorry."

"Her cancer is back," she cried. "And I wasn't here."

"Where would she go?"

Her mom would be scared, and alone, trying to deal with whatever the news was. A few years ago, a portion of her lung was removed. The last two years, she had been in remission following a nasty stint at chemo. When she promised earlier in the year to keep Mara updated, she reported in like clockwork. A couple of times Mara tagged along for the checkups. Her mom was religious about her lab results and MRIs and thriving at her new job. Mara hadn't thought about the cancer in months.

Curling her fingers into his shirt, she raised her gaze to the moonlight streaming through the kitchen window. "She would go to my dad."

"Let's go," Luke whispered. "She shouldn't be out in this cold."

Mara gave a quick nod.

"Can you take me to get my car? You don't need to come with me after all you've been through."

"Yeah, that's not happening. We're a team now, okay? Remember the life preserver we share? It has to make a quick turnaround tonight."

She didn't have the strength to argue. "Okay."

They found their way around in the darkness at the cemetery where her father was buried. The moon was full, and the air held a crispness, making the journey eerie and beautiful at the same time. Illuminated in the moonlight, her mom sat against his headstone, her head dropped back, resting against the granite. Mara hesitated, understanding in an instant how Luke felt not a week ago. Those things you want to know, but at the same time, don't want to know. She righted herself. This was not about her, not this time.

They squished across the wet grass until Luke stopped and squeezed her arm. "I'll wait at the truck. Holler if you need me."

Mara ran up the hill, collapsed, at the same time gathering her mom into her arms. They wept together and smeared each other's tears with fingertips. She didn't know what to say. How did her mom always know how to make things right, and she could come up with nothing?

"I'm so sorry I wasn't here," was all she could squeak out.

"It's back. Rolling around and creeping into other organs."

"We'll get a second opinion, and a third if we have to. We'll go to one of those cancer specialist hospitals. The one in Texas, or the Arizona one."

"No, not this time. I can't do chemo again. I was just talking it over with your father."

"You can't leave me," she cried.

"Sometimes we don't get to choose when to leave, when to stay in life." Her mom wrapped her up, planting aging, but strong hands on the sides of her face. "You're strong now, I'm going to be a mass of nothing, and I need you to be the strong one. The happy one, the one who makes my days worthwhile. I need you to be strong for

Charlie, so I can see as much as I can before I go."

"Don't, don't talk like that," Mara sobbed.

"Oh, my dear girl, you are the most resilient woman I know. I'm going to need every piece of you because I'm breaking inside right now. Let's just go home. Can you spend the night with me?"

Mara mustered every ounce of strength she didn't have. Pulling from years of her mom doing so much, conquering cancer, losing the love of her life, losing her job because of the cancer. She wasn't going to let her lose the support of her daughter and granddaughter. She stuffed her needs deep inside and lifted her head from her mom's chest, calming her erratic heart.

"Yes. I can do that. I can do anything." Words she had heard from her mother's lips most of her life. In the good and bad times, in the breaking in two times. Her legs didn't want to hold her up, but she fortified herself and eased her mom to her feet.

They looked together at the grave marker and blew kisses.

"Night, Daddy."

As they descended the hill, Luke jumped off the hood of his truck and rushed to open the back door of his cab. "Ladies."

Mara's mom touched his face. "So, this is your young man?"

He kissed her mom's hand. "Yes, ma'am. That would be me."

"I'm sorry to meet you under these conditions, but I am happy to finally meet you."

Her mom eased into the seat.

Luke's thumbs brushed under Mara's eyes while her mother settled herself. Wiping away the last of the wetness, she fortified just a little more.

Chapter Twenty-Four

Standing before the rich wood of the courtroom doors, Mara was unable to tame the shaking in her knees. Chase had thrown a fit about his weekend plans being disrupted with her late pick-up, but it was Vivian's satisfied smirk that put Mara on edge. As if she knew something, and could, and would, whip it out on demand. Mara ran through the entire trip, the entire night locating her mom. Rachel documented every phone call, downloaded Mara's phone, and printed out her text records for the lawyer to use if necessary. In light of everything that had happened recently, she needed her daughter in her arms, under her roof, more than ever before.

The judge took her place. Behind Mara, Rachel leaned over the rail and clutched her arm. "Whatever happens, do not lash out."

The admonishment sent her nerves all askew. Before this weekend, she'd been all forms of confident. Now certainty and determination were sliding out of her pores faster than she could keep up.

The judge glanced at both tables and flipped through the ever-thickening file. Closing it, she clasped her hands on top.

"I see there's a new development." She nodded at Chase's lawyer. "Everything seems to be in line for shared custody. I thought that's what we were working toward."

The skinny lawyer shot to his feet. "Last weekend Ms. Sawyer failed to show up at the assigned time to pick up her daughter. She was out of state with her current boyfriend…"

"Let me stop you right there," the judge said. "You know as well as I do, the paperwork for her trip was filed in advance. That's not a reason to deny custody. She is entitled to a life."

"But she was supposed to be back to pick up her daughter Friday. Her flight documents show her arrival on Friday. She didn't pick up her daughter until Saturday afternoon."

"Your Honor." Mara's lawyer was on his feet. "They know all this also. The flight was delayed by no fault of her own. Her mother was unavailable to help with the exchange. By the time Ms. Sawyer did arrive in town, it was well after midnight. She alerted her social worker throughout the day, who alerted Mr. Owens. Ms. Sawyer arranged to pick up Charlotte on Saturday afternoon. Which she did."

"Why not until Saturday afternoon?" The judge leafed through the paperwork as she asked.

The lawyer looked at Mara. She nodded. "Judge, Ms. Sawyer's mother was unavailable Friday night to pick up her granddaughter because she had received devastating news about her health. When Ms. Sawyer returned, she was informed of her mother's prognosis, and they were working on a plan. Mr. Owens was kept in the loop the entire time."

"That's not entirely true." Chase stood. "I didn't know about the cancer being a death sentence. I just knew they were dealing with a health issue.

Supposedly."

Chase's lawyer shot up. "This is even more reason why shared custody should be delayed. My apologies for her mother's health, but this is spreading her too thin. If she can't take care of her mother, then how is she going to take care of her daughter? Ms. Sawyer was on vacation in Texas with her current boyfriend. This could've all been avoided if she had remained in town."

The lawyers started yelling at one another. Mara held her head, the words taking root, manipulated to suit their cause of course, but they bit in accuracy. When she rotated in her seat, her mom and Luke were itching to stand up and join in the screaming match, but she stared them down. Chase's mom jumped to her feet, yelling across the aisle when the judge slammed her gavel down hard.

"Everyone settle down. Ms. Sawyer?"

Mara rose. "Yes, ma'am."

"This sounds like a lot of bad timing. I understand the delay of the plane was not in your control. Why the trip to Texas though with this proceeding hanging in the balance?"

"There was a death in my friend's family. If I knew my mother was sick, I wouldn't have gone."

"Your mother doesn't have anyone else?"

"I'm an only child. My father passed a few years ago."

"Do you think you can handle helping your mom, a full-time job, and shared custody? That would be a lot on anyone's plate." The judge shuffled through her notes again. "Is Ms. Cartwright in the gallery today?"

Rachel rose behind her. "Yes, I'm here."

"What do you think about Ms. Sawyer's capacity for

handling this? I'm worried the child will suffer. Perhaps, slowing the process down would give everyone time to adjust. Our primary goal is for Charlotte's schedule to remain intact and uninterrupted."

Chase's mom jumped to her feet. "Mara's never dealt well with anything that involved her mother. Her attention will—"

"Sit down. Now." The judge pointed at Vivian. "I've had enough of you and your speculations. None of us would do well with this kind of health crisis involving a parent."

Vivian huffed and sat.

"I'm sorry. Ms. Cartwright?"

"Ms. Sawyer notified me of every issue regarding her flight in real time. She was more than concerned about both her mom and her daughter, but she couldn't do anything until she landed and had more facts. Once she found her mother, they put together a plan to handle the logistics this unfortunate situation brings to the table. I don't foresee any issues with Mara's ability to handle her responsibility for shared custody. They are a tight family."

The judge scanned the crowd, cradled her chin in her hands, and stared at the back wall.

After a lengthy, soul-crushing silence, the judge nodded. "Alright, this is what we're going to do. Ms. Sawyer, first I want to assure you, you did nothing wrong here. I applaud that you want to help your friends and family both. But."

Mara's breath caught on the word "but."

"But" meant you disregarded everything you just said.

"My job is to determine what's best for your little

girl. I'm not denying the request for shared custody. I'm kicking my decision down the road sixty days. That gives you time to settle your mother into new routines. I'm not doing this to punish you. I'm doing this to help. As much as Ms. Owens gets on my nerves with her outbursts, I believe she genuinely has your daughter's best interest at heart and may be able to assist at this difficult time. Mr. Owens? Have you got yourself a job yet?"

Chase jumped up. "Yes, I started two weeks ago."

Mara huffed loudly, mumbling, "For his buddy's company."

The judge ignored her, and Rachel grabbed her arm. She shrugged away and shut up.

"Ms. Sawyer, you'll continue to have your scheduled weekend visits. Barring any issues, I will grant shared custody when we meet again. Please understand my primary concern is your daughter. I need to look out for your little one."

And it was over. Twenty minutes and her future had again been left dangling.

Chase grabbed her hand as she walked by. She shook her head and jerked away, walking outside to catch her breath, away from the confines of the judge and her power trip. Away from Chase and his mother. Away from her mom and Luke, who had caused all this. It wasn't fair to put blame on them, but she couldn't help herself. She did everything right. She could have called out Chase for not letting her have Charlie the weekend she was sick, but no, taking the high road got you nowhere.

Being strong meant you suffered, strong meant you hurt. She wanted to scream and yell, stomp her feet. Grab her daughter and head for the highest mountain, barricade them against the world.

At the edge of the parking lot, Mara turned back around. The plan was to go celebrate, but not any longer. The pain in her gut told her she was steadily losing control of herself. She let it churn away. What difference did it make if she did? Someone else always had control. Of not just her life—Charlie's life. She was furious with herself for going to Texas. She should have known.

On the courthouse steps, Rachel chatted with her mom. Luke stood at her mom's side, watching her. He cocked his head, his eyes soft and intense in his stare. The three of them, the ripple effects. Her mom and the devil of cancer. Luke, and his father in Texas. Rachel, and her inept advice.

The split she felt in her core ripped her in two. It was time for her daughter to come first. Not Luke, not her mom. What happened to her Charlie, Mara, mantra?

She weaved through the civil servants on their way to invade the hot lunch spots scattered around the courthouse. An hour ago, she planned on being one of those looking for lunch with friends. Now she just wanted to go home and eat a bag of cheddar flavored popcorn.

With wine.

Her mom hugged her as she straightened in front of the trio. "I'm so sorry, honey. At least next time…"

"Yeah, me too. Let's go. I want to go home."

Luke stared at her, cocking his head and squinting. "I was planning on taking you ladies to lunch. Don't disappoint me," he joked, feigning a pouty smile that would have made her laugh on a normal day.

She resented his calmness when all she wanted to do was break.

"Not in the mood." She spat the words and didn't really care what he thought, what any of them thought. They were talking and laughing while her daughter suffered. The humiliation of once again not being good enough to share custody with her moron of an ex, assaulted her.

"I just need to be alone, alright. Rachel, can you take my mom home?" She rammed her hands in her pockets. "I'll be by later to check on you, Mom. Right now, I don't want anything. From any of you."

Maybe if she had a few hours to herself, she could think rationally again.

"I'll take your mom home," Luke offered. "I can stay with her until you—"

Her face heated, and she couldn't stop. She just couldn't.

"No. I can take care of her myself. You've done quite enough, don't you think?"

"What?" His gaze never wavered. Hurt flashed, but he didn't look away.

"Mara," her mom growled.

"Mara, what?" She raised her eyebrows. "Mara, don't lose control? I lost that quite a while ago, don't you think?"

"Mara Elizabeth."

Middle name and everything. She would have laughed. Unfortunately, nothing about today even relegated a smirk.

"You can Mara Elizabeth all you want. When do I get what I want? I want my daughter. It's that damn simple. I'd take her and run away and never come back if I had the choice, but no, you have cancer and you—" Mara pulled up. She didn't want to be a rampage ridden person any longer. She just wanted to be alone. "You promised." She jabbed a finger in Rachel's direction. "You said if I conquered your list, I would get my way."

"I did not promise that. I can't promise that." Rachel grabbed her hands. "You did do everything right. Sometimes though, things don't work the way they should. But they will."

"Great. That's just great." Mara lifted her hands toward the building. "Looks like my prize is a social worker who can't do her job."

Luke grabbed Rachel's hand and motioned her mom forward. "Let's go."

"Too much family drama for you, Whitten?" Mara snorted. "Sorry. That's my world. Yay, me."

Luke stalled for a second and held his hands up. "I can't talk to you when you're like this. No one can."

She knew she was bordering the epitome of irrational, but she didn't want to think about all the shoulda, coulda, wouldas that made up the whole of her life.

Her mother was dead silent. The crowds stopped to stare. Chase, close to the building, stopped to stare. Chase's mother looked at her with a shit-eating grin because she had been declared the winner. Again.

Luke grabbed her hand. "If you need to get out of here and be by yourself, kick the black leather bag, I get that. Do what you have to do. Don't spout the first stupid, hurtful thing that hits your head though. Because some words, you don't get to take them back."

"Don't treat me like a child, and do not tell me how to treat my mother. You don't have any room, and I mean any room, to talk about relationships with parents."

The look that hit his eyes paralyzed her.

Luke rocked from side to side. "I won't apologize for loving my father," he said softly. "I won't apologize for wanting to make a relationship with him work. That's *my* world." His measured, controlled words hung. "If that's not good enough for you…"

Her mom started to cry. Luke took her mom's arm and started walking her toward the parking lot.

Rachel planted herself inches from her face. "You are your own worst enemy. Someday you'll see that." She turned her back on Mara and ran to catch up.

"Yep, that's me," she hollered. "Run home to help everyone, and I'm the enemy."

Rachel and Luke sandwiched her mother and helped her into the seat. He and Rachel talked at the side of the truck for a second, and he jogged around to the driver's side and left the parking lot.

"Mara, are you alright?" Chase was beside her, following her line of sight.

"You've taken my daughter away, again. I can't live without my daughter, and no one seems to care."

"I care." He pulled her into him. She straightened and forced him away.

"Maybe I understand, because she's my daughter too, because I can't live without her either. She binds us." He spoke with so much tenderness, Mara was on the verge of believing. "Why don't you come to the house, and we'll talk."

"I don't want to talk. I. Want. My. Daughter. Period."

She walked straight to her car and ripped out of the parking lot, squealing her tires like a sixteen-year-old boy.

After a quick stop at a mini mart to grab the needed

popcorn and wine, she sat in the parking lot at Veteran's Park. It was where her dad loved to visit, always saying the memories and quiet made him feel close to his own dad. They used to walk through the WWII airplane displays for hours. She wasn't interested in historical anything; it was the time spent with her dad. They had gone to the air shows too whenever they came to town. Seeing them always made her want to be a pilot, soar the skies, feel her stomach drop out in the whoosh. They took a ride in one once. He won the trip in some radio-show caller-number-twelve thing. She'd give anything to soar the skies in this moment, drop away from life in a whoosh.

The tears trailed. Memories of her father made her miss him so much. He was the only man she had always been enough for, who understood her anger, who always listened, even if she was irrational or unreasonable. The one who always taught her to be tough and strong. She thought being strong was a way to make her invincible to pain, but hurt wasn't ever that simple. Pain took everyone prisoner.

For once, just once, she wanted to let go, be weak and pitiful. Taken care of. Being strong meant feeling nothing, and she felt everything. The only thing to show for strength was a temper that flared at all the wrong times. It hadn't helped her get good friends or a good man. It hadn't kept her mother out of the oncology ward, and larger than all, it did nothing to help her keep her daughter. All strength did was make you break into a thousand pieces when times got tough.

The rain started pelting her windshield. The cadence of drops hitting the glass blurred everything into the realization that she had nothing.

Today, she'd probably hurt her mother as much as if she gave her cancer herself.

In a couple of months, she wouldn't even be able to say she had a mother.

Her phone pinged. She looked skyward, wanting everyone to leave her the hell alone.

When the notification flashed, she did a double take. It wasn't Luke, or Rachel, or her mother. It was Chase.

—*You alright?*—

Nope, not alright. Not in any way shape or form alright.

—*I have a solution to the mess*—

Mara stared at the screen long and hard. What kind of solution could he have? Barring dropping off the face of the earth, that is.

She thought through every solution he could offer and came up with nothing good.

—*I'm at Veteran's*— she finally texted.

He was a creative sort, at avoidance if nothing else. Jobs, relationships, all of it. Maybe he creatively found an answer for both of them. A girl could hope.

Thirty minutes later, he parked in the slot beside her. The rain stopped, and when he helped Charlie out of the back seat, her heartstrings snapped.

Leaping into his arms from the car, he passed her off with a smile. As she took Charlie and snuggled her neck with kisses, Chase looked at her like he used to. With love—not pity, not disgust.

She breathed the intoxicating smell of her child. That mix of cookie breath and the outdoors.

Putting her down, Charlie hugged Chase's leg. Mara strained to remember Charlie ever doing that. Their physical interaction normally relegated to the cursory high five.

"Why don't you go play on the playground, baby. Let Mommy and me talk."

"Okie dokie, Daddy," she yelled over her shoulder in her little singsong voice.

She stopped mid run and turned back around. "You okay, Mommy?"

Mara felt the tears well. "How can I not be good when I've got your sweet face in front of me?"

"You're silly." She turned and was off again.

"Thank you for bringing her with you." Mara leaned against her car, staring after Charlie as she climbed onto the structure made for toddlers. "I really did need to see her face."

Chase crossed his arms. "What if we made that a daily thing?"

She snorted. There was no way he was just handing her over. There was no way Vivian would just hand her over.

"What's going on, Chase? We've been duking it out in court, and you're going to stop the fight? Bigger still, your mom's going to stop the fight?"

"My mom doesn't know I'm here," he said, looking down.

Mara jerked at that. Chase never did anything without Mama's approval. He was the living, breathing embodiment of a mama's boy. In the worst possible way.

"Let's be a family again." His voice was so adorably lost, she thought he would break into tears. "I know I have a lot to prove, but we belong together. We always have."

Charlie squatted in the dirt, digging like buried treasure was just out of her grasp. "That little girl needs us both. You have made me a better father, and you are a perfect mother."

Mara forced herself to remember the cruel past, the hateful words, the late nights when she had no clue where he was. Taking his mother's side over hers. The destruction of her soul. Then she looked at her daughter and melted.

Every day. She could have her every day. Shared custody was on the horizon, but shared was still shared. What he offered was the whole. How long would he last before he spouted his venom? Did it matter? If she could snuggle and drink in the smell of her little girl every day?

"Chase…"

He held his hand up. "Just think about it, okay? I promise I'll be better. I know it'll take some time for you to trust me again, but…" He pushed himself away from the car and took her hands. "I still love you, Mara."

Chapter Twenty-Five

Mara did nothing but think about Chase's proposition. A real life with her daughter. Every day. The cost would be high, but nothing mattered except her daughter. Hadn't her own parents made sacrifices for her? Every day parents gave up everything about themselves so their kids could have a chance at a better life. Some of her older coworkers joked about how there would be nothing left of their marriages when their kids left for college. Perhaps Mara's whole life was meant to be a statistic in one way or another. It wasn't as if she would remarry Chase and give over to old, horrible habits, two divorces from the same man situation. Nothing mattered if Charlie was happy, and she could be a daily presence in her daughter's life.

Sacrificing the flip-flopping stomach of new love, the soul-searing sex with a man whose body she'd come to know as well as her own, the talks that were long and intricate, sensitive, funny, animated. A small price.

Who was to say Luke was the one she'd end up with anyway? Her track record in the romance and happiness department wasn't without scars in its own right.

She felt the pendulum swaying.

Arriving at her mother's house, she hoped for some of her mom's sage advice. That would help take this crazy but not so crazy idea of Chase's and put his solution to bed. Her mother compared all relationships to her own. Unfortunately, things had evolved since the happily ever after days.

Mara would let her plead her case, secretly craving someone to say, "You deserve happiness. You deserve the love of a lifetime."

The place where logic wouldn't let her go. Where logic didn't give her custody.

Her mother stared out the window when she walked into the kitchen. "Mom? Are you okay?"

When she turned, genuine tears glistened through her smile. "Of course. A little lethargic today. The pain pills make me woozy."

"Why don't I make us some tea, and you can tell me why you're tearing up."

Her mother sat at the scarred kitchen table. Stripped a half a dozen times over the years from the various stages of Mara growing up. Coloring with markers when she shouldn't have, Mara carving her initials together with her parents, trying to make them see she was supposed to live with them forever. That indiscretion, left for posterity's sake. Her dad thought the markings were adorable.

As she put the tea in front of them, using the dainty china her mother loved so much, she ran her finger through the engraving in the table, outlining the small heart wrapping up the three sets of letters. When her father died so suddenly, she had scratched at his initials in anger, trying to erase them from being. Her mother had stilled her hands, leaving a few hash marks, but their initials were preserved.

She burned her lip on the tea and almost spilled it all over herself. Her mom handed her a napkin. "Maybe put in a little cream. It'll cool it down."

"I know. I wasn't thinking."

"What are you thinking? Something has you all wrapped up in your head. You're not obsessing about the ruling from the judge, are you? You know the next time everything will go your way. The judge as much said so herself."

"I'm sorry for what I said after."

Her mom trailed a finger along the saucer of her teacup. "I know you are. Have you told Luke that? Rachel that? Your mouth got the better of you. Your father did a good job of eyeballing you. You don't seem to have that filter anymore."

Mara nodded. Her father could control her because she hated to disappoint him.

"I'm thinking of going back to Chase." There, she said it. She hesitated and couldn't bear to look at her mom and see the disappointment. "He proposed the idea. I could have Charlie every day. He's promised to be better. I really think he's changed. Charlie literally hung off him; you know that's not like her. I just want my little girl to have a happy life, have her little face in my line of vision every day. This gives me that. Even shared custody doesn't do the same, when and if that ever happens." She spilled out a flurry of words, trying to negate the past and rush her mom into understanding.

When she dared to look up, her mother stared out the window again to the clear blue. A puffy cloud drifted by. When her mom returned her gaze, Mara looked down, unable to go head-to-head with the intensity. Their old grandfather clock gonged in the other room.

"And what about you and your happiness?"

"I'm happy if my daughter's happy." Saying her thoughts aloud made her realize the situation really was

201

that simple. She really didn't matter any longer.

"From my side, I'm happy if my daughter's happy," her mom said.

Well, shit. Touché.

She felt like she'd been slapped. Her mother turning her own words around. Fair, but not fair.

Mara shrugged. "If he's trying, that's all I can ask. I can be happy."

"And what happens the first time he stays out half the night? The first time he calls you one of those disgusting words in his limited vocabulary? The first time he hands Charlie to his mother for consoling instead of you? What happens then?"

Mara shrugged again. "Maybe it won't go that way."

"Men who do those things, say those things, don't change, Mara. They say they can, but how many times has he said that in the past? Can you even count the times? Don't become him. You know better."

Mara walked to the counter and leaned against it. "Mom, I don't get the happily ever after. Some women do. I'm not one of them."

"You are not allowing yourself to be one of them."

There it was. Hope swirled in and around logic, taking up too much space in her head. She just wanted Charlie to be happy, with two doting parents. Her own heart she could sacrifice. Worst case, she could be one of those separate-after-your-children-graduate-high-school people.

"You have a man who could be that person, who already makes you feel loved and cherished, and you're too scared to grab hold and trust that he's the real deal."

She started to argue, but her mother held up her hand. "I know all the arguments. You'd have to be patient with the court's ruling. You'd have to give up being a full-time mom to Charlie, but that man would adjust the sun and stars to be a part of your life. To be happy together."

"You don't know him; he's as messed up inside as I am. We're a mess together."

"Two messy halves of a perfect whole." Her mom speared her with a gaze so intense, Mara's hands began clenching under the table.

She squinted her eyes, not wanting to give credence to the words. It did describe them, though. Two halves. There was beauty in that.

"I haven't decided yet."

Her mom swayed a little as she rose. "Yes, you have." She stalled at the countertop for balance and headed for the hall. "I need a nap; I have a headache."

"Here. Let me help you."

Her mother held her hand up. "No. There will come a time when I need your assistance. It's not today." She started down the hall and turned, looking like she would break into a thousand pieces. "I'm not one of those moms who tell you 'I told you so,' but mark my words right here, right now, because I may not be around much longer. Chase will never love you like you deserve to be loved. And you will never be happy with him. You deserve to be happy."

Mara started to respond, and her mother turned her back and escaped into her bedroom. The soft click of the door slipping into place followed.

The conversation ended exactly as she expected.

Her mother was a fine one to talk. Her parents were happy when they were poor, happy when they were comfortable, but they had never split and argued over their child.

"I'll see you tomorrow, Mom," she hollered down the hall as she headed out, careful to lock the door behind her. It took a full twenty minutes sitting in her car to determine her next course of action. She just wanted to hold her baby.

At home, she sank into the sofa and stared at the walls. On the wall, an adorable picture from preschool of Charlie, cocking her hip with her hand at her waist, her eyes rolled up dramatically. It broke her heart not seeing that face every day.

In front of her mirror, Mara stared at the tired, sleep-deprived eyes. With faint lines fanning, small indentations, she put her hands to her face, caught the harsh curves of her lips and mouth, the smile that still had to work too hard to make it to her lips, let alone her eyes.

Could she be happy? When cruel insults were thrust her way? When the arguments erupted? She touched the lines at her eyes as she worked herself into a smile. Did it matter?

She jolted at the ping of an incoming text.

Seeing the picture of Luke and her together with his name left her eyes fluttering shut.

—*Don't do this. You deserve so much more*—

How could he tolerate sending her a plea after yesterday? Because he knew she lashed first, processed later.

She grabbed her car keys and shot out of town toward the cemetery, needing her father. At twilight, the shadows loomed, but they weren't creepy. They were comforting and serene. Sitting and leaning against his headstone, she searched the sky above for his wisdom and answers. Usually, her father talked to her here when she was alone, not tonight. Maybe he was mad at her too. Maybe he had nothing to say.

As she sat, she remembered Luke racing through the airport and ripping out of the parking lot so she could get to her daughter, find her mother. Combing through the house like a madman looking for clues to her whereabouts. Handling the details of getting her mother home safe after her outburst.

She sent a short text to him apologizing for the aftereffects of court. He deserved that.

"God, what do I do?" she said to the night sky. "What does my daughter deserve?"

She found herself outside Vivian and Chase's house. From her car she could see them through the window, sitting on the sofa, Charlie tucked in close beside him. Charlie pointed at something on the television, and they both burst out laughing.

That could be her inside with them both. Every single night. The maybes were racking up, tipping the scales in Chase's favor.

She ran her hands over her face. "I'm sorry, Luke."

He deserved everything happy in life. Even if that meant moving on.

She looked again at his text.

—*You deserve so much more*—

Maybe. Maybe her chance at happiness was long gone.

—*Pick me*—

—*Pick us*—

—*Pick you*—

The notifications dinged one right after another.

Ripping her in two because she couldn't pick those

things.

She picked Charlie.

At the window, Chase swung Charlie into his arms and carted her toward the staircase. The light came on upstairs in Charlie's room. No doubt, he was maneuvering her squirmy butt into her favorite jammies, brushing her teeth with her bright purple toothbrush, and watching her grab one of her favorite books as she jumped into her bed. Patting her pillow so he would sit and read to her. He would make a long, drawn-out ordeal about how she could read the same story fifty gazillion times, and she would laugh and tell him how silly he was.

Luke didn't bother her again. He knew.

As she sat on the front steps, Chase came out and joined her, carrying two mugs of coffee.

"I'm choosing my daughter, not you," she blurted as he lowered himself beside her.

"I know. It's enough for now." He leaned into her, tucked his nose into her neck. "I hope someday you'll love me again, Mara. And I promise, I'll deserve your love."

She sat up straight, not wanting his body so close. His platonic, yet intimate nudge into her neck brought reality crashing in. This was not Luke, playful and loving. This was Chase, twisting her stomach. He had miles to go to get close to what she was giving up.

"And I'm not sleeping with you. Maybe someday, not yet though."

He jerked but softened within seconds. "I can deal with that. I'm a patient man."

She raised her eyebrows. "Since when? Like four minutes ago?"

Chapter Twenty-Six

Mara and Chase found a cute little house on the opposite side of town from Chase's mother. Close to the house Mara had been renting all along. Chase paid the fee to break her lease, hiring movers and a cleaning crew so the owners were ready within days to find new tenants. In their new home, they each took a bedroom, and together, she and Charlie redecorated on her days off. She went to work. Chase went to work. Charlie went to daycare. His mother didn't step foot in the house until seven days in. It shored Chase up, giving him confidence that he could indeed tackle life on his own. Somewhere along the line, he had become a pretty awesome dad. He may not ever be an awesome man, but Charlie was happy and oblivious.

Once they were all settled, they signed Charlie up for Max's soccer team. Without Vivian in her son's ear, Chase was just as excited to see his daughter branch out and try another sport. Mara went to every practice and loved every second of not only the soccer field, but having her daughter under her roof twenty-four seven, for three weeks now. For the last week she dropped the feeling that something would go wrong. Today was the day of new beginnings in more ways than one. Excitement ran rampant, and even Grammy V came to watch the first game. Probably to prove Charlie couldn't hang with the boys, but after watching the last few practices, Charlie would be proving otherwise.

All the little legs ran out onto the field amidst a thrall of cheers. Charlie had her own little cheering section with the chairs of both her parents and the two grandmothers running in a row down the boundary lines. Mara couldn't sit. She raced up and down the sidelines, watching the kids practice, listening to parents yelling and cheering as the whistle sounded and the game began.

"Looks like swarm ball." Chase joined her, his two fingers running in the air, to the left and then to the right. "Kind of cute, not very tactical or structured. Are you sure our coach is any good?"

A competitive statement had never come out of Chase's mouth. He just wasn't a sports guy.

"They're four. I don't know if the word structure is in their vocabulary."

His arm wrapped around her, and his hand fell to her shoulder, maneuvering her into him. It was nice to feel the companionship, being a part of a team. When Charlie made a run for the ball, Chase dropped his arm and watched in amazement. Their daughter was fast, faster than the others on the field. Kicking the ball hard from midfield, it bounced a couple of times and flew out of bounds, nowhere close to the goal posts she aimed for.

"Good try, Charlie," her coach yelled.

Charlie scowled and ran her hands over her face, took them down to her knees, and regrouped. Before she took off toward the ball being swarmed by a mass of kids, she yelled, "I'll get it again, Coach Max."

They watched her run back and forth what seemed like a thousand times. She managed to swipe the ball from a bigger boy by ducking under his arm and kicking it through his legs while he froze in place. When he regrouped, he went after Charlie with a vengeance, and she skipped along in her own little world, following the crowd. He barreled into her and knocked her flat on her butt.

"Get her off the field!" Vivian stood and pointed at the field. The game continued. "Chase, she can't do this. Go get her."

Mara held his hand, nodding toward Charlie, who swiped at her butt as she rose. Their tough little girl—who wasn't rough enough to play with boys in Grandma V's world—peered at her skinned knees and was off again toward the swarm. And she was mad now.

Coach Max shook his head and grinned at Mara. She had never been so proud. When Charlie took the ball again from the larger boy, there was no way he could catch her this time. She didn't score, but she somehow kicked it down the field to a teammate, who in turn kicked it into the net. The two followed the ball into the netting, rolling into the mesh, giggling, wrapping their arms around each other.

A mommy moment for the ages.

"Did you see me? Did you see me?" Charlie leapt into Chase's arms after the game. "I helped goal it."

They surrounded her, and when Charlie flew into Mara and snuggled into her arms, Vivian yanked at Chase's arm. "You need to take her out of this. She's going to get hurt. That boy probably had thirty pounds on her."

"More like fifty, but she was fine, Mom. Look at her."

"This time. Are you really okay with this, because I'm definitely not. She has a real future in ballet, and you're going to throw it away for a ball and a goalpost?"

"But Grammy V, I'm so good, and I hate dance."

"You don't. You just don't know what you like right now," Vivian snapped.

"I do too," Charlie yelled.

"Mom, please." Chase put his arm around his mother. "She really enjoys this, and soccer at this level isn't hurting anything. If nothing else, she's burning off a lot of her endless energy."

For the first time in his existence, Chase contradicted his mother. Mara glanced at her own mom, who was just as spellbound. Chase took her side. Progress in a monumental way.

"Chase, I'm taking you all out for dinner. Do you want to meet me there?" Vivian asked.

Mara raised her eyebrows. Coach Max waved her over to his group of excited parents. She headed in his direction. Chase could handle his mother. After games, the team met up for pizza. Charlie was looking forward to going with her new friends.

When she reached Max, the other parents headed for their cars with bouncing kids in purple shorts and bright yellow jerseys in their wake.

"I assume that was Grammy V?" Max said with a smirk. They had become friends while she dated Luke, sometimes landing at the same lunch table when he was on the night shift.

"The one and only."

"The other parents were talking about your little munchkin taking on the league bully. She'll be the talk of the next coach's meeting." He stooped down and imitated Charlie. Scanning his knees and brushing at his butt while looking for rips in her shorts. "It was priceless," he laughed.

Chase strode over with a scowl. Mara introduced the two and flinched when Chase put his arm around her possessively. Max got the hint and waved, hoisted his son up onto his shoulders, and headed to the parking lot.

"Did you tell your mom we're going for pizza with the team?"

"Yeah, but she wants us to come by afterward for ice cream sundaes."

"I have work tomorrow. And Charlie has school in the morning."

"I'll take her late. It's preschool. I doubt she's going to miss any great learning experience."

He had a point, but Mara didn't like to confuse Charlie's schedule. There were enough schedule changes with their divorce and separation to last ten lifetimes. And she was one of those children who required a full night of sleep so she could have the energy to run through the next day. Many nights she didn't get through the bedtime story, fast asleep before the first page was complete.

A long table overflowing with kids and parents rose and clapped when Charlie walked in. She climbed up into the end seat and took a deep bow, sat, and shoved half a slice of cheese pizza into her mouth. Once she finished, she worked the table, chatting to her friends about her heroics during the game. Mara concentrated on how happy she seemed, how animated, how wonderful it was to see her daughter as a normal little girl with two normal parents.

One of Chase's friends stopped at their table with his girlfriend and talked for a minute. The day and evening were so ordinary, making her heart swell. This was why she made this choice. As much as she adored

Luke, he couldn't give her a fully happy daughter.

"Are you meeting us at the High Five later on?" Chase's friend asked.

Chase shook his head. "Heading to Mom's for dessert and Mara has to work. I'm on princess duty."

"Aw, come on. Come hang. Jason's coming tonight. You missed him on Tuesday because you left early."

Mara scowled, looking away and pretending she hadn't heard. On Tuesday Chase called at quitting time and said he was working overtime. She hadn't questioned the explanation.

On the drive to Vivian's, Mara told herself she would take the high road and not mention anything about the Tuesday conversation, but she couldn't ignore the issue. She understood going out with the guys, but the lie wasn't sitting well. Chase lapsed into silence when confronted. He rolled the window down and ran his fingers through his hair, letting the cold air blast throughout the car.

"Daddy, I'm cold," Charlie whined, already half asleep in her booster seat. "Can you put your window up?"

"Please?" Mara turned and prompted Charlie.

Charlie mumbled a please and kicked his seat.

"Quit!" Chase turned and pointed at her. "It's warm in here. I'll roll the window up in a bit."

Charlie kicked again.

Mara fought an inner battle, wanting Chase to handle the situation. It was cold, but the classic signs of tired and cranky were spewing.

His answer was not only leaving the window down but mashing buttons on the radio and cranking up the music. Mara rolled her eyes. Four-year-old versus four-year-old.

"We should skip ice cream at your mom's. She's super tired," Mara said, trying to give him an out and keep the stupid peace.

"You'd like that, wouldn't you?"

"What?" Mara turned. Charlie nodded off again. "She's just a little girl, and she's worn out. Let's just take her home. I'll call your mom, so she doesn't get mad at you."

"I can handle my mom."

"Okay. You call your mom."

She angled herself toward him. He scanned her fashionably ripped jeans.

Turning back to the road, he squinted. "Yeah, dessert is probably not a good idea."

She didn't have the strength to wonder what he meant, what she hoped he didn't mean, so she turned back to her window and ignored him.

"The coach sure likes you. You shouldn't encourage him."

"Oh, my God, seriously?" Mara's head fell to the headrest.

"Maybe I'll start coaching. We can get Charlie on a new team."

She almost laughed. Almost.

"That's a great idea, Chase. Charlie would love you as her coach."

Chapter Twenty-Seven

Twenty-three days, four hours, and Luke wasn't quite sure of the minutes, but they became irrelevant as each day melted into another. She had texted and said she was sorry. He couldn't bring himself to be pathetic enough to respond. Truth be told, from the minute her mother let him know the decision she was trying to make, he knew he was going to lose. He couldn't compete with her daughter; he couldn't compete with the man who helped make her daughter.

Concentrating became difficult, and he needed to figure out a way to make it work. School was not going to wait on him to get his life together.

Losing track of time, he woke with a smooshed face in his desk. The law was fast becoming fascinating, intriguing, wrapping him up in a different sort of life he wanted to explore. He wasn't sure he would stay in Rock Springs. At the moment—the backburnered relationship was too painful—but being here worked for now. His savings was dwindling away, but the law office handling his case with Rowdy's family took him on as an unpaid intern, with the offer to hire him as a glorified receptionist in thirty days. At least an official office job kept him out of the oil fields and the mind games the trial created. The small firm was helping him gain a greater understanding of the case and everything involved. His trial would be the first, then Wyatt, then the big bucks one with Silverwood.

He tried not to think too much about the lawsuit. The firm assured him this case would go nowhere, and he didn't see how they could determine he could be at fault, but the anxiousness ate at his insides during the endless hours spent alone. Not knowing gnawed away no matter how many times his boss told him everything would be alright.

He wanted to talk to Mara about his uncertainty, and then he wanted to hate on Mara. He tried hard not to wallow in self-pity. He tried even harder to not imagine her head on Chase's chest, talking until all hours of the night. Sometimes the trying worked. Most times the effort made him sad. At least the law gave him somewhere to unleash all the energy. Constitutional law, criminal law, torts, all of it intrigued him. When his head hit the pillow at night, the energy and drive sapped right out of him, seeping into the feathery pillow she used to lay her head on. Pretending was easy during the day, not so much when darkness fell.

When his phone rang in the middle of the night, he blinked away tears when he saw the adorable picture of Claire and her boys.

She always knew. Always.

"I couldn't sleep," she said in a hushed voice. "JJ's still sick. He's finally snoozing. I'm hoping this time he's out for good. If anyone would be awake at this godforsaken hour, it would be you."

A small snore seeped into the phone lines. He couldn't imagine how much congestion caused a child to snore.

"You were right. I am awake."

"Schoolwork kicking your ass? You always were a

piss-poor student."

"Something like that."

The silence enveloped. He got up and roamed around his bedroom. Pictures of Mara were still crammed around the frame of his mirror. He fiddled with them and wretched them free, placing them face down in his sock drawer.

"What's going on with the 'phews?" Juvenile, like twelve-year-old juvenile, but his immaturity always got a laugh out of the boys when he would hold his nose and call them the 'phews.

"Same old, same old. Soccer, baseball, daycare, school. Same schedule, different day."

Perfection in his mind.

He could hear rustling, then quiet again. He could picture his sister in this moment, all beautiful, concerned, enraptured by her sick boy. So like his mom, wanting to make everything better for everyone.

"Why?" he whispered to Claire.

"Let her find herself, Luke."

"She's not looking for herself. She's only looking for her daughter. I'll never be able to compete with a mama bear."

"No, you never will."

She was right, just like always. He would never want to come between Mara and Charlie, anyways.

"She's not a stupid woman, and she loves you. I guess all you can hope for is she will somewhere, somehow, wake up and discover her own little heart that deserves to be happy. I'm not sure she understands she is worthy."

"I don't know what to say to that. I don't know it'll ever happen."

"Keep living your best life. Keep moving forward with all you're doing and accomplishing. It's the only thing you can do right now."

He smirked. "Maybe you're the one meant to be a lawyer. Always trying to convince people your line of thinking is right."

"No thanks. And you're the lawyer, one of those infuriating ones who inserts and weasels his 'aw shucks' personality into anyone who will listen."

He couldn't help but smile as he stared out the window, trying, with his sister's help, not to fall into the unhealthy thought realm. They hung up when JJ's scratchy voice let out a pitiful cry. Luke wondered if he'd ever have the chance to find his own love story again.

Chapter Twenty-Eight

A stumbling shuffle in the early hours, and Chase's body crashed to his bed in the other room. Mara looked out her window. At least his truck was absent from the driveway. One small win for the good guys.

A week after coming home drunk, his eyes wandered to the sugar infused fruity rings she ate with Charlie one morning. He cocked his head, shot a smirk. She reminded herself to focus on the adorable face counting out red loops, then counting yellow ones. The cuteness of their daughter hating milk on cereal, drinking it separate.

"Makes the loops mushy," she would say and fold her plump little arms and scowl at whoever tried to make her eat "mushy."

They were all three on the couch that evening, Charlie sandwiched in between them. They laughed together like a real family watching their favorite reality, team racing show, screaming at the people not to argue. Everyone knows if you argue too much on the challenges and speed bumps, you go home.

"Git along, will ya." Her drama queen flung her hand at the television.

They laughed more at their daughter than the idiot-arguing morons. Chase's hand wrapped around the back of her neck and wove his fingers in her hair. She stilled and tugged her head to the side, out of reach, unable to get used to him touching her. The slightest brush of his fingers still conjured up too many belittling phrases and actions still rattling around in her brain. As much as she tried not to compare the two men, Chase's fingers were a far cry from the revered, cherished, almost spiritual touch of Luke's hands.

She shook her head for Chase to back off, for herself to get out of her own brain.

"Sheesh." Chase removed his hand, yanking her hair in the process.

He grabbed his jacket from the chair, fishing his keys out of the clay bowl Charlie made for them both at a pottery birthday party last week.

"Daddy, it's not over yet."

"I know pumpkin, but I'm done for tonight." He glared at Mara and let his gaze drop to her feet and back up again. "I'm going to go see some of my friends."

"Night, Daddy." Charlie's gaze shifted back to the TV. "Mommy, look, Jenny and Ethan are in first place. I hope they win." She repeated her daddy's words from earlier. Mara was just glad she didn't understand the drama circling around her.

Chase slid out the door, and Mara closed her eyes, trying to keep the flow of tears inside. When Charlie stood on the couch and jumped into her arms to be toted off to bed, it erased everything.

They decided when they got back together, she would continue on nights, and he would work days. Allowing them to save some money on daycare expenses.

He hadn't come home after leaving their family night. She assumed he'd gone to a friend's house and to work from there. As she dialed the phone yet again, she tried not to panic that everything was upending.

Mara tapped her foot as the phone rang away. She had five minutes to make a fifteen-minute drive to the hospital.

When the phone connected, music hammered the background. Chase shouted at her over the noise. "Mara? Is everything okay?" He sounded halfway concerned, so she calmed down.

"Chase? Can you hear me? I've got to get to work. Why aren't you home?"

"You don't work tonight, baby." His words hushed and sweet, making her smile. An innocent mistake.

"Yes, yes, I do. You need to come home. I'll call and let them know I'm running a little late."

"You don't work on Thursdays. I'm at the bar with the guys. Just call out. I'll be home in a little while."

"Seriously, Chase? My schedule is on the fridge. We're six weeks in trying to make this work, and you're at the bar? Again? That does not bode well."

"Oh, for God's sake, Mara, it's one night. Just fucking call out like normal people do when they have something better going on."

Mara sat at their piece-of-crap dining room table and put the phone to her forehead. No answers came. She didn't want to yell and have Charlie be one of those traumatized kids in a therapist's office saying their mom and dad were always fighting, always angry.

She lowered her voice. "Normal people go to work when they're supposed to. Normal people have a handle on how to be an adult and make money. Normal people don't ask their significant other to 'call out' because they don't want to come home from hanging with the guys. I love my job. People depend on me—my patients, the other nurses, the administrators. I don't want to have to use a PTO day because you're drinking beer. I want to use my time off to take vacations, long weekends, extra time with my mom. I can't believe you would even ask."

"God. Drama queen. Always making a mountain out of a molehill. Call your mother. Hell, call my mother. Everyone deserves some time to themselves."

She went silent, knowing she had made the wrong choice for her and her daughter's future. Knowing this was her life. This was what she opted for. It took all the anger and angst right out of her.

"You're right. Everyone deserves some time to themselves. I'll call my mom."

He said something, and she just hung up, dropped the phone to the table, and pinched the bridge of her nose.

Charlie crawled into her lap, laying her head onto Mara's chest. The simple gesture so loving and innocent, Mara would melt into tears any second. She fortified herself. She didn't have the option of waterworks.

"Daddy is stuck at work. How about me and you walk to the park?"

"Yay. I love the park!" Charlie was off with her mounds and mounds of words about how amazing the park was, how much she loved every piece of equipment, while simultaneously holding Mara's hand, shoving her feet into red cowboy boots.

When Charlie was done playing on the jungle gym, climbing on the big spider, riding the horses with the massive springs for legs, she wore her little self out and settled into bed with a contended sigh, not even asking for a bedtime story. She closed her eyes, and Mara swept wisps of hair from Charlie's face as her little person curled into a ball, clutching at her precious purple blanket.

Mara planted a kiss on her cheek. Charlie's eyes popped open. "You sad, Mommy?"

Mara smiled. Her four-year-old daughter had more empathy than her grown-up father. "If I told you once, I told you a million times, I can never be sad with your sweet face in front of me," she said, shrugging dramatically.

"You're silly," Charlie said, closing her eyes again.

No, Mara thought. *I'm a fool.*

She meandered into the living room and saw the DVD she'd watched with Luke amongst a dozen cartoon flicks scattered throughout the bookcase.

"What the hell. Everyone deserves some time to themselves, right Chase?"

Plugging the DVD in would be a mistake, yet it didn't stop her. The ripe emotions conjured up a picture from the not-too-distant past. The song, and its emotion, breaking through to every cracked and crippled thing within her. How Luke understood without her saying a word. Luke, wrapping her in his arms, dancing, knowing she didn't have the ability to explain the emotion of dams breaking down.

She sobbed into the bright and cheery throw pillow, not wanting Charlie to hear her pain. Hear how her mother was so broken it sometimes seemed impossible to get her feet up under her.

Her sobs continued into the night after she settled into bed. She clutched at the sheets, remembering Luke discovering her body for the first time. Tasting her body, loving her, loving her body. The thoughts made her bury her face in the pillows so no one, least of all herself, would hear the cries.

She could have had everything. Instead, she sacrificed the most important of things.

When she woke to the sun streaming in the window, her cheeks were stuck to the sheets in the salty remnants of last night's tears, making her eyes puffy and scratchy.

When she rolled onto her back, she stared at the ceiling. "I can't do this anymore," she whispered. Somewhere inside, her strong self woke up.

"I can't do this anymore." Her words, sure and confident.

She sprang out of bed with no idea how she would resolve her situation, but last night had broken a part of her. Last night made her realize she had once again lost pieces of herself on the journey. Chase's reality may be everyone deserves some time to themselves, but her reality was everyone deserved to be true to themselves. More important, to stick with the decision.

To know who she was. Not as a mom, not as a daughter, not as a friend or significant other.

Mara Sawyer could have it all.

She dropped Charlie off at daycare, returned home, and called her old landlord to see if she could get her old house back. Fortunately, it remained empty since the day she left. She called and booked movers, disconnected and reconnected utilities, and texted Chase. Ignored his replies.

Little tremors broke over her when she found her mom curled into a little ball in the middle of her bed. "Mom? Aren't you taking your pain pills? Let me get them for you."

Remnants of throw up floated in the toilet. Dropping the toilet seat, she flushed it and shook a couple of pills into her hand. She filled a glass with water and helped her mother sit against a mountain of pillows.

"I'm going to leave him again." The strength of her words made her smile.

Her mother trembled for a second. "For good this time." Statement. No question.

"For good this time," she repeated. "Yes. I was a fool to think things would change. And I want more for me, more for my daughter. If I have to wade and swim through hell and high water in the court system, then I'm going to have to do it."

"About goddamn time." Her mother pounded her fist into the bedding.

Mara laughed.

Her mom struggled to sit, and she pressed herself under Mara's arm and into her chest, shaking. "You lost too much control all at once."

"Not exactly the problem, I think your drugs may be too strong."

Her mom held her hand up. "You're a control freak. Tell me you realize this about yourself?"

"I am not."

"You are. And you lost too much control, making you break. You make stupid-assed decisions like going back to your deadbeat ex-husband." A strong emphasis on *ex*.

"I didn't lose control, but yes to the stupid-assed decision."

"Listen to your doped-up mother. You lost control of me and my cancer returning. You had no control over Luke's father and the impact of his father's words. And you lost control of the court system. In turn, you lost control of your daughter's future. Chase is something you could control, so you grasped on with everything in you and took advantage. Now you've paid the high price of regaining control, and where did it get you? Absolutely nowhere. Relinquish control and live."

Her mom nodded off with her wisdom spouting. Even when her mom's words resonated and banged around throughout the day, her most important thought?

"I've got nothing to lose. I'm going after what I want."

Chapter Twenty-Nine

Luke glanced at his watch as he left the office, shifting his satchel to his other arm. With the workday over, a light evening with friends from school could now get started. A little trash-talking their professors. With Mara out of the picture for more weeks than he cared to count, he'd settled into school and found a small group of friends in similar situations. Same as in oil-filled Texas, plenty of people were looking for something new and more stable. Lots of older students like himself, hitting the books again.

Luke clicked the fob unlocking his doors and paused. All of him. Heart, legs, arms, eyes. Legs drawn up, head resting on her knees, Mara sat on his tailgate. Trying to work himself into stone, his heart hammered away. When it fell into a normal rhythm again, the damn organ pulled in pity. Her eyes were puffy and shadowed. He took a second to fortify himself before stepping forward. Loading his bag and files into the back seat, he slammed the door and stood at the tailgate, arms folded. Her lip lifted upward for a moment in a halfhearted smile, then fell from her face again. A loose ponytail fell at the back of her neck, strands escaping and lifting in the wind, settling again before she wiped them from her face.

When she breathed deeply, her breath pulled her head back and she held it in. He wanted to look at his watch, let her know he wasn't just sitting around pining for her, but he waited anyways. Knowing she needed to let herself roll on out of those dark caverns of her inner self.

When he could bare her gaze no longer, he leaned against the tailgate, staring at his office across the darkened street.

"I know I have no right to be here. I really do know that." She blew out a deep breath. "And if I were you, I'd tell me to scoot along."

"Are you putting words in my mouth again?"

"No. Shit, maybe. I really do understand I screwed up, and screwed up big, but…I could really use a friend right now, Luke. I've got nothing. No one."

He looked up and down the street, returning his stare to his office. He didn't want to look at her. He didn't want to fall again. Falling hurt.

"I picked Charlie, and I know I hurt everyone else with my choice. I was wrong. I understand I didn't pick you, but worse, I didn't pick me."

"You could have had you, me, and your daughter. Everything. You could have been patient; it would've worked out. Now, I don't see how it can. I told you once before: in this game, I don't play for second place."

"Can you play for friends?"

She broke his heart with her pitiful ask. That was his heart. His head didn't want to give.

"I'm a pathetic mess. All I want is my mom, and she's dying. The cancer is moving so fast this time. I can't dump all this on her."

There were long moments following her words. Moments where he thought it was low to piggyback her mom dying into the conversation. Moments when she should have known where all this was headed when she made the choice she did. But then there were the other moments, where she was offering at least the friendship he missed. Moments where he wanted to melt when she said his name.

He sat on the tailgate. "I can't take any more hurt from you. Some scars just don't want to heal, okay?"

Her head shot his direction, and he gave her a stern look. It was hard to be angry when she hurt this badly. Her slumped shoulders, shaking hands, curling into herself.

"I never slept with him," she blurted, looking down at the street, her feet dropping from the tailgate to hang off the edge. "I couldn't."

A slam hit his insides.

"I don't know why. No, I do know why. The ice just wouldn't thaw. Any time we brushed hands cleaning up dishes, or whatever, I would turn to stone. I would remember…all the horrible things he would say about me in those moments. He didn't respect, appreciate…me."

"You don't respect you."

"I know." She dropped her head. "It was just like you said. All that confidence and coming back into myself slipped away again. My dad would be so ashamed of me." Her words drifted off.

"I think…do you want to know what I think?"

She nodded. "Yes, I do. You're the one who gets me, who gets all my hopes and dreams. You're the one I let in. So yes, I want to know what you think."

He lifted her chin. "I think you need to start living for Mara. Not what I think, not what your dad would be ashamed or not ashamed of. Dads don't have all the answers either. You do have a daughter, and yes, you need to consider her, but on being a mother, you never stopped. What you stopped, what you quit on, was you. You quit me, you quit Rachel, you quit your mom and justified the decision by saying you were doing it for Charlie, but that was just an excuse. You quit on you. Just like you did when you left him in the first place. You always want to blame someone, but it's just anger at yourself. The venom you spewed hurt, I'm not going to deny that, but the real people in your life? They know your hateful words were disgust with yourself. Chase was the easy way out, because he fed you the lies you were already feeding yourself."

She was crying for the second time in their short history. Whether she acted on those tears was a whole other story.

"I wish I could go back, not say those things. I'm sorry."

"I don't want your apologies. I'd much rather you figure out where those words come from, why you continuously feed them to yourself. Until you work your way over that hurdle? Your apology means nothing. You, and only you, can change this. You and only you, can start a new chapter and deal with life. Quit hiding behind your daughter, go out and get what you want in life. I know you can; I keep seeing glimpses of the real you in there. Go find that girl."

A car drove by in the silence, and the overhead streetlights clicked on.

She nodded. "I'm sure you have somewhere to be. I've got to go find that girl."

He smiled and tapped his finger on her hand. "Bring her on by when you end the search. She was fun to hang out with."

Mara hopped off the tailgate, and he locked it in place, glanced around to make sure her car was close.

"Hey, Whitten?"

He turned and rolled his eyes.

"That Luke guy? He was the reason I turned to ice with Chase. Because you make me feel…like me."

He probably wouldn't sleep tonight, but those words. Coming from her mouth?

Two peas in one messed-up pod.

Chapter Thirty

The first thing Mara noticed when she walked into the bar three weeks later was his downcast head. A half-drunk beer and an empty shot glass sat in front of him. Even then, he looked good—better than good—outfitted in his new law office job wardrobe. Khakis and a button-down shirt. Even the sleeves were rolled up his forearms, just so. She wondered with the new look whether the weekends were still for sweats and old Texas-something T-shirts.

The upscale bar on the square was empty for a Thursday. The threatening spring storm undoubtedly left most people hunkering down. His Texas ass still hadn't learned lesson one. His was a fine-looking ass, but still a stupid one. He glanced at the muted television above the bar, looked down again. The bartender, bored with his singular client, pointed the remote at the TV and swapped around the channels.

The interesting thing about this bar was the interior looked exactly like the one in one of his favorite '80s flicks. She had watched the movie twice with him, the older one of course, listening to him fight himself not to recite every word, knowing it irritated her to no end. She didn't have the same adoration for his number one movie, but there were some great lines there.

The bartender looked at her, nodded, and returned to his channel surfing.

She eyed the jukebox against the wall and couldn't help but smile.

The jukebox looked retro, but she doubted it was. Probably had never spun an '80s song.

Hunkering over the flashing monstrosity, she scanned it as she dug in her purse. Not a coin slot to be found. Or a card slot. But hell, you could stream from your phone. Jukeboxes had come a long way. She loaded the app, and the wheel spun at a painstakingly long pace. A list of choices popped up, and she tried to decide how to play this out. The best way to woo him back.

It read the device and threw up a search bar.

Go with one of the movie soundtracks? Or go with their song? What she believed to be their song.

Hell, he got his movie scene. She was picking the song.

The bartender looked in her direction when the machine came to life. When she nodded at Luke, he found something to do in the back. Luke continued his stare at the amber liquid in his glass, swirling it aimlessly.

The song kicked in, and his head jerked, his body going from slumped to straight as he caught her gaze in the mirror over the bar. He spun in his seat, shooting a quick look at the jukebox, and slid from the stool.

"You stole my movie with your song," he said in his sultry, curl-your-toes voice.

"Our song."

"Still my movie."

She cocked her head. "I feel the need."

He grinned like a stupid fool. "The need for speed?"

They met in the middle of the empty floor, dancing to the song that initiated the best relationship of her life.

One she had given up, but she wasn't giving up things anymore. She was worth more. They were worth more.

His eyes were closed when she looked up, and she wasn't sure she had ever seen anything quite so beautiful.

A simple man. A complicated man.

Hers. He was hers.

"I need you to be my wingman again." She looked directly at him and stroked his cheeks.

He raised his eyebrows, grew serious. "No room for this cowboy if it's second place," he whispered.

She tucked her head against his chest. "Took a little bit for me to realize things. Thank you for being patient."

He gathered her tight against him, and every misstep melted away. The silence was killing her.

"Talk to me, Goose."

He tried hard to hide his smile. The harder he tried, the more his lips lifted.

"No." He nuzzled her neck. "I just want to take another look at you."

She leaned back, his arm tight under her shoulder blades. "The boy has some moves of his own."

"Twelve notes. Let's not repeat the last octave."

"Deal." She grabbed his hand. "Take me to bed or lose me forever."

They both cracked up. He slung down the rest of his drink. "Show me the way home, darlin'."

"Is that the Texas version?"

"That's my version, and you're my star who has been reborn."

She groaned and looked skyward. "God, you're hopeless with the sap."

The night air bit when they stepped onto the street. "Sappy and crazy for you. Problem with that?"

"Not a one."

They left his car and took hers to his house. The wind bit when they shut the iciness out, slamming his front door with his foot, his mouth on hers before she could shrug out of her coat.

"God, I missed you," she said.

"Same."

With the movie reference foreplay, nothing else was the same. A frantic need instead of the slow unraveling. A brief thought of stupidity swept through as she wondered how she could have given Chase another chance. This was life. Luke was real life. Her Luke, who's own life hadn't been easy. Her Luke, who loved her from the inside out. A million thoughts floating around and filled her up as he set into an easy motion on top of her, entering her with a deep and throaty sigh, and she understood being home. When he settled himself between her legs, all was right with the world once again.

The life preserver encircled them, tethering them. She never wanted to lose her grip again. As she fell into racking spasms deep, deep within, she forgot about life preservers and settled into the suspended moment when she rose to experience strong and soft at the same time.

Merging wants and needs was what Luke Whitten did for her.

They woke to the sunlight streaming in the window. The still howling wind caused her to settle into his chest, tugging the blanket up to her nose. She wasn't cold, not with all the heat of his body, but she found herself shivering inside as everything rotated into rightness. Flashing to the indescribable feeling she had last night when strength and softness met; the deep emotion wrapped in physical embodiment was how his body felt in this moment. Strong, ready to take on the world, but willing to mold and sculpt to whatever life threw his way, her way. She liked—no, loved—he had both, the strong and the tough. But could pivot and become a pile of sappy mush.

"I want to introduce you to my daughter," she said as her finger roamed up his side, around the U of his armpit, and down his arm. He drew in a breath as her finger hit the juncture on the underside of his elbow. She kissed his sweet spot.

"I would be honored." He pressed her head and lips to his chest, shuffled his body to wrap around her and cup her bottom, trail his own finger up the small of her back. "Be prepared. I'm amazing with kids."

"I know you are. But this kid's a little special to me."

"I think I knew that."

They were the last words as they mingled skanky breath with sweat and sheets.

Chapter Thirty-One

Charlie's face was stuck at the front window, chubby fists at her cheeks. She began jumping up and down and clapping her hands.

The front door opened before Luke could walk around the truck to the sidewalk.

Mara stroked Charlie's hair. "She's a little excited today."

Charlie crossed her arms over her chest, scowling. "You're late."

Luke glanced at his watch, raised his eyebrows at Mara.

"She's been at the window since she rolled out of bed."

"The fair is going to start, and we're not going to have enough time to see all the animals." She stomped her foot and pouted.

"Drama much?" He squatted to make himself eye level. "I apologize, madam, for my tardiness."

She broke into the biggest smile. "Silly boy."

He looked up at Mara, back to the same amber eyes in smaller proportions. "How're we all today?"

"Ready, we're ready to go," Charlie said, ramming sparkly sunglasses into place, outlining her eyes in glittery stars. "Mommy has snacks for the road."

He kissed Mara's nose. "Shall we?" He swept his arm toward the truck. "Your chariot awaits."

Charlie rolled her eyes.

The chatter ran nonstop from the back seat. Mara flipped through her phone for a while and then closed her eyes—rested her eyes, she said. Luke managed to hold his own in the conversation, understanding quickly how much a four-year-old could truly talk. And yowza, this girl could yack with the best of them. His older nephew, JJ, was not a talker, but Luke didn't think Claire would get that lucky with Cole. Engaged with everything, he kept his gaze on the rearview mirror, watching her facial and hand expressions as she talked about nothing in particular. She'd taken to calling him Uke, her little voice sounding just as adorable as Cole's.

"You have a nana, Uke?" she asked, but didn't seem to think he needed to respond as she rambled on again. "My nana, she's sick. Did you know that?"

Luke eyed her. After a second of staring out the window, looking a little lost, she was back on all cylinders. "She does the Upchuck Chuck."

"That's not nice to say," Mara said behind closed eyes.

Charlie flung her hand. "She thinks it's funny. And she says there's not enough funny right now, so I think…" She was back to staring out the window. "Is Nana going to die, Mommy? I don't want Nana to die, then she won't make me peanut butter cookies anymore."

Luke eyeballed Mara as she, too, watched the scenery slip by. Having no clue what to say, he fiddled with the radio.

"And how will you live without your cookies?" Mara flung both her hands, using all her drama stops to teeter Charlie into a new conversation line.

"I don't know. But you better learn to bake, because you're a mom, and moms bake. Grammy V says so."

Charlie hoisted herself up as far as she could in her booster seat, craning her neck when Luke exited the highway. Before Mara could get out of her seat, Charlie unbuckled herself and waited on someone to open her door. Jumping to solid ground, the dirt spit up around her red cowboy boots.

"Is that a pig? That is a fat pig." She pointed at the animal pens lining the entrance gates.

Mara grabbed her hand as Luke lowered the tailgate, putting the stroller on the ground.

"I'm not riding in that." She scrunched her nose up. "I am four, you know."

"And you will get tired at some point and be begging for a ride," Mara reminded her.

"Will not," she said, stomping her adorable, booted foot yet again.

Luke put the stroller in the cab. "We can come back for it when the princess decides she needs a chariot."

Charlie's little head dropped back, and she sighed heavily. Mara took a hand; Luke grabbed the other. And then they were back to wide-eyed wonderment. And nonstop words, sentences, paragraphs—hell, full-on novels spewing out of the diva's mouth.

They all tried unsuccessfully to land a stuffed animal at the ring toss. "It's so not fair." Charlie stomped away, and Mara spun her around. "You need to thank the man for letting you try."

Charlie scrunched her eyes, trying to outmaneuver her mom, but there was no finagling being done in the manners department.

"Okay, Mommy." She thanked the man ever so

sweetly. Stuck out both her hands for Luke and Mara. "Next?"

"Baseball toss?"

Charlie tore her hand from theirs and skipped ahead. Luke picked up Mara's hand, kissed her knuckles, and looped his arm over her shoulders. She laced her fingers into his. "I wish I had her energy." He nodded at Charlie.

"Oh, she'll go until she drops, so you better strap on those big girl panties, Whitten."

They rode the Ferris wheel, the swings that flew out from a circular tower. Mara and Charlie rode some kind of floating Arabian carpet thing rotating on a track at a painstaking pace. The smell of popcorn drew them to the food booths.

Charlie skidded to a halt in front of a cotton candy vendor. She touched the pink poof, her eyes widening as pure sugar hit her tongue. "It's like a cloud. It tastes like a cloud."

"And how, pray tell, do you know what a cloud tastes like?"

"Oof," Charlie grunted, throwing her head back. "Men!"

"I know, right?" Mara squatted and lifted a piece for herself before they set off again.

They raced around a mini track in baby race cars, relaxed for a whole fifteen minutes while riding the open-air train around the fairgrounds. His world was about wrapped up in perfection when Charlie clambered into his lap and kneeled on his thighs, scoping out the bulls and horses, chickens and goats. Luke was quite sure he would burst from the inside out when she smooshed his cheeks together and told him today was the best day ever.

Kathryn Beck

Bouncing off the train, her little hands dragged them toward the twirling cups. Like the old school Tilt-A-Whirl, but without the tilt part.

"Oh, man, these are just like the teacups my sister and I rode when we were kids," Luke said in an overexaggerated voice, matching her drama head-to-head.

Her little face lifted, sparks flying in wonderment from small person eyes.

Lord, he was a goner. Charlie looked at him with utter hero worship because he'd been to a Florida amusement park. He must never have daughters; they would be the epitome of spoiled.

They retrieved the stroller in the early evening before they settled in the open-air amphitheater to listen to music. Every time they imagined the child was whipped, she kept on running. Long lasting battery commercials were front and center. A battery in red boots. Waiting for the music to start, Mara settled in between his legs on the blanket next to the stroller. Charlie clambered out of the contraption to sit between Mara's legs.

"Like a choo choo, Mommy."

Luke nuzzled Mara's neck and whispered how much he loved her. It was quite possible he enjoyed today more than Charlie. When Mara settled back into him, molding into his chest, he inhaled a deep whiff of sweaty coconut suntan lotion and realized life was pretty damn perfect.

When they were on their way home, the back seat, dead silent. Hair sprouting loose from her ponytail. Her head flopped to the side, corrected itself with a jerk, and falling again.

Mara was half asleep in the passenger seat when he

felt, as much as saw, Charlie's head pop erect. She stared out the window for a second and looked directly at him in the rearview mirror. The image made him melt with her cheeks all flushed, her eyes full of glassy sleepiness.

"If you and my mommy get married, what do I call you? You can't be my daddy because I already have a daddy. Amy has two daddies, but I don't know…" She returned a perplexed stare to the road sweeping by.

A smirk crept onto Mara's face. He slapped her hand.

Charlie leaned forward. "I could call you Uke, of course. Or, my mommy calls you Whitten sometimes, maybe that?" Charlie's hands started flinging at the road, at the front seat, over her head as she ran through her ramble of naming options.

"Your mommy calls me Whitten when she's making fun of me, or mad at me. I don't want to be called Whitten."

Charlie snorted and giggled. "That's kinda true."

"And Chuck?" Luke did a full-on belly laugh. "Hey, I'm going to call you Chuck."

She scrunched up her nose. "But I'm Charlie."

"I need my own name for you. Chuck is a nickname for Charlie. Ha, you can be stuck Chuck, maybe duck Chuck. There's so many places to take this."

A tired smile hit her face. "Or when I'm sick and throwing up, I can be like Nana and be upchuck Chuck."

He made sure she was still awake. "Maybe we stick with Uke for now and see where it goes."

"Okay." She bit the corner of her lower lip. "But if you got married…" She let the thought trail off. "Then you will have another kid with my mommy, and they would get to call you daddy, but I wouldn't. That would

241

make me mad."

"I don't think we have to solve this tonight, Chuckie."

She speared him in the rear view again. "Amy calls her other daddy, D2. I could call you D2."

Mara smirked and still seemed intent on letting him handle things all on his own.

"D2 huh? I like it." he asked.

Charlie scrunched up her nose. "Why?"

Luke sat up straight in his seat, took his hands off the steering wheel, and banged his palms on his head. "Because? Because it's…" Charlie would have no frame of reference. "That's just sad."

Mara nudged him and laughed. "She's four, Luke. Good Lord, what do you expect?"

"Oh, girl. Date night, me and you." He settled a hand on the top of the steering wheel. "Space ship movie marathon, next Friday."

"You're silly. Dates are for grownups." She giggled, settling back in her seat with an exhausted sigh, making Luke wonder if she might finally be running out of steam. Her eyelids fluttered and fell shut. He watched every second of her winding down and knew, without question, he should never, ever have a daughter.

Chapter Thirty-Two

The courtroom was a hive of activity. Luke's heart began racing at the wide-open double doors. He fought to get one foot in front of the other to cross the threshold.

"Babe?" Mara questioned.

He nodded, stopped again when he spotted Rowdy's teenage son sitting in the front row on the aisle. The same one he caught with a beer earlier in the year, the same one Rowdy swore was a baseball phenom. "Made for great things, my kid." Luke heard Rowdy's voice as if he were standing beside him. Luke went to see one of his games and had to agree with his proud papa regarding his talent. He smiled in his direction, but Rowdy's widow caught the exchange and tugged on her son's hand.

Luke stopped at the barricade separating the people from the lawyers and defendants. His hand turned white clutching Mara's. He mumbled a "sorry" and kissed her hand before stepping through the gate where his lawyer and now boss read through a notebook full of reports, stopping to jot down a few more notes. He threw an unsure smile at Mara, knowing any courtroom was the last place she wanted to be. Though last week her own experience had gone her way, joint custody now her reality.

His stomach did a flip-flop as the doors whooshed shut at the back of the room. The room settled into silence, and sweat soaked through his new shirt, making him claw at his tie and brush nonexistent lint from his jacket. Today was just an evidentiary hearing, but it would set the tone for his old employer, the contractor, and for himself, his own future in or out of a jailhouse. His lawyer was confident the evidence was on all their sides, but the judge was well known to be on the side of whoever opposed big oil. Knowing this, the plaintiff requested a bench trial. This wasn't about money—this was about making someone pay for the loss of a father, husband, son. At the opposite table, Rowdy's wife sat ramrod straight, her hands clasped tightly in front of her. Her lawyer patted them, and she continued her steady stare at the seal of Wyoming behind the judge's head.

Luke removed some of his own notes, studying them as he had every night since they drafted them. As much as they were in the right, knowing he told everything that happened to the best of his ability, his stomach continued to turn. The antacid regiment for the last month did absolutely nothing today.

When the judge called the courtroom to order, a memory surfaced of his father in a Texas courtroom. An accident on their property left one of their employees paralyzed. That man's family also wanted someone to pay. But mostly they wanted money. His father offered a generous sum as a settlement, but the amount hadn't been high enough to stop the family from going to trial. His father sat proud and straight, spoke sincerely, confidently. Luke was just a teenager then, but his father told him later how scared he had been, how it would be foolish not to admit your fear, but you couldn't ever let people see you as weak, giving them the upper hand. And he told him something that resonated with every step in preparing for this battle.

If you're on the side of right, son, justice will always prevail. No matter what your name, what your bank balance, how many acres you own. All a man really has is his truth.

Luke straightened, picking up a pen and pretending to write something down. His drawing was only a doodle of the word Texas in chunky block letters, but it settled his stomach and calmed his throbbing head.

All a man really has is his truth.

He nodded to the words while the judge shuffled papers around in front of him.

"We're here to review the Pump Forty-Nine accident on May fifteenth of this year where Mr. Finch was killed." He nodded at the widow. "I'm sorry for your loss, ma'am."

She wiped at a tear.

"I see Mr. Whitten is here with his lawyer. This is a trial to determine negligence on his part. Trials with Silverwood Oil and Wyatt will follow. All three hearings will be separate, with different legal teams. The trials will be kept independent of one another."

"Judge. If I may." The lawyer on the other side of the aisle popped up.

"No, you may not. I won't have any grandstanding folks. I know this is a big deal here in Rock Springs, lots of national coverage, but we're talking about lives. There's not going to be anyone jumping on high horses or bashing in the social media world. This hearing is a legal proceeding, not a circus for a media feeding frenzy. Am I understood?"

Luke and his lawyer nodded their heads. The other lawyer sat down and mumbled.

"Alright, any new evidence to present?"

"Your Honor." Luke's lawyer jumped to his feet. "We would like to request the case against Mr. Whitten be dismissed. There's no—"

The judge flung his hand. "Sit down, Mr. Adams. My question was a simple one to get things rolling."

Adams dropped into his seat with a huff.

"Again, any new evidence?"

"No, sir," at least four voices echoed at once.

The court reporter's tapping nails broke the silence. When she stopped and looked up, the judge gnawed away on his pencil.

"I have clawed and clambered through this report, combed through the evidence, the procedures, steps taken by not only Mr. Whitten, but also the various companies involved, and I'm honestly compelled to do just as Mr. Adams jumped the gun to request."

Luke barely had time to register the words, relish the words, before the widow and her lawyer were on their feet shouting at the judge. The judge allowed them to run through a whole host of admonishments until they wound down.

When they sat, the judge leaned forward. "I am truly sorry for your loss, but I can't bend the law. As much as big oil exerts their considerable influence at times, and their lawyers drag things out, there's nothing here. Mr. Whitten did his job. He reported the malfunction a week before the accident. He ran into the burning fire. Risking his own life was not in his job description, but he raced to help anyways. I have read countless reports from workers, and no one disputes anything he has said. I have photographs of the burns he received trying to make the best of a horrendous situation. He did his job, Ms. Finch.

I can't find anything to implicate him."

The judge patted the stack of paper in front of him, and the courtroom hung in silence. "And I'm going to go a step further. These other cases against the contractor and Silverwood, your lawyer may have an alternate plan, but oil law is very detailed, very intricate. The contractor took Mr. Whitten's advisement, reported the safety deviation to Silverwood within the forty-eight hours mandated. Silverwood reacted swiftly. A maintenance engineer was ready to fly out to the site. This is a terrible tragedy, but legally you're talking a tough sell in any of the cases. The only case you may have is against the manufacturer, and they are overseas. Anything off American soil gets into a whole lot of international court systems. And I will tell you, they have very deep pockets. They can drag this out until your children and your children's children are gone from this earth."

He stacked up his papers, straightening them from the top and bottom and again from each side. The tower was perfect. "I understand Wyatt is withholding life insurance until these cases are settled, but they are still willing to pay if the cases are dropped. I know you don't want to take what you consider blood money, but you are entitled to it. The money would help ease the financial loss of your husband. It does nothing for the emotional pain, but at least it removes the day-to-day battle of maintaining a home for your children. Please take this into consideration." He nodded at the bailiff. "We're adjourned."

Luke dropped his head to the table while his heart gained normal footing. He'd stressed for so long, been a mass of conflicting emotions, to have it reduced to being dismissed left him empty, depleted. Like everything drained out of him in a single moment. At the same time, life could set itself in motion again.

His shoulders shook in relief, his biceps trembling and quaking. A comforting squeeze from his lawyer returned him to reality. "It is as it should be. Congrats, Luke."

Luke raised his head and shook the older man's hand with both of his own. "Thank you for believing in me."

"Thank you for trusting me. I hope you'll continue to work for us until you finish school and come on board once you pass the bar. We could use a good oil law expert, not to mention the hardest working man I think I've ever met."

Luke nodded while searching out Mara. "I'll do that."

At the back of the room, he locked eyes with her. Her head cocked with a small smile on her face. He closed the distance and fell into her.

"You're a free man. I think you need to buy a girl a drink to celebrate."

"I can do that. It'll be nice to sleep tonight. It's been a while." So many nights the ceiling was the only thing he could concentrate on, driving himself crazy with unknowns. Not knowing was worse than knowing. He'd faced that fact a couple of nights ago. He collapsed into her chest. When her fingers stopped stroking his back, he raised his head. She smooshed his cheeks and kissed him gently. Her touch elicited a powerful, gut-level pull, making him thankful to be alive, thankful to be in love, thankful to be a part of a team.

Thankful for his father's words, but mostly, thankful for her, and his truth.

Chapter Thirty-Three

Luke thumbed the red dot on his phone and settled back into the couch. His heart hammering, he closed his eyes and waited for it to calm down. The needy little boy in him was smack dab in the middle of a boy, teenager, man, wanting his father's approval.

His father had called.

His father needed him.

The thought settled in his gut and carried a complexity of extremes. Making him want to weep with joy, at the same time, filling him with anger and an intense desire to smash something. So much time lost on nothing more than Evelyn taking away everything. His father disregarding everything precious in his need to appease.

A monumental moment in Luke's sad little happy life. He wanted to shove it in someone's face. He wanted to roll up in a little ball and grasp on.

Everything with Mara was moving into the what-comes-next stage, and his father picks this moment to pick up the phone and call the son he abandoned a decade earlier. Luke wanted to sling the phone into the wall, then sling it against the other wall, but the real thought was how much he loved his dad.

How much he needed his dad. And always had.

The ranch was failing, Claire said earlier. Two steps away from declaring bankruptcy and selling off their assets. He thought she was being dramatic when she asked him to come home.

No—his answer.

The words were super easy to say.

Not only had Ward Whitten picked Evelyn for a good portion of Luke's life, then he picked someone not even related. Luke never expected Evelyn's hatred to rear its ugly head after she was six feet under. His father could have finally stood up and made things right, but he let him down. Again.

Why in the world would he subject himself to whatever other mud could be thrown his direction?

Because then his father asked.

Because his father had finally called.

Mara knocked and let herself in, and he smiled despite the heavy conversation not fifteen minutes old. His Mara, bright and sunshiny with a mid-summer tan, torn jeans, and a hugging tank top that sent his mind roaming down the hall.

On the non-Charlie weeks, she'd taken to spending weekends at his house, going to work, checking on her mom, and then back to his house.

"I come bearing gifts," she said, propping her foot to hold the screen door. At the same time, trying to lug in some reusable bags full of something. "A little help?"

Luke jumped up, kissing her as he grabbed two bags, and took them into the kitchen. Setting them on the table, he peered inside, scoping out the contents. "Looks like a mountain of vegetables. Where's the beef?"

She rolled her eyes. "It's some broccoli and a bag of salad. Not even a hill, let alone a mountain. And if you dig farther, you'll find two beautifully hand-selected fillets for tomorrow night." She removed a baggie filled with fluid with hunks of meat swimming around. "I thought chicken for tonight. Do you have charcoal for the grill?"

"Yes, ma'am." He took the baggie from her hand and set it in the sink. "How about an appetizer?" he said, nuzzling her neck and moving to stick his nose down the V of her tank top.

Her breath caught as her nails dug into his forearms. "A better appetizer than cheese and crackers, I suppose."

"I'm all about furthering your appetizer palate." He nudged her breast up and out of her bra, loving the moan slipping out more than the bare breast in his hand.

"Oh, Whitten. Down the hall, now!"

"Yes, ma'am."

She giggled and grabbed his hand.

When they came up for air, long shadows were looming as he stroked her hair away from her face. He closed his eyes, wishing for a simpler life than the one he had. He wanted to be here, with her, more than anything. He wanted his father's respect and acceptance, too. How did the two ever merge and become one?

"My dad called me," he whispered.

Her head popped up off his chest and scoured his face.

"You've waited a long time for this." She interlocked her fingers on his chest, propping her chin on them. He couldn't help but lean in and kiss her now swollen lips.

His head fell back onto the pillows. "The ranch is failing. Claire called earlier, but I chalked it up to her overly dramatic self."

"Claire's never been overly dramatic. And those are your words. How bad are things?"

He shrugged, stared at the ceiling. "Bad, I guess. I don't really know."

"Liar." She settled her head into his armpit, ran her hand across his chest. "How long until you leave?"

"I don't know that I am," he said, already knowing. Just like she did. He wanted to think he put up a good fight first.

She held herself over him, forcing him to look at her. "I know you are. You know you are. No matter what he's done, he's still your father, and you still love him. You still crave his acceptance, and this is a way to right a whole lot of wrongs."

Her bare breast hovered over his chest. Touching, but not touching. "I don't want to leave you."

"You're not leaving me, Luke. This is just a pause."

He wrapped her up in his arms and full-on ugly cried. For the lost years, for the uncertainty of what was to come, for the beauty of Mara and that she understood him so well.

"You come back to me though, Luke Whitten. I'm lending you to your father, not giving."

He smiled though his tears. "God, I'm going to miss you."

"Pick me, Whitten. Please pick me."

He didn't quite understand what she meant, but she said it so emphatically he acted like he understood.

"I will always pick you," he said, touching a whisper of a kiss to her earlobe. "Always."

Chapter Thirty-Four

This was the homecoming Luke dreamed of experiencing. The one where he was welcomed and hugged heartily by his father as soon as he reached baggage claim. The one where his dad clutched tight, clinging moments longer than necessary. The one where the conversation on the drive to San Angelo was continuous, the laughs, endless. And finally, the one where they hit the orange-and-white awnings of his favorite burger joint for patty melts and chocolate shakes. Some traditions just never wanted to die.

The gates flung wide when they arrived, no codes necessary. No pleading or begging necessary.

"You didn't pack much." His dad pulled the truck to a stop in front of the house, nodding at the canvas bag that had seen more miles than he could count. Following him into war zones, college zones, visiting friends across the country zones, and as of now, coming home zones.

"Dad, I can't stay long. I have classes."

"I know classes are done online these days. We'll see how things go."

Luke stopped, determined not to be manipulated. "No. I came to help—I'm happy to help—but I will be going back to Wyoming within a week. If a week isn't good enough, then tell me now, and I'll head on back to the airport and go home."

His dad flinched at the word "home."

"Whatever you say, Luke. Your terms." He nodded. "I am just glad you're here."

"Me too, Dad." He softened at the momentary distraught look on his dad's face.

When he stepped inside, and made his way upstairs, the waves of emotion were like nothing he'd imagined. All those years away, all those wanting years.

He automatically stepped over the fourth step from the top, knowing from too many nights trying to sneak in, the creak was the worst for giving away curfew infractions. His old room had been freshened and smelled of hay and springtime. A new dark gray comforter lay on the heavy wood bed. Snapping open the curtains, he lifted the blinds, opened the window, drinking in the smell. Something like manure and sweat, a hint of mesquite. The air didn't have the same purity as Wyoming, but many of the memories and history evoked warmth and contentment.

The room itself was filled with thoughts of his mom. Lying by his side reading when he was in grade school, helping him paint his room lime green, and in this room his mother told him about her cancer. Looking out the window, down the road leading to the house, his knees buckled, remembering standing at the end of their road. Without a doubt, he wouldn't be able to stand ever again if his father rejected him this time.

He let the curtains fall. Not this time.

That man who had waited at the end of the road wanting to come home was gone. The room softened something jagged in him, smoothing out the nicks and crevices of disappointment and betrayal.

The next morning, they sat in the home office. It too had been redecorated with masculine, old leatherneck

Texan decor. Navy curtains hung at the wall of windows, open wide to an expansive view of Whitten land. The room encapsulated his father so much, it almost hurt to sit here. Luke shook himself away from thoughts of the last time in this room, forcing himself to focus on the new décor, new beginnings, and a bright new future.

After dinner last night, complete with whiskey on the porch in old rockers, he was filled with more hope than he wanted to admit. Luke started to talk business, and his father brushed him off and said there was plenty of time in the morning for those discussions. They shared a funny conversation about a fishing trip gone horribly askew when he was nine. One story led to twelve more.

He scrolled through his phone. Mara had texted a video of she and Charlie singing some hokey hoedown song about Texas, leaving him rolling his eyes. But those same eyes melted, together with his heart, when they both blew kisses to him at the end.

Claire swept into the room and leaned forward for a hug. She held him at arm's length. "Dude, you look good. Better than good." She walked around him, pointing up and down. "Must be a good woman involved."

Like a first grader, he raised his hand, a sloppy grin on his face. "Guilty."

"I am so happy for you. You cannot rely on me and me alone to give this man grandkids."

"Whoa, whoa, no one said a word about kids."

"You were made to have kids. You and I both know it."

Across the desk, his father took in the two of them and listened to their banter. His craggy, old features softened with a look of contentment.

"Let's get going on this. I've got a return ticket for a week from today," Luke said.

"I'm not sure that's going to work, but tickets can be rescheduled."

"Two weeks max," he blurted before he thought. "Let's just have it. What can I do?"

"We need to make a recovery," Claire began. "And fast. And I need ideas. Anything we can think of to keep the land. To make the land work for us."

Luke leaned forward. "What do you think of wind energy?"

His dad scowled for a second. Claire prompted him to continue.

"You see those wind-farm things all over this area? We have natural gas leases. Why not wind?"

Claire jotted something down. "I'll check into it. I think you can get energy companies to survey your property to see if the location is suitable. The Suarez brothers have some on their ranch. It's a matter of where you sit in wind tunnels."

His dad nodded. "It's worth checking out."

"We need to talk about Justin," Claire said, removing a piece of paper from a folder. "He was told to tone back the expenses and to cut three hands. He cleared some bodies, but he cut the long timers. So now we have no experience and no leadership, and still, the higher payrolls."

His dad shook his head at whatever paperwork Claire was handing him. "Justin needs to go."

"Yes, he does," Claire said. "The problem now is we need someone to take his place. It's going to be difficult to find someone with managerial ranch experience."

"Luke can handle it until we can replace Justin

permanently."

Claire stopped him with a hand. "No, Dad. We need to nix Justin now. Find this particular someone and let him work alongside you and Luke while he's here. Hopefully, they can be up and running in a few weeks. We're going to have to throw a lot of money someone's way, extras no one else offers. Sign-on bonus, the house on the back side. We're going to have to sell some of the useless equipment Justin bought and did nothing with. There's some decent money there, and the funds can float us until things get rolling again. Our line of credit at the bank is tapped out, so if we want to make this work, we need to find the money in assets or sell off some land."

Their dad rose and stood at the window. "What have I done?"

"We're going to fix it," Luke said. "The three of us are going to dig in and come up with a plan. Hopefully, the equipment will do the trick, and your land won't have to be sacrificed."

Claire and Luke looked at each other in the silence. It hurt to watch their father accept what he had done.

"Our land."

They both jerked when he spoke. A reminder of the old Ward who built an empire.

"Whitten land."

"Yes, sir," they both said simultaneously.

"We need Mikey back," Luke mused. "How do we get Mike to come back?"

"With a whole lot of fancy words, and I'm not sure that'll be enough." Claire let the thought sit.

"I'll go," Ward said, nodding at the same time. "First an apology and then a job offer. But it has to come from me."

In the silence, Luke thought how alike he and Mike were. Both rebuked, cast aside by the same man. They could commiserate. He had a front-row seat to the abandonment movie.

"I disagree," Luke said, glancing at Claire, then at his father. "Let me wedge my foot in the door, then you can come in and do your thing."

"Okay. We'll do it your way." Ward walked around the mountain of a desk and kissed Claire on the cheek. "Thanks for your help, honey. The rest is on us."

****

A blast of cold air hit Luke as the door opened. Mike looked like he'd aged a decade since he'd seen him at Evelyn's funeral. His face unkept and straggly with more gray than black scrub. Wearing the beginnings of a beer gut over the waistband of his shorts.

"Luke? Good God, boy, bring your ass on in out of the heat. What're you doing here? I thought you saddled up and moved on to greener pastures?"

The room was dark and chaotic, with soda and beer bottles on the coffee table. Newspaper strewn about. It was a mess, but he hadn't worked alongside the man and not learned a little about how he ran his life. With a sweep of his hand, Mike cleared a chair. Their old dog padded in and sat at Luke's feet.

"Oh, man, Cody's still roaming around." Luke scratched up under his neck. Cody flopped over onto his back, fully expecting a belly rub. He needed a dog. He wondered if Mara and Charlie liked dogs.

"So, are you home again? What do I owe the pleasure?"

"Naw, I'm heading back in a week or so. I really like

Wyoming. Not the ball-chilling cold, but the rest of it."

"My guess would be the woman at your side. You look happy, deep down happy. It's been a long time since I've seen a look of contentment in you."

"She makes me a better person. Like the old movie line, 'she completes me,' " Luke said, stalling, trying to figure out how to lead the conversation, get the topic headed in the right direction. "So, how's Zack? I should call him while I'm here, see if he wants to grab a beer." He'd grown up with Mike's son. A lot of time had passed since he'd seen him, but they still communicated a few times a year.

"Not so good. Emily left him. Rightfully so after he stepped out on her. He knows he's at fault, and it's ripping him apart. He's gone on a little bit of a wild binge."

"I'm sorry to hear that. I will for sure try and roust him up for a beer and see if I can lend an ear, if nothing else. Those women, they break us, then we break ourselves. Makes you wonder how any relationship works."

"Well, you know better than most about women breaking us. I'm glad to see you're recovering from what your father and Evelyn did to you."

Insert wedged foot.

"We both know about rejection and abandonment at my father's hands."

Mike nodded. "That we do." He sat silent for a second. "How is he? Not sure I care, but you know us Southern boys, cordial to a fault."

Luke laughed, then they both laughed. "It's getting better, him and I. Granted I've only been here twenty-four hours, but he seems to be understanding the impact of Evelyn, and then Justin." Luke looked up to see Mikey's eyes directly on him. "He's going to lose the ranch," Luke finished simply.

"I've heard rumors."

"We'd like you to come back."

Mike's head was already shaking back and forth. "I can't, Luke. I'm sorry, but old Ward…he wouldn't listen to anyone, least of all me. Justin and his buddies did whatever they wanted, whenever they wanted. Justin laughed when he told me my services were no longer required." Mike laid his head back against the sofa. "I couldn't believe your dad would be so ball-less to not tell me himself, so I double whammied myself and asked Ward myself. And nope, he just ducked his head like he used to do to you and said he was sorry. Twenty-five years and bam, you're done, no discussion, no nothing. Then I hear rumors I'm using the ranch's accounts to buy things. Oh, and I drink too much." Mike shook his head. "It hurts, man. What hurts the most is he believed it. I was lucky. Old man Weathers passed away, and they needed experience at the Triple R. So, thanks, but no."

"This is for your old job before Justin. We'll double whatever they're paying, give you the house once we clear him out, and a 25k sign-on bonus."

Mike blew out a long whistle. "That's one hell of an offer. But, if you're in as bad of shape as Angelo gossipers say, I have a hard time believing there's any bang behind the offered buck. So again, thank you, but no."

Luke racked his brain, trying to think of anything else he could offer. He settled in with good old-fashioned honesty.

"Listen, Mike. I know how much he hurt you. Hell,

I know exactly how it feels. He wants you back, and he wanted to be the one to offer it, but I convinced him to sit in the car until I talked to you first. We need you. You want to slap him, punch him, do it for me too, but just come back and help us recover, straighten out the damage he's done. The damage Evelyn did."

Mike looked out the window, rubbed his chin. "He really is out there. You're not just blowing smoke up my ass."

"No, I'm not. Please, just hear him out."

"I don't know how this can work. I'm going to work for you, and you're going to work for him. And I love you like a son, but you are so eager to please. You'll do whatever he says, and then where am I?"

"No, you will not work for me. You are going to run the place. I'm going home, and my home is Wyoming. You and he are going to have to make this work or not work."

Mike took his time and mulled over the offer. "Will the discussion start with an apology?"

"The discussion will most assuredly start with an apology."

"I'm not agreeing with anything, but for you, I'll hear him out."

Two hours later, the two geezers were hugging it out.

Two days later, Justin was throwing his shit in the back of his truck.

Two days after that, Mike was moving in, and he and Luke were making a plan.

Chapter Thirty-Five

There were long days and longer nights. As the rain pounded the roof, Luke lay in his bed wishing he was at home, with Mara next to him. The two halves of him were ripping apart. One week turned into two, two was now turning into three, and he still didn't have a homeward bound plane ticket booked. For a few hours each day, he'd creep away and work the classes he could online. The participation and mock trial classes would wait until he returned.

Last week, they had run into some of his father's old friends on the downtown streets. All of them launching into little-old-lady mode, sharing gossip, talking about the charity event coming up at the club. His father smiled for days after the encounter. Last night, the house was alive with cigar-smoking, whiskey-drinking, name-calling old farts. Poker nights became a thing again.

"Hey, babe," he said when she answered.

"Hey yourself."

A chair scraped across the hospital's linoleum. A smile crept onto his face as he imagined her putting her feet up in the break room, a cup of their toxic coffee dangling from her fingertips.

He rolled onto his side and stared out the window. Lightning set the sky aflame with brilliance. A loud boom echoed in the distance, igniting a wail of coyotes.

"Damn, is that rain? Sounds like a hurricane or

something."

"Naw, just a little Texas storm. They're pretty if you're lying in bed and not having to drive in them."

The line grew silent. Another rip of lightning and thunder splitting the sky apart.

"How's your mom?"

Another long silence, making him wonder what she was doing. Rubbing her head, warding off a headache? Taking a sip of coffee? Anything that would give her a moment to gather herself. When his mom was sickest, the helplessness, the emptiness, continually assaulted, leaving a blank, hollow feeling inside. The wondering what comes next. The same, and yet, very different. Mom, son, as opposed to Mom, daughter. Twelve as opposed to double that. The feelings of loss were as fresh today as they had been back then.

She sighed. "I'm losing it. I swear I'm losing it. My brain is telling me to keep moving, keep doing. At the same time, I know I'm not handling this right, but if I keep doing...I can trick myself into thinking a miraculous healing is on the horizon. When Charlie settles in beside her, she cuddles and reads, and that's when she's happiest. I want to slow down and enjoy, but...I know I'm holding on too tight."

"I remember the feeling," Luke said, staring at the ceiling. "Thinking if you just do everything to perfection, it'll drag things out. Maybe it won't hurt as much because you were able to postpone the inevitable a minute longer."

"I want to quit, but I'm so desperate to hold on. I don't know how to let go. I don't know how to do anything."

Luke nodded in the darkness. "That was the hardest

thing for all of us when my mom was sick. Letting go. I'm not sure my dad ever did. Maybe it's why he was so messed up when she died. There was never a time when her hand wasn't engulfed in his. He never let go." Luke stopped and could picture his mom's bedside as if it was yesterday.

"When he finally did, she was gone," he whispered.

The moment his mother died, he bolted upright in the dead of night, crept into her room to check on her, finding his dad already there, crying, his hands stuck deep into his armpits. Rambling that she said she was ready. When he let go, as she asked, she slipped away from them all.

Claire had come into the room and crawled into the bed, curling into their mom as the body grew cold. His father hadn't had the strength to pull her away until hours later.

"I should have never let go," his father said continuously, hauntingly, back then. Like he was stuck in an endless loop.

There were times when Luke's emotion had been thick, when Claire needed consoling, and they were alone. He blamed his dad for letting go during those dark times. Time marched on, but it was a painful parade.

Mara would have to go through the same. For now, she was caught up in the grieving process before there should be grieving. The land between life and death. He wasn't sure he could help, that anyone could help.

"Tell me about when you were little, your favorite memories." Diverting her attention was the only thing he could offer up.

She sucked in a deep breath, and he could almost see the tears falling. Mara never ugly cried. She was beautiful when she allowed the tears to flow, like her heart was escaping through her tears.

She coughed and sucked in another deep lungful of air. "Oh, man, there're so many. Where do I start?"

"I've got all night marveling at this beautiful light show, so I'll hear as many as you can tell." The words were barely out, and someone turned up the intensity. A crash of thunder shook the house.

She laughed deep and throaty. The laugh he missed, her genuine one, the one that rolled up and out of her, the one he could feel if he lay on her belly or chest. Whatever the memories were, they were good.

"Unfortunately, I've only got twenty minutes left."

"Then you better talk fast."

"My favorites are the simple days and the simple lessons. I'm not sure why I try to make life so difficult when the uncomplicated moments make life beautiful."

"Tell me."

Luke waited out the long silence, the comforting hospital Muzak penetrating the line.

"My parents never had the kind of money to take big vacations, but we always went somewhere. One year it was the Grand Canyon. The next year it was the Redwood Forest. I remember standing inside that tree you drive through with my mom. There's a picture of us somewhere my dad took. I just remember having both of them to myself for days on end. There are advantages to being an only child. We'd camp in an old tent trailer my dad borrowed from a friend, have campfires, make s'mores, the whole thing. And Whitten, it's where I learned how to beat asses like yours at poker. We played every night."

"Damn, poker at what, eight, nine?" He smiled into

the darkness, thinking about a wild little girl, getting all excited with a good hand and trying to smother her poker face.

"One year we drove into Canada and saw so many beautiful things. Mountains bigger than Wyoming, campgrounds filled with us Yankee folk. Oh, and then, one night we splurged and spent a night at a beautiful, high-end hotel at Lake Louise, in Banff. We ate at this amazing restaurant overlooking the water. Then we drove farther west to Vancouver Island, to see their gardens. My dad was big on flowers." She grew silent.

"Mara?"

"I was just thinking I should get out those old photo albums, go through them with my mom. She would like that."

"I think you would like it too."

"When are you coming back, Luke?"

The hard left slammed his heart to a stop. Stammering, he shut up. He had no answers to offer. She needed him. His dad needed him. His father had finally seen the light, seen him, and Luke jumped in with both feet, lapping it up like a stupid child. He closed his eyes, feeling the jagged edges of his soul ripping, not knowing how to answer.

"It's okay," she said quietly.

"I miss you." He wanted to give her something, and that was all he had right now.

"Charlie misses you."

"Oh, yeah, throw the kid card out there. That's just cruel."

"I might miss you too."

"I love you. You know that?"

Silence.

"I can't wait to get back there to both of you. I just need—shit, I'm not sure what I need."

"You keep needing people to love you, to accept you. We're right here, Luke."

Chapter Thirty-Six

Luke rattled the old fence, eyeball straightened the post, then re-pounded it into the parched dirt. Two posts down, Mike and his father fortified the property line fences with more wire. They set out on the western perimeter this morning, somewhere Justin hadn't sent anyone in weeks, maybe months. Luke took his hat off and wiped his face. The sun beat down, and not for the first time, he pictured himself in the beauty of a crisp, eighty-degree temperature in Wyoming. Their horses chomped nearby, sauntering their way to the creek bed, happy to be doing nothing more than eating instead of working in the brutal heat.

A smile continually lit up his father's old, weathered face. More often than not, his eyes crinkling into a grin as he talked. Every day he became more the man Luke remembered. Remembering the past brought thoughts of his mom. The twinge hit, same as memories did every time he thought about her.

Nearing the creek, he crunched through the rocks and gravel, listening to Mike and his dad argue about the number of cattle in the lower pasture. The smell was sweet and fresh, despite the putrid stench wafting from his body. He became even more sentimental the longer he stayed. Feeling everything, just as his mom taught. Not the Texas-man way, but who his mom wanted him to become.

Be Texas, be all the Texas proud you want, but don't become a strong can't-express-how-you-feel Texas man.

It may have been the sun, but everything about her goodness hit at once. How he strove to become what she envisioned before she was taken. In spite of the grief he caught back in the day about wearing his heart on his sleeve, the good-natured harassment his Marine buddies and coworkers in Wyoming gave him. Even the joking Mara and Claire both doled out. Though she was gone, it meant something to know she would be proud. She may have been taken way too young, but the lessons and instructions she left were branded on his insides. He smiled to himself. He planned on enjoying every second on this land before he returned. His father was still old school, and old school in Texas meant strength would never be equated to feeling.

The water gurgled over the rocks and trickled downstream, brushing the banks, carrying twigs and leaves.

Life goes on. And keeps going on.

"I love you, Mom," he whispered to the rocks, the water, someone.

"What's that?" His father clapped him on the shoulder before he bent down and cupped his hands to get a drink.

"The land makes me miss Mom." He tossed some pebbles in the water. They clinked when they hit the bottom of the stream.

Looking across the creek to the shade wafting through the old live oaks, revered and cherished memories cascaded in a different way. Whitten land was sacred, not a church sacred, but sacred in its own right. A respect for the generations before them, who worked and hoped, and believed this was the best place a Whitten could possibly be. In all his selfish wanting the acceptance of his father, Luke forgot how much he missed the land. And now, how robbed he felt at all that had passed.

"Remember when you, me, and Bo camped here," his dad said. "I think he was about seven."

Luke walked closer to the water, losing himself, remembering everything about those ending days of happiness. "Dad, I remember everything. All the good, all the…"

His father dropped his head. The simple movement caused Luke to roll into anger. One mention of the past and his dad goes all suck inside, silent cowboy.

"We need to talk about this. You don't get to check out again. I want to know why. Why did you hate me and listen to her? Why? Can you give me an answer?" Luke held his head; it pulsed in the heat and unresolved pain.

The welling wanted an escape, and his dad was still hanging his stupid head in shame.

"I deserve an answer. You've made my life a living hell trying to be accepted. This is not the old days; you don't get to be the strong silent type any longer. You want to know what I was just thinking? Why I said, I love you, mom? Because I was missing the hell out of her. It twinges from time to time, and I need you to step up and tell me it's not a bad thing. This has nothing to do with Evelyn. Evelyn's fucking six feet under. Let's at least give ourselves a chance to have a relationship. I hated Evelyn; I really hated her. But do you know what I hated most? I hate that she took you from me. And you." Luke poked his index finger into his dad's chest. "You went along with it."

"Don't disrespect Evelyn when she can't defend herself," his father said, looking off in the distance.

"Evelyn is dead. It is not disrespectful to talk about these things. It's disrespectful not to. You don't want me to disrespect Evelyn? Then don't disrespect my mom either. I was young, but mom ingrained lessons of becoming a man who could talk about the real things in life. She didn't want me to become the clichéd desperado cowboy. I have a heart that really, really wants to heal because she didn't want me to become a loner, but you know what? That's what I became because I had to go at life on my own." His mom's worst fear, realized. Loneliness bred strength, but loneliness also bred pain, and distance.

And here he stood, pleading with the one person who caused the pain, to please accept him, please love him. Again.

"Please, just tell me why you didn't want me anymore?"

His father's head snapped up. "You think I didn't want you?"

"What am I supposed to think? You took Evelyn's side in everything. I was a good son. I stayed out of trouble. I got decent grades. I liked all the things I grew up doing with you, hunting and fishing and studying the stars." The tears were trailing down his dusty cheeks, and he rammed his hand over them, smearing the wetness. "You had two sons. Did you even realize that?"

"She thought you were at fault. You left." His dad rose, dropping his head again.

Luke stomped around in a circle like a child. "Do you even hear yourself? I was a good brother. You know I was. I was gone when Bo died. I left because, well,

Evelyn couldn't stand the sight of me. I left long before the accident. I was overseas when it happened. How in the holy hell can it rationally be my fault?"

"I know," his father whispered.

"Will you please confront this like a man? Yell and scream, but don't do your dropped head, whatever-you-say thing. We are both grown men, and I hate you right now. I don't want to. I want everything we used to have. I want to become the man you were before Evelyn ripped up your insides. I want to learn from the best, because until that point, you were the best father I could ask for. So, stand up, face me, and tell me what in the hell I did wrong here."

His dad leaned over, grasped at his chest, and Luke faltered. His dad put his hands on his knees, straining to draw in a breath.

When he stood up, Luke pushed at him. "I want my father. Can you be my goddamn father?"

The swing came from Luke's left and smashed into his cheek. Warmth radiated where the fist hit. He launched at his dad, dragged him into the dirt, and pounded a fist into his face. He heard a crack and halted before he let loose another. They rolled around in the dirt, and his father pinned him, and then the fight went out of him. That, too, made him angry. Luke flipped his dad onto his back and stood, pressing his foot into his chest, then pulled him standing.

Luke held his hands out and thrust his face forward. "Do it again. Please to God, let it out."

He had one second before he found himself flat on his back in the weeds.

"Why?" he screamed from the ground.

His dad spun away from him, pounding in the air.

The tears ripped from his eyes, cradling in the wrinkles, then running in little rivers. His dad screamed at the sky and threw fistfuls of dirt like a two-year-old.

"I didn't love him the same," his dad yelled into his hands. "I didn't love him the same." He screamed at the world.

"What?" Luke gave his head a tiny shake, trying to follow the train of thought.

"I didn't love him the same." His father dropped to his knees in the dirt.

Answers.

A decade in the making.

His father collapsed. Beside the creek bed, Luke heard a hidden, pain-filled story. In all his dad's "bowing to Evelyn," it was guilt he didn't love Bo as he loved Luke. Losing him had eaten him up, and his penance was letting her control everything. It wasn't Bo's artsy side, his soft side, but his dad was a Texas man through and through. He wanted the strong son, the hunting, fishing son. The son who played football under the Friday night lights and loved camping. Bo was none of those things. Everything Luke loved, treasured, desired, had been sacrificed for his father's guilt. The heavy burden dropped, escaping into the wind, turning to dust. Liberating his insides with the relinquishing words. It was just gone.

"I'm sorry. I wish I could go back and do it all again." He turned away and stared at the now setting sun. "My God, I miss your mother. To this day, I miss your mother."

Luke stared at the creek bed, wishing time to go backward, wishing for more than his father wished for, but there was just the going forward part.

"I'm thankful you listened to your mother's words. I'm proud you didn't become a man who doesn't talk." He rubbed his face. "Wish I could have avoided getting slugged by my son, but..." He shrugged.

Luke rubbed his own eye and the shiner that would require an explanation.

"I know you want to go on back to your life, but I hope you'll consider staying just a little longer. I've missed everything about you. Selfish, I know. But there's a lot of making up for me to do, so there you go."

They walked to where the horses were grazing. "Mara really needs me, Dad."

Luke was running out of time. But for this? Would she see the delay as another lame excuse? He wasn't sure how many more of them would fly before he would lose her completely.

His dad nodded, his eyes saying he wanted to understand. The final rays of the sun dropped into the horizon, lighting up his dad's eyes. One of them may be a little purple or yellow by morning, but they were happy eyes, content eyes.

Luke tipped his hat to the sunset, to his mother for making him not afraid to feel.

Chapter Thirty-Seven

In the baggage claim area of the San Antonio airport, she waved like a mad woman from the top of the stairs in an oversized T-shirt falling over jeans so faded they were now white. The doubts about whether Luke had done the right thing flew away with the next airplane taking off. After listening to her heart breaking over the phone two nights ago, he'd set to working with Rachel to arrange a kidnapping of sorts.

Mara hit the bottom of the escalator and rushed to him, did a quick tap dance in her bright flip-flops, and launched herself into his arms. Holding her, touching her, weaving his fingers into hair cascading over her shoulders—well, nothing compared to that.

"I'm so mad at you for this, no luggage, no anything? I'm wanting to scream and yell and give you what for…but—"

Luke dropped his mouth onto hers and wrapped her up tight. She was flushed when they came up for air.

"You were saying?"

"I said many foolish things. I love you comes to mind right now."

"Exactly what I wanted to hear."

They headed to the hotel he booked on the Riverwalk. There wasn't anything to drop off except his own bag, but they checked it out just the same. He draped his arms around her, hugging her into his chest as she stared out the window to the channel below. One of the floating boat tours drifted along the river, so close you could hear the announcer talking about the historic hotel they were staying in.

"Can we do that?" Mara pointed and latched on to his forearms at the same time.

"We can do anything your heart desires, but first we have to get you some clothes; me, some alcohol; us, some romantic ramblings along the water."

She spun into his arms and kissed him gently. "I needed this. I'm excited and anxious and so in love right now, I can't quite see straight."

His confidence slipped a little when she said anxious, but he understood. "Let's delete the anxious part for this weekend. There will be no talk of obligations or parents from either of us. These three days are all about you, me, and we. Deal?"

A battle waged in her eyes as she fought herself. Eventually she made a halfhearted attempt to smile. Luke clamored to give her an out, because she needed a little one. He kind of needed a little one too. Maybe they could share battle scars on the needs of parents. Later.

"Let's just try, okay?" He kissed her nose. "I want to watch you laugh and let go. I want to make San Antonio come alive. I want to enjoy drinks with stupid umbrellas, and I want to make love to you in our little escape from the world."

"Then let's go find ourselves some umbrella-laden cocktails."

The rooftop of their hotel opened up as they escaped the elevator. They had shopped and drunk, and walked, circled the Riverwalk loop on the pontoon style boats twice. Mara talked nonstop. Every time she got excited and would grab his hand and bring it to her heart, he made another promise to himself to settle up in Texas and get on back to this amazing woman who kept setting his heart aflutter.

On the rooftop, there was an empty pool and spa on one side, a bar with scattered conversation sitting areas on the other. Many couples and families were settling in to enjoy the transformation from day to night. They found a small table tucked against a rail with comfortable armchairs. Small potted trees flanked them, giving a small degree of intimacy.

An hour and a couple of drinks later, she was still running so many words though her more than buzzed mouth. The conversation wound its way somewhat into the what-comes-next-for-them category, and he was curious enough to take advantage of the situation.

"So, just to be clear." Luke looped his finger in the air, halting her next Charlie story. "In the spirit of an honest and nonbinding hypothetical conversation, being that you're downright drunk and I'm a little more than buzzed. Are you saying you wouldn't want more kids?"

Mara propped her elbows on the table, then she put her chin in her fists, her eyelids falling and rising slowly again. "I was talking about what a handful a little girl is."

"No, you said sometimes it's all too much."

The bartender interrupted, and Mara started to order another drink and waved the waiter away and began to cry. Luke dropped on his knees in front of her, wondering what foot he had put in his mouth causing such an abrupt pivot. It melted him into a man who wanted to right every wrong in her life.

"Your mom?" he asked.

"I don't know. Maybe?" She straightened and pulled

her legs up on the chair. "You said we weren't talking about parents. I can't do heavy today. Please? I just want to enjoy all of this, having fun and being young, and being with the man of my dreams who…Thank you so much for doing this. I really did need something happy and didn't know I did."

"You are very welcome." Luke followed her lead and switched gears. He could easily keep going with fun and lighthearted, not having thought about his father for a single second. They needed to talk about things, but it didn't have to ruin today.

"Feeling pretty loopy, Whitt. You may get lucky tonight." She stuck her foot into his lap, wiggled her toes in his crotch.

"Oh, I'm getting lucky alright. Your boobs are calling my name. Among other things." He motioned for the waiter to come back, telling him they'd take a couple more of their amazing margaritas.

She hiccupped back a laugh, lifting her boobs and smooshing them together, so blessedly unashamed. "Huh, they kind of are."

"You're evading, albeit with a great visual. But focus, woman. Back to the question at hand, because now I'm more than curious. In the most lighthearted of ways, is Charlie enough, or do you want more?"

Mara raised her eyebrows. "Not exactly lighthearted, more in the where-is-this-relationship-going discussion."

Exactly.

He shrugged.

"Nonbinding and hypothetical, remember. Besides, you're three sheets. I promise not to hold you to anything."

The drinks arrived, and she sucked down a generous gulp as the potted trees flicked on small dancing lights. Mara's cheeks were downright rosy and her eyes now glassy, but her words were only the slightest bit slurred. Just looking at her made him want to look at her every night, every morning. She tugged the elastic out of her hair, and it cascaded onto her shoulders. He bit his lip, wanting to tell her all the ways he loved her, but he'd save those for later. Right now, he just wanted to bask in watching her, letting her voice penetrate where all the sacred things lay.

She was still trying to stifle a drunken giggle about his three sheets comment, making herself snort, and then they both laughed.

"Can't take you anywhere," he whispered, touching her hand to keep her from putting her hair back up. "I like it down, all tousled and messy."

Her hands weaved into her hair and rubbed it back and forth, making it the epitome of messy. They both laughed more.

"Kids, huh?" She stared off, gathering her thoughts from the tops of the trees rising from the Riverwalk and grazing the roofline. The wind swished through the branches, and the fading sunlight filtered into their eyes for a second. The wind quieted.

"Charlie is a handful, but I wouldn't want to miss any of her little quirks. I do want more kids, but I don't want to go it alone. Being a single parent is tough, maybe tougher than anything I've ever done, but I think I'm a good mom. I'm doing the best I can anyway. So, yes, my handsome and very hot man. Given the right partner, I'm game."

His gaze locked on to her long and hard, seeing the

sincerity, and more than that, feeling the openness. Though he'd never given the single parent thing more than a passing thought, it would not be a job for the weak at heart. Put in this light, he kind of somewhat understood her willingness to give Chase a second chance. Not an answer to a problem, but it was the easy choice.

In spite of her glassy eyes, she kept them riveted on him. "You?"

"I do. It would be super scary, wondering if you're screwing anything up…but I'd like to think I'd be a good dad."

"You would. What would you do the same? What would you do differently?"

Luke dropped his head back, hitting the top of the chair. The music played at the cafes and bars below, drifting up, swapping from Tejano to classic rock, to country. Diversity was one of those things he loved and appreciated about Texas.

"I would want to eat dinner together every night. I would want to do my share of the bedtime story routine, the bath routine. My father always ate with us, but he left the rest for my mom. Winding down time is important. I want to do the hunting and fishing thing." He shrugged. "I think it's something Texas men do well. Quality time with no distractions. Whether your child is into hunting or fishing or not. My brother Bo wasn't a hunting sort of kid, but he loved sitting around a campfire. Video games are not always the answer for entertainment. Being out in the open, experiencing the land? That's pretty entertaining, too."

"What if it's a girl?"

"What do you mean?"

"Girl. You know, a female type of child?"

"Girls hunt, girls fish."

"Did your sister?"

"Sometimes. She wasn't really into it. But she would always come out for a little while. Filling up a thermos with hot chocolate and toting it to wherever we were, or sometimes helping us cook our fish. Claire was into horses. Sometimes her love of riding overlapped. Sometimes it didn't. My parents were good at letting us find what we loved, what we were good at. It bred confidence. It may be why Bo…" Luke stopped, never having considered the situation this way. Evelyn wasn't the type of mother to let Bo find his own happy place. There was no safe place to fall like he and Claire had.

"It must've been hard," Mara said, spinning her straw in her drink. "Wanting to be something he wasn't. It's sad when parents try to live…vi-car…"

Luke laughed as she twisted the word out of her margarita mouth. "Vicariously?"

"Yeah. What you said."

"You?" Luke asked. "What would you do the same or different from your parents?"

Staring into her drink, she plugged the straw and released the trapped liquid onto her tongue. "I would do everything the same." She turned to him and smiled. "And all they did was fill me up with love. Every hour of every day."

Her eyes danced with happiness as she floated through various memories.

"But I would give me a sibling. I hated being an only child."

"Ah, and there we are. Back at the original question."

Kathryn Beck

She stuck her feet up on his chair, and they listened to more of the music, laughter below intermixing and floating upward. When he glanced over, her eyes were closed, and she wore a tiny but very beautiful smile as she rested. Peeling her flip-flops off her feet, he began massaging her toes, the balls of her feet, circling his fingers around the soft skin of her ankle. How was it that even her feet were beautiful?

"Can you just talk?" she whispered. "About nothing, about everything, I just want to hear your voice and know you're near."

So he did.

Chapter Thirty-Eight

His breathing woke her. Not in a bad way. Sometime during the night, Luke had turned sideways and used her back as a pillow. His breath was even and steady. His presence comforted her. Thinking of waking like this day after day, knowing she'd get to repeat it all again at the end of the workday, left her smiling.

A kiss hit her bare skin. "You awake?"

"Mmm, just thinking I could be quite happy to stay right here, maybe forever."

Repositioning himself, he rolled her onto her side, gathering her tight.

"I would love to make that happen for you, but…we have plans."

"Okay, so, the Alamo was great, the Riverwalk was fantastic, but I don't know if I can do it again." She rolled to face him, kissed him long and hard, skanky breath and all.

"That's good, because that's not what we're doing." Luke kissed her nose, leaned over her to look at the clock. "And we better get moving. You're spa'ing with Claire, and I'm going golfing with Mitch. And, sorry, but we'll probably hit the Riverwalk again, find some more yummy margaritas and maybe a little dancing. Texas style, of course."

"I'm going spa'ing?" She flopped onto her back. "Like facials and massages and mimosas?"

Luke laughed, climbed over her all naked and beautiful. "I'm not sure what my sister has planned. I let her handle those arrangements."

"Oh, my God. I'm dying. I'm seriously dying right here and now."

"Don't die yet. You're looking all gorgeous and tousled in my bed, so I'm going to do you real quick, and then you can die." He shrugged. "Or go for facials and mimosas. Your choice."

He dropped on top of her.

"You did me twice last night."

"And?" he said, squeezing her breast and running his hand down her stomach to the tender skin at the juncture of her thighs.

"And we may be late meeting Claire."

****

The spa was appropriately called Escape, and it lived up to its namesake. High end, with rich teakwood lining the walls and girly chandeliers. Eucalyptus-laden air wafted throughout. Mara sank into her thick robe, settling herself into the wicker lounger. A young woman in a teal blouse and a flowy wraparound skirt placed a cool champagne glass beside her. Mara held the flute up to the light before she took a sip. Bubbles snaked up the inside of the glass, the liquid a pinky orange. Exotic.

This weekend was already perfect, better than perfect. Yesterday, between getting her new clothes, toiletries, stopping at too many bars along the Riverwalk for a "to go" cup, and even a little touristy remembering the Alamo, she forgot her duties left at home. Rachel had texted earlier all was well in her absence, settling the twinge that hit in the early morning. Exactly what she needed to enjoy being away from the day-to-day cycle of watching her mom waste away into nothingness. And now, waiting on a quiet voice to call her name for a facial, her heart fell into a peaceful tranquility.

Over the last hour, the massage, with musky oils and soft instrumental music, slowed her thoughts to a standstill. The long strokes from fingertips to shoulders, hands cascading from her bottom, sliding the length of her thighs, to her ankles, and then up again to stroke her back and knead the knots in her shoulders. Wrapping her up and taking her to a place she didn't know existed. Like Luke's Zen place she could never find.

"Mara?" A voice floated her direction, begging her to follow.

The swirling fingers along her cheekbones, stroking her neck and ears, left her drifting off. A sharp scent of oranges hung as cool circle wedges were placed on her eyes. The tantalizing fingers did their thing again. She wanted to cry when her thirty minutes were up.

"Let me get you another mimosa and take you to your sister-in-law so you can get started on your pedicure."

The correction hung on her tongue, but sister, even with the added in-law, sounded so pretty.

"Look at you all exfoliated and glistening. You look like you could float away," Claire said, studying her as she entered yet another room filled with warm woods and sagey colors.

"I think I will," Mara said, sinking her feet into the tub, collapsing into the heated seat. The massaging action of the chair started as a warm wrap was placed around her neck.

"I suppose I have you to thank for this amazing experience?" Mara said from behind closed eyes. "Not like Luke would know what an exfoliated anything would be."

Claire laughed. "No, he would not. He would understand glistening though. As in a horse's glistening coat."

Mara smiled as the women at their feet set to snipping at cuticles and scraping away dead foot skin. A tender rub at the balls of her feet left Mara sliding farther into the cushions.

"If you must know though, I had to wrangle the invitation out of him in the first place. He wanted you all to himself. Sweet, yes, but I worked my magic on my sap of a brother and used you and your desperate need for all things spa to get myself away for a weekend. Thank you for that."

Mara waved her hand. "No problem. Happy to help."

"Mitch and I used to do more weekend getaways before the kids came along."

"Who's watching your kids while you're gone?"

"My sister and brother-in-law. Mitch's family is huge. All it took was a phone call with a drop-off time."

Mara thought about Claire's larger, in-law family, the closeness. The champagne did an amazing job of championing all her hopes and dreams, launching them to the surface. She imagined Claire enjoyed Luke being home as much as their father.

"And your much smaller family?" Mara ventured. "Your father seems happy Luke's home."

"He is. Sadly, a long time coming."

The tone of Claire's voice was distant and lost. Mara didn't know what to make of it.

"I love having him home." Claire tapped a newly

manicured finger on her current drink. "For the stupidest things. Him walking in and helping himself to the pot of coffee, or, by chance of course, coming to visit the kids right at dinnertime. But with that, I can usually get him to handle bath time for me. I have to bitch and moan for appearance's sake, but I do love it. I'm going to be a little lost when he leaves again."

Mara stayed silent, not knowing what to say.

"I'm sorry. I didn't mean anything more than I miss my brother." Claire squeezed her hand. "But no, he has to fall in love with Wyoming, and doubling down, fall in love with a woman in Wyoming."

They laughed together. It was sad and sweet at the same time.

"I'm sorry, kind of anyway." Mara sank farther into the chair as another scoop of smelly beads was dumped into the water.

"Don't be sorry. You can give him the happily ever after he's been looking to find for a very long time."

Mara stared at her feet, bubbling away in the lavender-scented water. "I hope so. I miss him so much, and every time I try to talk to him about when he's coming back, he goes dark. I'm trying to understand, but I'm not sure I do."

"Oh, Mara." Claire threaded their fingers together. "He is so in love with you. There's not a doubt in my mind where he'll lay his head when this is said and done."

"I wish I was that sure," she said, polishing off the rest of her mimosa. In the time it took to put the empty on the table, a fresh one, purple this time, appeared.

Claire kept hold of her hand and sighed. "My brother is experiencing everything with my dad he has wanted for a very, very long time. When he would visit while on leave from the Marines, it almost got to be too much for me. He was so hurt and lost. He would scream, literally, throw tantrums better than any two-year-old. Right now, he's capturing all he lost. That's on my dad—not on me, not on him, most definitely not on you, but Luke needs the closure on what he lost. Almost like he's going back in time and recapturing."

"I know, I think I know." Mara remembered the broken man rolling into Rock Springs.

"I don't know if it's possible to understand how close they were before Evelyn did her thing. To Luke, it wasn't just losing our dad. He lost his best friend. He was not only at every game Luke played, but he was at every practice, every awards banquet. Even volunteered for snack bar duty. On weekends, they'd work the ranch together. While they worked, the chatter never stopped. If there was a pause or silence, it was a comfortable one. Their relationship was almost not a parental one. Luke was not a perfect child or teen; he hell raised with the best of them, with everything that entails in small-town Texas. My dad never overstepped and did that 'I want to hang out with you and your friends' thing, but my dad was always where Luke landed. His soft place for literally everything."

Their many conversations didn't do Claire's emotion justice. Her voice ached for her brother. It made Mara feel selfish and petty when all he was asking for was time with a parent he adored, just like she needed time with her mom.

"Luke's a grown man though, Mara. I'm happy he's finding himself through all this. I'm happy my dad is enjoying all this. I don't even know or care what the reason is anymore, but my brother is a beautiful human being. You are the lucky girl who has landed smack dab in the middle of his heart, so that makes you an amazing person, too."

If she hadn't thought of Claire as a sister before, the urge overwhelmed her now.

"As much as I love my brother, he's relishing in my dad, and he takes family obligations too seriously. You are the future; it's been beaming out of him since he arrived. Please don't worry he won't come back. Wyoming is in his blood now, and you and your little girl are a part of the whole equation."

"Thank you," Mara said, meaning it. The words gave her hope she was overreacting.

Claire rose from her chair and wiggled her beautiful-looking toes on the plush mat, stepping into her rubber spa shoes.

She pulled Mara into a tight hug.

"You are his happily ever after," she whispered.

Chapter Thirty-Nine

She was losing him. The loss sat in the middle of their stilted conversations, in the evasion of simple questions.

In spite of the amazing weekend in San Antonio, two weeks later all he offered now were ambiguities.

As she looked at her phone, the frustration built and then…just sadness. She wanted to have a pity party, eat BBQ chips, drink beer, but looking out at her little yard, with Charlie playing with her friend from across the street, there wasn't anything except the stupid hope word.

Hope he picked her.

Her mother continued her decline, making Mara feel pathetic and unstable. The old her would shrivel up, go back to begging someone to see her, love her. She wasn't that person any longer. It should make her proud. Instead, she felt nothing. Another look at her daughter, the joy of seeing her blossom into a happy, content, smart little girl, that was what kept her standing strong.

No pity parties, not today. Maybe some chocolate, but no pity parties.

"Mommy. We're going to get Brittany's animals. We're making a zoo." Charlie rose from the blanket, checking little plastic fences outlining her pretend farm, making sure they were straight and erect.

"Show me how you cross the street like big girls,"

Mara hollered as they opened the gate.

They grabbed hands and stopped at the curb. Simultaneously, they looked to the right, to the left, and back to the right before skipping across the asphalt.

They disappeared into Brittany's house.

Mara looked at her phone and typed out texts in quick succession before she lost her nerve.

—Pick me—

—Pick us—

—Pick you—

They were the same words he sent to her not too long ago. She added one of her own.

—Pick happiness—

Wrapping her arms around her knees, she wallowed in the silence of her phone. They talked not an hour ago, and he had rambled on and on about everything he was involved with on the ranch, with his father, until she couldn't hold back the inevitable question any longer. "Are you coming back, Luke?"

He'd laughed and thickened his voice. "Course I am. Just need a little more time."

That became a fill-in-the-blank statement—I just have to…

Mend this fence, train this horse, take my dad to the club, etcetera, etcetera.

He'd sounded happy, carefree, burdenless. She didn't begrudge him anything, she knew he was finally getting the relationship he'd always needed, but…what was the but? She wanted him, she needed him. She wanted to feel his heart beating under her hand, feel life, feel the love. Then she could relax again.

"Pity party," she whispered.

Charlie and company jumped from Brittany's porch,

each of the girls hauling armloads of stuffed animals.

When they dumped the animals on the blanket, they set to placing them in distinct places on the grass, somehow knowing what their vivid imaginations were creating.

Charlie's nose hit the air. Chase's truck rumbled down the street through the long shadows. It was very sweet how she was so in tune with her dad, but Mara didn't want to think about sweetness and light tonight. Her separation from him months ago quieted him in a way. He had sucked inside himself and become a recluse, at the same time blossoming on the dad front.

Running to the fence, Charlie waited for him to pick her up. He nodded Mara's direction, and the gate squeaked shut before he hung Charlie upside down, her little pink panties wide open for the world to see as she fake walked on her hands. She wailed in delight when he dropped her on the blanket to join her friend. They went back to zoo-land, yacking away in sweet animal voices.

Chase sat at her side and was silent while the girls played. Charlie held out her favorite stuffed pig for her dad's approval. "Uke won it for me at the fair."

Mara looked sidelong to see how he took the comment. There was no reaction; she'd take the win.

When Charlie skipped back to the blanket, he turned to her. "I need to discuss something with you."

"I'm not in the best of moods. Please be gentle."

He smiled. "I know I'm not first on your list, but I'm learning to be a good listener. Trying, anyways. And I promise, what I need to discuss isn't bad." He took in her slumped posture and sad eyes. "Your mom?"

A tear crept out. "Some of it. I want to be brave, and all I am is a mass of emotion. I see every inch of her pain.

Feel every inch of her pain."

"I can't even imagine," he said, staring out at the street as dusk descended and the trees cast their shadows. "I'm sorry."

"And I miss Luke."

He didn't jerk. He didn't really react at all. Not what she expected. She expected a condescending comment, not acceptance.

"You?" she asked. "Little weird you are here on a Wednesday."

"I know." He stretched his legs out and crossed his ankles. "First, this is going to seem like it's flying in out of the wild blue yonder, but…I want to say I'm sorry. I'm sorry for everything I ever said, or did, or did and you didn't know about. I'm just sorry."

"Okay…" She dragged the word out and scrunched her eyes together. "Not in any way, shape, or form, words I thought would ever come out of your mouth."

He smiled at something Charlie whispered to her friend. There was a softness in him tonight, taking away all the harsh, mean memories.

"About a year ago, I received a letter from an uncle I never knew I had. My dad's brother."

"Whoa."

There had been one of those small-town mini scandals when his father left his mom. She never remembered anything about an uncle.

"Exactly. I'd never met him. When my dad died a few years ago, you were there. It didn't bother me. I hardly knew him. But this letter opened a floodgate of anger and hurt. All my harsh words at you were probably part of that. I didn't know how to deal. It wasn't like I had a stellar role model or anything. And my mom, she just did what moms do, overcompensated, trying to make it all better."

"What did the letter say?" Mara asked.

Chase continued his stare at the street.

She backpedaled. "I'm sorry. I have no right to ask."

"You do; you really do." Chase looked at her. "He told me how sorry he was he never asked about me. He acknowledged his brother was a son of a bitch, but my dad, till his dying day, never changed. One of those people who blames the world for their problems. So, I guess, I was one of those problems." He stopped and pushed his palms into his eye sockets. "I've been seeing someone, a counselor. It's helping and hurting at the same time. Pretty painful to know your own father doesn't want you."

"I'm sorry you missed out on having a good dad. But you've risen above." She nodded at Charlie. "You're great with her, breaking the daddy cycle. Our little person adores you."

"Thank you for saying that." He looked happy, then serious. "I didn't mean to break her mom in the process."

Mara stiffened. It was quite possible she could be knocked over by a cotton ball right now. He nudged her with his shoulder. His beautiful words only made her wonder more about the other shoe.

"And I sincerely mean all of that. It should have been said a long time ago."

She thought about Luke fighting the same battle. What was it with fathers and sons? Wanting the connection but pushing away the opportunity at the same time. "Why don't you tell me why you're here, so my imagination will quit running wild."

Brittany's mom hollered from across the street.

Mara waved, telling the girls to clean up.

The animals were shoved in bags, and the girls hugged like they'd never see each other again. Charlie dumped her toys on the porch next to Chase.

"Can I watch a movie? Daddy, you want to watch a movie with me?"

"Not this time, sport. I will this weekend though."

"Okay," she said, chewing on her lip, looking at one and then the other. "Are we moving back to the other house with Daddy again? I love you, Daddy, but I would miss Brittany."

Chase held his hand to his chest. Charlie giggled.

"Why don't you start a movie? I'm going to talk to Daddy, then I'll order the pizza."

Rolling her head back, her face erupted into her adorable smile. "I love pizza night."

Blowing kisses to them both, she banged in the screen door, and the TV clicked on. The familiar music played.

"Ugh, I'm sick of that movie." Chase said.

"The song runs on repeat in my head, I'm usually humming all things beneath the sea my entire shift."

"God, I know." He sighed.

Mara cocked her head. "The teenage years are going to be bad with our little drama queen extraordinaire."

Chase propped his elbows on his knees, grew quiet. "I've been corresponding with my uncle pretty regular. He's in Alaska and working on the pipeline, and he wants to hire me. They're looking for welders, and well, it's about the only thing I've ever completed in life, so…"

Mara's heart slammed to a stop. What did any of his ramblings mean? She panicked for a second and remembered he said it wasn't anything bad at the onset of the conversation.

"It's a chance to do something worthwhile for me. Change of pace, get out of my mom's house, and not live off a job that is handed to me—" He stopped and laughed. "Well, I guess it kind of is, but the pipeline is good, honest work. I need to be on my own and figure out me."

The streetlights blazed to life, setting bugs flying in circles, running into each other in their quest to be the closest to the light.

"The schedule is six weeks on, two off. I'm hoping we can work this out without going back to court. I don't want to fight, and really there's nothing to fight about. I'm giving you what you've always wanted. Temporarily I mean."

"I don't understand."

"Custody, full for the most part. I'd like to have her the two weeks I'm home, maybe take mini vacations, at least until she starts school. But those six weeks in between...all yours."

Mara didn't even feel the tears start falling. They just did.

"It's very generous. If you want to have your lawyer draw it up, I'll sign." Inside, she was freaking out in excitement, wanting to get up and do a happy dance, squeeze her daughter, but there were too many other things at hand.

He grew quiet again. "I'd appreciate it if my mom could have her on Friday afternoons. I know my mom's not your biggest fan, but she loves our little girl."

"I know she does. That's not a problem."

"It'll give you time alone with your mom, too. And

I'll send support, whatever you want. Whatever you need."

"Wow," was all she could think to say.

Everything finally falling into place. Except the man you wanted, the man you needed, at your side.

They were silent for a long time. A song from Charlie's movie leaked through the screen door, seeping into the night.

He patted her knee, took her hand. His touch didn't turn her stomach like it had a few months ago. Maybe because she knew herself better now, knew the relationship would always be a part of her life, but wasn't her life.

"He's going to come back, you know," Chase whispered.

"When?" Mara couldn't help blurting.

Chase laughed. "When he can be everything you are to him."

She closed her eyes, wanting to hold on to the simplicity of the statement.

"And because unlike yours truly, he's not a fool." He turned and touched her cheek. "He loves you. His heart will always win out over everything else."

"I wish I had your confidence. And with my mom… Shit. I hate needing someone, but I need him."

"Just when you need him most, he'll come rolling on up to catch you."

Chase stood and smiled. A genuine smile, not the placating one he normally shot her direction. He hopped onto the porch and banged into the house. He told Charlie goodbye and that he had some big news this weekend. There was no response, so Mara assumed he interrupted one of her favorite parts of the movie.

As he got halfway down the walk, he turned and stopped. "When you need him most, he'll be there." One quick nod added emphasis to his words, like a big old exclamation mark.

Chapter Forty

A tear escaped, sliding down her mom's cheek as she pressed her finger to the picture of her dead husband's smile, making Mara's own eyes swim. With everything in her, she wanted her parents' undeniable, enviable love. The love her mom carried for her father outlasted even his time on this earth. The intimate smile in a photograph of her father left her mom sucking in her lips, moving inside herself. As if she knew she would be with him soon.

Earlier, Mara watched her sleep, clenching the sheets at each wince of pain that faded and washed into smiles as she dreamed.

"Should I put them up?" Mara whispered, tugging at the edges of the photo albums.

Her mom hugged the album to her chest, faltering as the weight was too much for her emaciated arms, laying her head against the top of the pages.

Mara curled into her side, wanting to be as close as she could, as long as she could. The loose, crepey skin of her mom's hand reminded her of Luke talking about his father not wanting to let go of his mother's hand.

The pages fluttered open on their laps, and together they burst out laughing.

"You and your tie-dye overalls."

The pages fell open to one of those Fourth of July parties at the lake. She had been ten or so, excited to sport overalls that were more than patriotic—they were a monstrosity. They made them together from remnants of an old skirt from her mom's hippie days. Looping around her forehead, topping off the horrendous outfit, was a string of thin rawhide. A hemp tattoo, like the anchor one she wore now, displayed on her arm. Her dad had picked the anchor, claiming he wanted her always firmly fixed to him. In the days following, laughingly telling her to drop anchor and sit in his lap for a story. She touched her dad's face. Maybe all of this was God's way of righting the world of good versus bad parents, taking the good ones too soon. Like a choice. Do you get amazing parents for a short period of time? Or do you get shitty ones for decades upon decades? She would take amazing ones in a heartbeat.

"I hated tattoos."

"But Dad had one."

"I know. I learned to live with my prejudices. I'm a victim of my conservative upbringing, I guess."

Mara smirked. It was why she hid her own all these years.

She scooted to the edge of the bed and stood, unbuttoning her jeans. Dipping her jeans in the back with her thumb, she showed her mom the one above her crack. "Kind of why I never showed you mine."

They both laughed again. Her mom touched the outline. "I like it."

"Liar."

"Well, I like that you like it."

Mara buttoned her jeans up and crawled back into the bed. "Sounds like one of those mom placating things."

"Tell me what it means? Tattoos mean something

these days. It's not the same as back in your dad's and my day."

The image arose vividly. The tattoo parlor lit up brightly against the night with flashing neon signs. Mara sat outside the storefront, excited and restless, craving everything since she had left Chase. Everything she hadn't become. Everything she had been too scared to become. The lights of the tattoo parlor pulsed, daring her to step inside.

"I got it the first night I made the decision to leave Chase. Strong, like no one could touch me. No one could hold me down. Maybe that's why the anchor." She swung her head from side to side. "Or maybe because of Dad, I don't know. But the anchor seemed right, felt right." She looked down at her dad's picture, touched his face. Strength, security—her father's words echoed in her mind about his anchor fixation. "He was the strongest man I knew. That night was the first time I acknowledged I was my father's daughter in that way."

"You've always been strong. Maybe too strong."

Mara shook her head. "You can never be too strong."

"Yes, yes, you can. Maybe you don't understand that because of what Chase took you through. But at some point, to feel love, to be loved, you've got to let yourself be a little vulnerable. Be strong on the backside, but be open, mushy in the front. You don't want to be a crusty rock. With the right person, love doesn't take away your strength. You're strong for each other. Strong because of each other. The beautiful thing in life is strength multiplies when you tether it. You can take on the world and all its messiness together."

"I don't know how to be strong except by myself."

"That doesn't always work on the heart. The heart still wants what the heart wants. Cliché, I know. You can't stop feeling, not ever, or you're going to miss out on all the joy and hardship, pain and downright insanity. If you don't let someone in, it is a very lonely world."

Mara didn't want to be lonely; she wanted Luke. By her side, forever. Everything her parents enjoyed for the whole of their marriage. Their love wasn't always perfect, but it was happy and good.

"You're thinking about Luke."

"I am." A tear trailed down her cheek, and her mom brushed it away.

"He'll be back."

"I wish I was as sure as you seem to be."

"Don't you see he's doing this because he wants to be the best man he can for you? Because if he's not whole within himself, then he's no good at being part of a team. He's still searching for a happiness within. You make him into a better man, just like he makes you into a better woman. If you don't see that, then I'm happy to point it out."

"You're supposed to be on my side."

"I'm always on your side, but I like him. Relationships are not perfect, Mara."

"I know. I'm scared, really scared. I miss him so much, and I hate that I miss him. A stupid, endless cycle."

The last conversation raised so many confusing questions. "Every time I talk to him, he sounds happy, content. Authentic, maybe."

"He's waited for this relationship with his father for a long time."

Mara nodded, adjusting herself closer to her mom.

"I could really use his arms around me."

Her mom nestled into Mara's shoulder. The role reversal reminding her of the grim reality of the last doctor's visit.

"His arms will be here when I leave you, baby." She nudged her nose into Mara's neck. "I feel it in these messed-up bones."

"I don't want you to leave me."

"The time is coming. And I'm going to need you to let me go. I want every second with you and Charlie, but the pain is eating away little pieces of me. There's going to come a time when you're going to have to release. And then you're going to have to put yourself in motion again. Allow yourself to grieve, but don't stay there. You need to live."

Mara shook her head, letting the tears escape. "I can't."

"You can, my sweet girl. When the time comes, you'll understand what I realized when I lost your father. The pain you feel at someone's passing is hard, and the loss hurts like nothing you've ever felt, but if you've experienced the blessing of a special someone in your life, then the pain can become bittersweet. And when you're a mom, you keep moving. Your daughter is going to require every ounce of the strength you've built. And it will be easier when your gorgeous man wraps his arms around you and lets you know there's still so much beauty in life. So much messy to make into good."

Chapter Forty-One

Messy did not work for her right now.

Last week, Mara received a screenshot of a returning airline ticket. His arrival should be tomorrow. Yet, when she texted and then called to let him know she took off work to pick him up, her phone had been silent. Three dots popped up, disappeared, popped up, disappeared. And then nothing.

Nothing prepares you for the word hospice being thrust into your working vocabulary. Knowing you can do nothing more than make your loved one comfortable as they return home for the last time. The finiteness of it. The reality of hospice being so synonymous with the end. Last week that day had come.

Inside the house, the hospice nurse performed her monstrous tasks. Most days her mom slept while Mara sat at her bedside. Even the simple act of breathing caused her breath to catch over and over again. The endless battle to sweep the oncologist's words into the street.

Her plan had been to take a leave of absence to handle the care herself. Unfortunately, her mom's mind had gone nowhere, even with the pain meds, reminding Mara they already discussed her wants at the end.

Back when things didn't seem altogether real. Back before hospice care entered the picture.

The fight to do something remained. The empty

remained.

Her emotional strength waned in equal measures to her mom's physical. Each day emptied her. The endless sting of being alone, of not having the life preserver Luke always talked about, tore her gut apart. Twisting her stomach and heart until they were mashed up together into a lump of…She didn't even know what to call the desperation of it all.

She wanted his arms around her. Wanted him to fill up all the lonely places inside. She wanted someone to lie and tell her everything would be okay. In the same vein, someone to tell her the truth. Everything would be okay because her person was standing at her side. They would be her strength while she tackled life's messiness until she could do it on her own again.

Their individual alone. Back on the table.

The door closed softly, and the hospice care nurse smiled in her direction. A smile reeking of pity. If there were any words at this point, they were empty ones. The nurse offered the only thing she could, a touch at Mara's shoulder, a two-fingered wave. A sore replacement for Luke's arms, Luke's endless hold on her insides. The arms that refused to turn the world back into its proper rotation. If he would only understand, she needed him to take away the alone.

Mara worked herself into sad, then depressed, then into downright mad.

—*Are you coming back?*—

—*Oh, babe, of course I am*—

Followed by three little emoji hearts.

The three dots were back, faded again. She dropped the phone into her lap, curling herself around it.

—*Rebooked my ticket. Wind survey team is coming*

tomorrow. After that, they're on their own for the auction. Can't wait to see my girls—

He couldn't be serious. The wind people? She began scrolling through their text trail, swearing the wind people were last week. Closing her eyes, she wrapped her hands around each other. What did it matter? Another excuse. Another "I've just gotta." All she wanted was his arms for one moment, maybe two. Then she could make it through another day, another evening.

A screenshot of a new ticket pinged. The purchase date, two days ago.

He called after a few seconds, and she had enough self-respect to ignore him.

—Seriously?—

—You know what this means to me. My dad needs just a little more help. It's only a week—

Then some stupid throwing-up-your-hands emoji.

—Yay you. My mom's dying. She needs a little more help too—

In her anger she wanted to throw out a coffin emoji, but it would make things too real.

Instead, she powered down the phone and chucked it across the room.

He could live in three-dot land now.

Chapter Forty-Two

The Whitten ranch outfitted a small, no-nonsense office in town. After finishing breakfast at their favorite local diner, it was where Luke and his dad headed. The first cold front had hit West Texas, and unlike Wyoming, the first fronts in Texas were always a good sign, another brutal Texas summer simmering into humane conditions. They both nodded and tipped their hats to old Mrs. Summerlin. She'd been old when he was in grade school. She still trucked along, dressed to the nines year-round. San Angelo offered so many things that never changed. Usually, the status quo grated until you couldn't see straight. Good or bad, there was a comfort in knowing what to expect.

They walked past their cute little receptionist. She'd been flirting relentlessly with him, no matter how many times he repeated he was here temporarily, and there was a girlfriend in Wyoming. She would smile in her knowing way, or his sister would say it was a knowing way. He didn't understand what it was she knew.

Luke scrolled through his phone as they waited for Claire. His home screen lit up with an adorable picture of himself with Mara and Charlie at the fair. She hadn't texted since her mini rampage yesterday, then hadn't answered any of his calls to talk out the argument. Luke touched the screen, touched her face. He'd become enveloped in helping Mike with the branding process, hadn't forgotten how things were left exactly, but hadn't put her needs on the front burner either. Everything with his dad and the ranch was almost where he wanted to leave things.

Except there was no Mara here.

Claire rushed in, and he blackened the screen, set the phone on the desk.

"How goes it, kiddo?" he and his dad said at the same time.

They both got an eye roll.

"I've got one hour. You two may have all day to meander around town, but some of us have things to do, and a specific time to do them."

Ward cocked his head at Luke. "Hear that. We get to meander today."

Claire began shuffling files out of her briefcase. "I'm serious, alright? Cole's at home with Mitch and an ear infection. I've got a ten o'clock with the bank's transition team, then I've got to relieve Mitch so he can go on the field trip with JJ. Then I go back for a four…" She looked from one to the other. "Never mind."

"Whoa." Luke held his hands up. "Can I help with anything? Cole? I can babysit. He can meander with us."

"Sick." She thumped her forehead. "See, you weren't listening."

"I was. I can coddle with the best of them."

She was silent, her mind somewhere else. Shaking her head, she opened the file.

"What do we have, Claire?" Ward leaned forward, propping his elbows on the desk.

"Recovery looks good, actually. Since Luke and Mike have been here and Justin hasn't, expenses are way down. We're starting to see a recovery, and we're in the black. Not a lot, but we cleared a lot of dead weight off the payroll, and the ones who stayed have remembered you get paid for working. They're saying beef prices are going to be up for auction, so as many head we can put out there, especially the higher breeds, the better. But I know we don't want to jump the gun; we're building for year-over-year growth. We just need to produce enough to get us through the year. I don't think the oil leases are going to be helping out much, at least for the near future, so we need to lean heavy on the livestock."

"What about the horses Mikey's been working?" Luke asked.

"Are any of them ready to sell?" Claire thumbed through her stack of paper.

"Not sure. There may be a couple. It may be better to have an open-house type thing, so ranchers can see what we've done. We should still have a decent enough reputation to have a good draw." Probably an unhappy conversation. Mikey was a big child at times, knowing the animals had to be sold, but Mike didn't have to like it. But ranching was more than "playing with the ponies" as Mike so eloquently called it.

"You've done a real good job, son," Ward said, glanced at Claire. "You too, peanut. Being together again, working together, has made us a powerful team."

Claire and Luke looked at each other. It had been a really long time since their father spared any compliments their direction. It had to be good, especially for Claire to hear. Always here, always unrecognized as others ran them out of their own legacy. He did a quick shake of his head. This was not his legacy. He was a lawyer. Or, would be someday.

"Now. Point two," Claire said after a long silence.

"I love having you here, Luke, but when are you going back? You need to get these guys able to function on their own. You've got to start delegating."

Ward's chair squeaked as his weight shifted. A full minute passed before they heard any sound other than the hum of the computer tower, Alaina's chipper voice down the hall. Luke opened his mouth, didn't know what to say, so he shut it again.

"I don't think there's any rush. We're enjoying ourselves; we've got a lot of time to make up for. Maybe your little lady can come on down for a spell."

"She can't, Dad," Luke said, the words hitting right at his heart. The emotion of the words from his father froze him up with happiness. Then he thought of Mara, the last text, her needs.

"I really need you here, son. At least a few more weeks. Maybe you can take a long weekend and go visit. Then come back, get us through the spring auction, and then you can go."

Luke's stomach did flip-flops. He ran his phone along his jeans, and the screen flashed with the fair picture. Maybe they could make the long-distance thing work. At least temporarily. Maybe she could leave after her mom…He made himself stop.

Claire stared at him with a look of honest to God disgust.

"Are you kidding me right now?" she yelled Luke's direction.

The silence hammered and encapsulated the whole office.

She began pacing, stopped in front of her father's desk, and leaned into it. "And you!"

His dad scrunched his thick eyebrows together.

"You think this choice is even yours? It's so good of you to give your son permission to go after the spring auction. That's mighty big of you. He's thirty fucking years old, Dad."

"Claire," Luke growled. "Dad knows I'm going back to Wyoming. He was just throwing out ideas."

Ward opened his mouth and thought better of it.

Claire flung her hand, looked at Luke. "Does he? Have you told him 'that little lady' "—she flung air quotes right in front of his face—"was who helped save you when the times were the toughest?"

"I saved myself." Luke glared at her.

"Yes." Her voice skidded to a halt. "You did that without him, and now you're going to throw your happiness—her happiness—to the wind because he commands it?" She knelt down in front of him, put her hands on his thighs. "I get this is the relationship with Dad you have always wanted. It's everything it should have been all along. And trust me, I love seeing it blossom, but this?" She did some kind of a crisscross motion with her hands between him and his father across the desk. "This doesn't have to land on one or the other. You can have both. Your relationship with Dad doesn't end because you're not here."

Luke stared at his dad, and then out the window. The conversation had remnants of the same one he'd had with Mara when she went back to Chase. Was that what he was doing? This wasn't a choice between two men; it was a choice between a woman and his father.

Claire's voice elevated again. "Isn't she wondering when you're coming back? Six weeks you've been gone. Six weeks! Or have you avoided telling her? Worrying about what Daddy will think?"

"Claire, don't." His dad shriveled before his eyes.

He wanted to open Mara's last pain-filled text, but he didn't dare.

Claire continued to rant, then she stopped and began slamming her files and papers and whatever else into her monstrous bag of a purse, not even taking the time to open her thousand-dollar briefcase.

She walked to the door and stopped, looked at him and then his father, back to him. He looked away; he'd never been able to go head-to-head with her when she was wound up.

"Am I the only one getting the irony here? Are you both so dense you're not getting the full gist of this?"

He and his dad looked across the desk at each other. He didn't see any notes of irony in this whole rant of hers.

"God. Luke, come on." She stopped, and he didn't know what to say.

"Dad chose." She emphasized *chose* with a huge punctuation mark. "Chose Evelyn. Every single time over you. Now you're making the same, stupid, hurtful choice. You are choosing him instead of Mara. He who hurt you." She turned to their dad. "You left rejection scars in both of us, and now you're asking him to do the same thing. You're playing Evelyn now. You can have it all, Luke. Everything. This relationship with Dad you crave? It's not location specific. That's what airplanes are for. That's what phones are for. Don't sacrifice yourself. Please don't sacrifice yourself."

With her words hanging, she left, her heels clicking away on the hardwood. The front door squeaked open and closed. The office returned to fingernails tapping away on a keyboard.

The tears burned, and he refused to let them fall. He flipped his phone, and two beautiful smiles stared back at him. She who helped him breathe again.

He touched the screen and read her last utterly painful text.

The pain behind his eyes shot somewhere into his brain and down to his heart. How could he have not run to her side?

Looking across the desk, his father openly cried. He removed a genuine, old-school hankie and blew his nose.

"Your sister was always smarter than both of us put together."

Luke smiled. So much truth.

"I'm going to miss the blazes out of you, but she's very right."

Luke nodded and remembered his perfect wingman, battling a painful part of life alone.

—Yay you, my mom is dying. She needs a little more help too—

He was an idiot.

They raced home, and he packed while his father looked for the fastest flight out.

"I love you, Luke," his dad said from the door as he threw his bag in the spare car his father kept.

He turned and saw more tears and ran to the porch and threw his arms around him.

"I love you as big as Texas," Ward said into his hair.

Luke laughed and gathered his dad into him as best he could. Words from when he was a little boy, sitting on tailgates staring at stars, sitting on docks fishing, sitting in deer stands, lapping up every ounce of his father he could find.

"I love you as big as Texas, too. Just gotta throw a

little Wyoming in there right now."

He hopped down and was on his way.

A text pinged once he was on the highway. He glanced at the screen on the dash. Rachel?

—*Mara's mom passed away yesterday. Please come*—

Luke pushed the accelerator.

Already on it.

Chapter Forty-Three

Mara had mistakenly thought the pain of losing her father was the greatest agony she would ever experience. She was wrong.

How did a daughter survive when her mom left this earth?

Mara stood achingly still, staring across the gaping hole to an aunt she hardly remembered. To neighbors, coworkers, countless friends and family. Even Chase and Vivian were here to pay their respects.

Chase caught her eye and nodded her direction.

"He'll come rolling on up, just when you need him most." His words from the not-too-distant past slayed her. Because they weren't true.

The minister droned useless words holding no meaning for how much her heart hurt. An attempt to offer something bordering on hope in the hereafter, make you feel better, feel something other than pain, when nothing could. A million memories ran on fast forward. Playing princess, having tea parties, transitioning into a tomboy and skateboarding, right alongside her mom, her mom indulging her whim with horses and taking her riding. Entering the tween and teen years and begging her mom to explain why her boobs weren't growing. Bawling after she left Chase, sure no one would ever love her again. Mara's stomach turned at the thought of helping Charlie understand all those things. The things her mother could explain effortlessly.

The pulleys clattering to life left her looking skyward. The tears began for the fifty-third time today.

As people mingled, she touched her neck, her chest, feeling a hammer sling into her heart. The life preserver of his arms wrapped her up, and he rested his chin on her shoulder.

"Damn you," she said, hating the crack in her voice.

"I know," Luke whispered into her neck. His rich, emotional voice beat her heart into a pulp of something she couldn't begin to describe. "It's okay to break now." He tugged her tighter.

She straightened for a second, maybe two, and gave over to the pain encapsulating the last of her mother's time on this earth. So beautiful and agonizing at the same time. Watching her fight like any prize fighter for one more coherent moment with her daughter and granddaughter. Wanting to hold them both before the medication made her life swim away from the shore. Mara shook uncontrollably and wanted to break free, but she didn't. She just wanted to lose herself in his firm arms and solid body. She was a mass of confusion, and he held on tighter, until she couldn't squirm away. She twisted to face him and couldn't lift her gaze, so she beat on his chest.

And he pulled her tighter still.

"I don't want you here," she cried.

"I know."

She sobbed into his chest and his fingers curled into her hair, laying her next to his heart. Her labored breathing turned into gasps. Tired of fighting, she let her body melt in his and collapsed.

When the cars of all the mourners disappeared, they

still clung.

He helped her settle inside the limo. "Your family will be waiting. I'll be right behind."

Logic eluded as she studied the floorboard. In real world terms, her mother's passing changed nothing. He couldn't leave his family; she couldn't move her daughter.

"I still can't go," she finally said.

He took her face in his hands and touched her lips with his in a whisper of something bordering on intimate and at the same time, so chaste. "But I can."

She blinked. What did he mean?

He shut the door and pounded on the roof.

More tears slid as the driver pulled away. Whether his words were metaphoric or literal, she didn't have the strength to analyze or second-guess the vagueness of his statement.

****

People stuck around the house long into the afternoon. Her mother touched so many lives. But with each and every conversation, something slipped away. Every person who wanted to comfort, instead, brought silent screams. Luke circled, watching from afar. Every shift of her legs, every word she shared, every hug clinging a little too long—he saw it all.

Her exterior hardened, and the walls fortified. There was nothing to do but greet and meet and hope tomorrow, the pain would ebb just a little.

Charlie launched into a full-on run from the porch, slamming into him, attempting one of those hit-and-run hugs, but he hauled her up and threw her high, letting her drop into his arms, giggling. She wanted to be comforted by the sight, but finding anything reassuring about life right now felt hollow.

Luke could help with Charlie—if Luke stuck around.

Together, Charlie and he sat on the grass, picking at the weeds and flowers. His fingers wrapped and tied, patiently showing her how to make a chain of dandelions. As she worked her little fingers, his gaze scanned her mother's yard. Just like her life, a neglected mess.

Could he help with that?

Again, was he staying?

As they huddled together, Mara was comforted by the innocence of childhood. Maybe her daughter wouldn't remember any of this, but then she would never know how precious the time shared with her grandmother was. Charlie maneuvered herself into Luke's lap, and they talked like they'd been apart for years, not months.

Her mom's best friend became hysterical, leaning into Mara, causing Luke to look up and study her. Mara hugged the woman hard and froze up, turning her eyes to stone so he couldn't see, couldn't read.

While she walked people to their cars on autopilot, Charlie and Luke shifted from the grass to the porch. With a small wave, she closed the car door on the last of the visitors, stalling as she stood, weaving as a wave of dizziness overtook.

She was done.

Mara turned to the two of them, sitting tucked together.

"But I can." She thought of his words, still not knowing what they meant, and had no energy left to explore the statement. All she wanted was to curl up and die herself. Crawl into the casket with her mother and be lowered into the ground. The mom thing was something you couldn't contemplate until you were in the midst of being one. Who to call when your daughter throws a tantrum? When your ex calls you a fat ass for the twenty-third time in a week's span? When your friends leave? She looked at Luke as he brushed a strand of hair from Charlie's face. What about when you lose the love of your life?

He lifted his head as if some unspoken words captured his attention and looked in her direction. Touching his lips with two fingers, he sent them toward her with a sad smile.

Charlie scampered inside, the old wooden screen door slamming behind her as she shouted she was going to watch a movie.

Mara dropped her head to her chest and breathed heavily, lowering herself to the bottom step. Luke said nothing, and it was okay; she didn't want to hear anything. Her strong insides were scooped out and lying in a heap on the cement at her feet.

A happy song spilled out the screen, making her want to throw up.

Silence stretched into dusk, and dusk turned over to darkness.

Tears fell in streams, tears dried up, tears fell silently.

She made no move to be closer. He made no move to comfort. Even that scared her. He knew her so well.

Charlie joined them and sweetly patted Mara's head, asking for a story. Luke took her little hand and disappeared.

When he came out, he sat closer. Not touching, but

his warmth invaded.

"Chuck says her daddy's going away," he said with a flip of his head, throwing his bangs skyward before they settled.

"Alaska."

He nodded at that.

She circled the air with her finger. "Finding himself, something along those lines."

"You're not going?" he asked, cocking his head.

Silence.

"My life is here." The wind hushed through her mom's trees. She didn't want to be anywhere else.

He nodded with a small smile. "Finding himself, huh?"

Silence.

"I still can't go," she reiterated, in case he forgot.

Her hands were encapsulated in his own. "I know."

He looked inside her, contemplated her, maybe trying to decide whether he could handle her and her mess of a self.

A calloused fingertip touched her face in a whisper of a caress. "I wish I could do something to help right now. So much."

She nodded and fought the lump of another round of waterworks.

"I don't have all the answers," he said, brushing at some gooped mud on the toe of her shiny new pumps. "But I'm working on them. Okay?"

"Why do you throw out all this vagueness?" She flung her hands and slumped. She couldn't even work herself into the good-and-mad, yelling-and-rage category.

He pressed her face between his palms, stroked

beneath her eyes with his thumbs. "I love you. And I know you love me. You know I don't make promises I can't fulfill. I'm working on answers. Once I get those answers, I'll be back so you can yell at me, beat on me, kick me, whatever your little heart desires. But I'll have answers."

"Your answers."

He kissed her fingers and set her hands in her lap. "Our answers."

Chapter Forty-Four

They sat in the distance, not quite at the shoreline, but close enough Charlie could run and play in the water, run back to the safety of her mother. Four-year-old laughter drifting his way left Luke smiling. From her beach chair, Mara stared at the lake, at the mountains beyond the lake. He loved life here in Rock Springs, and he loved this woman. The sight of her by herself, and as a mom, made him yearn and want.

And hope.

Today, some of their answers and decisions tumbled, jostling themselves, and falling into place.

Meandering through his crazy life, there would always be times where one or the other would be splintered, broken. At one time, he thought at least one of them needed to be whole to come together and make this relationship work, but he wasn't sure anymore. He had been wrong about a lot of things. Ironically, when talking to his father last night, a piece of life slipped into place. There were enough of life's trials and tribulations, complexities, twists, turns, and downright wallowing in the dregs of life to not grasp on to the good when you had the chance. Every relationship deserved a whole lot of happy to counter the messy.

Mara lifted her head as Charlie squealed at something crawling on the sand at the beach. Pulling up her knees, she put her cheek on them. She was smiling at this moment, seeing her mother in her little girl. How far they had come from the night at the bar when they were both broken, not having anyone to call their own. The life preserver they had been passing back and forth needed them both to grab on tight and never let go.

"Uke!" Charlie spotted him and was off, pounding into his knees before he could stop the collision. He hoisted her and nuzzled her neck.

"How's Chuck?" he asked as Mara held a hand over her eyes, looking in his direction.

"Chuck's uck." She giggled.

"Ew. Yuck."

"You're silly." She squirmed, done with him for the moment. She ran to Mara, screaming excitedly. "He came, see!" She pointed at him. "I knew he would 'cause he loves us."

The words made his heart melt.

Yes. Yes, he does.

Mara's lost look was back in place. She looked beautiful and vulnerable and ready to break into a thousand pieces. At the same time, strong and steadfast and ready to take on the world for everything she loved and believed in. He took her hand, standing close enough to smell her drugstore shampoo. Nothing had ever smelt so good. Nothing ever looked as good.

Charlie tugged on the bottom of his shorts, forcing him to pay attention.

He squatted down in front of her. "Can I help you, ma'am?"

She huffed and crossed her arms. "You need to 'pologize to my mommy. She really, really missed you because you didn't come back for, for like forever. You can't do that to my mom, because she's the best mommy in the—" Charlie spun, slinging up dirt in her awkward pirouettes, then stomped her foot, making the sand jump onto his loafer. "It's not right."

"I agree. Thank you for bringing these things to my attention." Luke squeezed her hand. "Before I give a shot at a decent ''pology' though, I have something for you, ucky Chuck." He fished the tiny box out of his pocket.

Charlie could barely contain herself, jumping up and down on the balls of her feet, no longer interested in decent apologies. "I love presents. What is it? What is it?"

He draped a little bracelet over her wrist, watching her eyes light up.

"You did me purple. I love purple." Charlie counted the interlocking hearts. Miniature eyes, glassy like her mother's, when she got excited. "It's so pretty."

Luke fastened the clasp on her wrist. With his finger, he held the hearts away from her skin. "This one's Mommy, this one's you, and this one is me."

"Ohhhhh." She linked her arm with his. "Like when we hook our arms. The hearts are like when we hook our arms."

Mara finger combed Charlie's hair, concentrating on the bracelet.

"Did you get Mommy a present too?" Charlie said, poking her finger at her heart.

"I did get Mommy a present too."

"Can I see, can I see?" Charlie was back to dancing on the balls of her feet.

Mara shifted her gaze from Charlie to him. He rose, brushing her hair from her eyes, tucking it behind her ear where the strand refused to stay. The wind kicked it skyward. She looked down at her bouncing daughter and back at him.

When their eyes met, he knew it was time to live, and live well. His father's words, learned after a lifetime, but still learned. And the woman before him couldn't hide her love any better than he could.

"Pick me up. I want to see."

"You know what, Chuck? You're going to have to wait a minute."

He removed the necklace from his other pocket. It too held three heart charms. Not connected, but loose.

Holding the ends apart, he took in eyes, swimming with emotion. "May I?" He nodded at her neck.

Mara's eyes were glistening. Her lips, silent. But she pulled her hair to the side so he could fasten the necklace. The little hearts clinked together, settling just above her heart.

"I am sorry for hurting you," he whispered. "I was being selfish, and I wasn't here when you needed me most. It'll never happen again."

She covered her face with her hands. Her shoulders shook.

He grasped her hands tight in his own. "This man who has done so many things wrong in life, somehow did the most important thing right. The end of my road wasn't a raging river, or a hydroplaning car. It wasn't even Rock Springs, Wyoming. The end of the road was a barstool, in a run-down trucker bar. In front of you. The end of the road was everything I'd been looking for all along."

Luke closed his eyes and opened them to stare at the woman he wanted to share every waking moment with from this day forward. Picking up the chain, he fingered the charms, leaned in, and touched his lips to each in turn.

"I'd like to add a couple… or five, to this someday."

Mara raised her eyebrows and smirked.

"I accepted a lawyering sort of job in town while I finish school, so I hope you like having me around."

Charlie circled them up, her arms around their thighs and hugging them both tight. Like the little life preserver she was.

Mara's head fell to his chest, and his heart stopped. He kissed that perfect little place where her earlobe met her neck. The place where he could feel the pulse of her heartbeat against his lips.

"You're the breath I didn't know existed. The breath I didn't know I needed."

The end of the road had never been a definitive place. It was perfection now. With his father's words guiding, his soul standing before him.

A word about the author…

Kathryn Beck loves writing stories about strong females, morally gray characters, and the messy relationships they tackle along the way. Born in Eastern Canada, raised in California, Kathryn now makes her home in Texas. More than anything she enjoys time with her family and friends, her husband of thirty-five years, and her children and adorable grandsons.

To find out more, visit
kathrynbeck.com.

Thank you for purchasing
this publication of The Wild Rose Press, Inc.

For questions or more information
contact us at
info@thewildrosepress.com.

The Wild Rose Press, Inc.
www.thewildrosepress.com